Sh

Mark Timli................ent of hardboiled British crim............. He has also been described as the only writer in the tradition of genuine pulp this side of the Atlantic. Born and brought up in Tulse Hill, he has worked as a roadie for The Who and T. Rex and now writes full time. Following the successful TV pilot based on one of the Sharman novels, Carlton Television are to screen four more, starring Clive Owen, to be screened during late 1996.

mark Timlin

SHARMAN
AND OTHER FILTH

VISTA

Published in Great Britain 1996
as a Vista paperback original

Vista is an imprint of the Cassell Group
Wellington House, 125 Strand, London WC2R 0BB

This collection © Mark Timlin 1996

A catalogue record for this book is
available from the British Library.

ISBN 0 575 60101 9

Typeset by CentraCet Ltd, Cambridge
Printed and bound in Great Britain
by Cox & Wyman Ltd, Reading, Berks

96 97 98 99   10 9 8 7 6 5 4 3 2 1

Contents

This book is dedicated to
my friend and editor
Richard Evans, who
tragically died during
the preparation of it

Introduction

Most of the following short stories were written for one or other of the excellent anthologies edited by Maxim Jakubowski. So it's him you've got to thank or otherwise.

There's a whole lot of other people to thank too, and this is a great opportunity: fiction writers rarely have a chance to speak in their own voices, as their characters always seem to take over. Which, I suppose, is the whole point of fiction.

Here goes. First there's my mother, who helped out with big breakfasts and large steak and kidney pies. My wife Robyn Timlin and my good friend Robin Cook, two more examples of the fact that living is losing those people we love most. Then there's Hazel Griffith, who encouraged me to write all those years ago, and who sadly died soon after my first novel was published. No more than a few minutes have gone by when I haven't thought of her, or missed her.

On a happier note, though they may not share the sentiment, I thank my book editors: Colin Murray, Oliver Johnson, Jane Morpeth, Peter Lavery, Mike Bailey, Penny Phillips, Julia Wisdom, Faith Brooker, and, of course, my mate Richard Evans, who rescued me from oblivion, took me to Headline Books and saved my skin all those years ago. Cheers, pal. You've got a lot to answer for.

A big mention has to go to Heather Jeeves, my agent and buddy. And I mustn't forget all those at Casarotto and Co., especially Tracey Smith, who made it her business to get my books on to TV – and succeeded. Serena, too, who took the books into ICM and got the whole works rolling there.

Then there's the World Productions team who actually put the books on the screen: Tony Garnett, Wild Bill Shapter, Suri Krishnamma, Jim, Fleur, Valery, Bob Bierman, Matthew Evans, Nigel, Danielle and too many others to mention, except, of course, for Clive Owen who *is* Nick Sharman now.

Who else to mention? Lucy Ramsey, who keeps annoying people into writing about me. My two daughters, Amy and Charlotte, of whom I am inordinately proud. All who worked at Keables in West Norwood – it keeps turning up in the books and films in various disguises. The staff at *A Shot in the Dark* for all the coverage and all those free books. Maxim Jakubowski (again), his wife Dolores, and the Murder One crew who sell the books when they can get them. Gerry's club should be in here, too, plus Kathy, Nick and Angus, Gerry and Pat, Kerstan and Maxine, Philip Miles, Piers Allardyce, Milton and Stewart Homan who keep the wheels turning, my friends from Cropredy, Martin, Polly and family, Geoff, Angus and Anthea, little Annie Ival and Barbara, Dirk, Charlie Grima, and, finally, anyone else I've forgotten to mention. There must be hundreds of you.

I've also written a pompous little introduction to each story, just like a real writer. Christ, I'll be having my teeth fixed next.

Ai No Corrida

This is the first short story I ever wrote. It was originally intended for a collection by a bunch of crime writers gathered together under the umbrella of *Fresh Blood*, which was also going to be the title of the anthology. Unfortunately, in a classic 'piss-up' and 'brewery' scenario, nothing ever came of it, and eventually the story was published in 1992 in *Constable New Crimes 1*.

It's actually an extract from the original manuscript of my first novel, *A Good Year For the Roses*, and explains why Sharman left the police. Eventually, some kind editor pointed out that if this was how Sharman left the force, he'd've ended up in jail for twenty-five years, so I changed it. But I still liked the idea and kept it in a drawer until I could use it. So in a way it *is* a Sharman story, and reminds all us writers never to throw anything away, because one day it could be worth a bob or two. 'Ai No Corrida' is a hefty hunk of eighties disco funk by Quincy Jones.

It was the kind of midsummer's night that never really gets dark. Some memory of the day remains in the sky until dawn, and the city shimmers like the skirts of a girl's white dress seen out of the corner of your eye as she vanishes through a closing door.

Any mist was burnt off by 5 a.m. I was in an all-night drinker in Peckham with Eddie. The place was quiet. Just us and the barman, who wanted us to go but was too scared to throw us out.

Even though the curtains were tightly drawn there were enough cuts and holes in the material to allow a few rays of the early sunlight through. They lay like gold coins on the filthy carpet. I saw Eddie watch them move slowly across the floor. He checked his watch and, with one smooth movement, leaned down and picked up the black leather bag that stood next to our table and flicked it in my direction. I caught the bag one-handed.

'Time to get changed,' he said.

I headed for the toilet. On the way I picked the raincoat I didn't need for the weather off the coat rack. Inside the gents' there was just one filthy stall. It stank of old shit and vomit overlaid with the sharp tang of urine and the sharper smell of cheap bleach. The floor felt sticky underneath the soles of my shoes. I stripped naked in the confined space, folded my clothes neatly and piled them on the closed toilet seat. Then I removed the outfit that was in the bag. Eddie had done me proud. I struggled into a clean jock-strap. Then pulled on a lilac satin running vest and tight black shorts. There was a new pair of white tube socks, still in their plastic bag, and finally a pair of Nike trainers with thick rubber soles. I put the suit and shirt, boxer shorts, socks and plain black loafers that I'd been wearing previously into the bag and zipped it up. I pulled on the raincoat and went back to the bar. 'I've always admired your legs,' said Eddie when he saw me.

'Shove it,' I replied with what felt like a sour look.

'Lighten up and have a quick one,' he said. The idea made me want to puke. We'd been up all night, drinking and smoking too many cigarettes and snorting too much coke so that we'd stay awake. My throat was numb but I could feel the rawness underneath and my eyes felt as if they were full of ground glass.

'No more. I've had enough,' I said. 'Let's do it if we're going to.'

'OK,' he said.

So we did it.

That's how it began. But it seemed to have begun so many times. So maybe that was just the beginning of the end.

It had really begun a few weeks earlier when Eddie found the girl.

The pair of us had been temporarily seconded to Kennington Nick Crime Squad. There had been a spate of queer-bashing in Kennington Park, which had culminated in a double murder on spring Bank Holiday Monday.

Then, a gay man who jogged around the park every morning looking for talent and combining his two favourite sports, sex and running, literally had to run for his life when he approached a young guy sitting on a bench. The young guy turned out to be carrying a flick knife, and had a friend with another, hiding in the bushes. When the jogger made his intentions clear the friend came at him and slashed his arm so badly he had to go to hospital. If he hadn't, I doubt whether he would have reported the assault. Eddie and I interviewed him. I think he talked because he realized that his sexual predilections didn't bother us. Eddie didn't care that he was gay. I don't think that Eddie cared that much for sex at all. He had another love in his life. As far as I was concerned the more guys that were gay the better. All the more women for me. We moved in mob-handed for an undercover operation. I wasn't known locally so I was the mug who got dressed up as the decoy. I'd been pumping iron all winter and looked pretty fit, even if I do say so myself. I was supposed to be a gay jogger. All pastel running gear with tight shorts and a butch haircut. I drew the line at growing a big moustache, but did look the part when I was all dressed

11

up, as the rest of the chaps took much delight in telling me.

The idea was that I'd cruise around the park as if I was looking for early-morning trade. If the bashers were around and took the bait, the squad would leap out of the undergrowth and nick some bodies. If I collected a spank, too bad. It was up to me to duck and dive until the lads appeared. I spent four mornings poncing around the park like a prat. The fifth morning, the Friday, things changed. I was swanning around like I was looking for some swift buggery in the bushes, when Eddie crashed out of a small copse of trees looking as grey as last week's shirt. I swerved in his direction, picking up speed. He grabbed my arm when I got close. 'Back there,' he said in a gagging kind of voice that I hadn't heard from him before. 'I'll get the others.'

'What's up?' I said.

'Take a fucking look,' he said. 'And stay with her. I've called an ambulance on the R/T.'

I pushed my way through the undergrowth and found her. She could have been any age, but I later found out she was fifteen. Poor little bitch. She'd been raped, beaten and left. Some of what had happened was obvious. Some I guessed, and some I found out over the next few days from the doctors at St Tommy's. She'd been pretty well hammered. At first, in that shady clearing, I thought she was going to die on me there and then. There was a lot of blood. More than you'd think could possibly be contained in her small white body. When the doctors got through with her, their reports showed that she'd been the victim of a multiple rape, perhaps by as many as five or six men. Portions of her hair and scalp had been torn from her head. She'd been punched and beaten around her face and head, which resulted in a broken cheekbone, two breaks to her nose, severe bruising and lacerations around both eyes, a broken jaw and the loss of most of her upper front teeth. One arm was dislocated. Both her breasts had been savagely bitten and her right nipple had been hacked off. Her vagina had been chewed raw. Some of her clothes had been torn off, the rest had been cut off with a saw-edged knife. Someone had carved the letters SKAG on her stomach. One finger had been chopped off with the same knife to facilitate the removal of an antique gold ring, too small to take off by more reasonable means. Her panties had been stuffed in her mouth to act as a gag. There was a quantity of semen on her face, in her hair, inside her vagina and over her thighs. At first all I could see as I bent down beside her were her two black eyes, one totally, one partially closed. I gently eased the flimsy material from between her lips. Her battered face was covered in blood and come. She moved the hand with the stump of a finger to try and hide her damaged cunt. She was either having a heavy period or haemorrhaging badly. By the time the ambulance arrived, bouncing across the grass with its siren yelping, and the attendants were carrying her to it, the rest of the squad had gathered round. There were some hard men watching her taken away, but more than one excused himself to throw up behind the trees. Me included.

The uniforms found the rest of her clothes, her nipple, her finger and seven teeth in the grass when they came in to do a close search. One morning, in the canteen, some joker called it a fingertip search, within Eddie's hearing. If I hadn't stopped him, Eddie would have killed the bloke. No one called it that again. At least not when we were around.

Eddie and I went with her to hospital. I held her good hand. About half-way there she opened her less damaged eye and said through lips swollen to the size of sausages one word. Beneath the scream of the siren it sounded like 'Dago'.

13

'What did she say?' asked Eddie.

'It sounded like Dago,' I replied.

'Christ, I should have known. This has got that little posse's mark all over it.'

'You know him then?'

'You mean you don't?'

'No,' I said.

'You're lucky.'

'Sounds like it. Who is he?'

'I'll tell you about him later,' said Eddie. 'The bastard's gone too far this time.'

'We'll get him,' I said.

'Bollocks,' said Eddie. 'We'll never get him for this or anything else.'

I didn't reply. We just sat in the back of the hot ambulance and didn't say any more.

Later I checked on Dago in the files. He and his little crew were a collective pain in the arse to the local force. With his mate Maggs he ran a gang of hotshots who lived on the Aylesbury Estate, SE11. It was one of the nastier corners of South London. A part of the city that had no past, no history, no future. Around that way, what the blitz didn't knock down during the war, the council did during the fifties. In the sixties they flung up a maze of interconnected blocks that hadn't been too hot on day one, and had deteriorated badly since. It was a no-go area for milkmen and postmen and even us lot were a bit wary.

On the scale of council estates it wasn't as bad as North Peckham and slightly superior to St Martin's. Which meant that the cockroaches were safe, but the junkies went around in pairs.

There were six in the gang.

Dago and Maggs were the top dogs. Dago's real name was Owen Whittaker. He had a white mother and a black father. The old man hadn't been seen since the night of conception. He and Ms Whittaker were just ships that passed in the night. Nine months later, a bonny brown-skinned baby boy was born in King's College Hospital. After nineteeen years, the baby had turned into a mean-mouthed half-caste who bounced his mum around the walls of their slovenly living-room when she wouldn't turn tricks in order to supply his pocket money.

Jimmy Maggs aka The Junkie was just that. A glue sniffer at twelve, he'd graduated to mainlining smack by the time he was fifteen, with a touch at most of the stops along the way. When times were hard Maggs had been known to snort Brillo powder just to remind himself of the real thing.

The other four weren't much better. Johnny Crawford had begun his criminal career nicking fruit from barrows down the lane whilst in his pre-teens. Then he'd moved on to shoplifting from Woolies, until eventually he'd made the quantum leap to specializing in robbing sub-post offices run by Asian families. He'd done one short stretch for ABH, but that was all. For some reason the Asian postmasters could never give a description of the robber. Johnny told them graphically what would happen to their wives and children if they did.

Jason Ford, Little Jase to his mates, was an angel-faced twenty-year-old black youth who looked about thirteen. He was small and slim and handsome, with a mouthful of white teeth that smiled all the time. He liked rap music and stabbing people. Not necessarily in that order.

Alan Bird was a white-haired half-German, who'd been born to an army sergeant father and the wife he'd met in Dortmund and brought home to London. Mrs B. wasn't too keen on the Aylesbury, and soon hopped it after her husband dragged her there to keep house for the trio, and Sergeant Bird's incontinent mother. The German lady had been a real beauty by all accounts, and ended up living with a pop star in Cheyne Walk. Alan ran wild when his alcoholic father gave up the contest between the booze and being a daddy. Alan was a hard sod. He wasn't big but he fought like a demon. He was a jack of all trades, but preferred robbery with violence, preferably if the violence was meted out with a pick-axe handle.

That left Peter Parker. A large, moon-faced individual with an IQ about the same size as his dick. And he wasn't called Tinymeat for nothing. His one asset was his ability to drive, repair and steal any make and model of motor car he'd ever come across.

So that was Dago's bunch. They were all hard except for Parker, who was as soft as a fresh doughnut. They were all young. All used soft and/or hard drugs to some extent. They all had a history of juvenile crime. All had been on probation. Some had done community service or short, sharp shock. Only one had done adult time. All had been known to carry firearms at some time or another, and a blade was just another fashion accessory. But they moved as one round the streets. They protected each other. Their world was concrete and glass, and when trouble loomed they vanished back into the safety of the estate. They were clean and clever. But not for long. Eddie and I made sure of that.

When we got to the hospital the girl was rushed into intensive care. We hung around until some uniforms arrived, but as I was getting funny looks from patients and staff alike, still dressed in my sports rig, we thumbed a lift from a squad car and headed back to the nick. I got changed, and the pair of us pushed off for a drink at The Early Hours. We were both walking a thin line in our careers by then. We were hanging on to our jobs by the skin of our teeth and we both knew it. They say, whoever *they* are, that all villains could be coppers and all coppers villains. In Eddie's and my case they weren't far wrong, especially Eddie's.

Eddie was a hard man. As hard as they breed in the badlands of Essex. He was big too, and made even bigger by the look in his eyes. He even scared me sometimes when he glared up from underneath his eyebrows and his eyes went as cold as drops of January rain. Yet underneath the hardness, if you looked long enough, was something else. Only when he relaxed did it show, and he was a very tense individual who didn't relax often. But I'd seen that something else when we shared a squad car together for eighteen months. You don't have many secrets from your partner in a white Rover with a blue light on top. Eddie was just Eddie. Maybe he was half mental like some said, but there was no one on the force I'd sooner have covering my back in a bad situation.

He'd been married for a while, but it hadn't worked for one reason or another. The job mainly. But that was about par for the course. By that time his mum and dad had moved to Norwood. He'd moved there himself after his marriage broke up and his father died. That was when he transferred to the Met and we got together. He took over the basement of his mother's house and made a pretty good job of converting and decorating it. He put in all kinds of security devices to protect his little toys. They were the love of his life that I told you about. Eddie was a gun freak. Had been since he was a boy. His first weapon, he told me, was a Daisy air pistol. He'd moved on since then, collecting any gun he could get his hands on. Guns were the main reason he'd joined the force. He could learn more about guns, use the shooting range for free, but most important of all, he could appropriate guns for his own use.

I suppose we were like a little firm ourselves. Me and Eddie and half a dozen or so others. But me and Eddie were the ringleaders. Where we went the others followed. We charged up and down the town from Putney to Rotherhithe and back, and they acted like they loved us in the pubs and clubs we frequented. Did they fuck. They hated us. We screwed their wives and girlfriends and didn't pay for our meals or drinks. We could have gone on like it for years. But me and Eddie started taking backhanders. No big deal. Just a few quid for looking the other way, and we soon spunked it away on women and booze and nice clothes. Then the two of us got into coke. It was easy to get round South London in them days. Still is, I suppose. Specially if you had a warrant card.

The other faces dropped out pretty quick. No one seemed able to keep up, and the few that tried soon got the good word. We were on a one-way journey to deep trouble, but I don't think anyone guessed how bad it was going to get.

Of course Eddie was right about Dago. We never got him for the rape. The girl, whose name turned out to be Sarah Campbell, never mentioned him again. She had a round-the-clock police guard whilst she was in the ICU. Hardly any visitors, just immediate family. What the hell was there to see? Just a hank of hair sticking out of a swathe of bandage. But by the time she could talk, she wouldn't. I even interviewed her myself. Dago? Never heard the name. Some fat chance. She lived on the Aylesbury herself. Dago's mum was her aunty's best friend. Sarah had been got at. Just like the rest, and it pissed me off.

It pissed Eddie off too. One night he and I were in the boozer near Kennington Cross. Eddie was drunk and snorting coke and ranting on about Dago's mob. 'They'll never go down,' he said bitterly. 'Unless we put them down ourselves.'

'How?' I asked.

'Fit the fuckers right up.'

'It's been tried.' I was an expert on them by then.

'Fit them up permanent.'

'Tell me about it.'

'Those prats are laughing at us.'

'Them and a thousand others,' I said.

'It's them I want.'

'What, for your collection?'

'I'm not kidding.' I could tell.

'How?' I asked.

'Set the fuckers up, and blow them away.'

'Are you serious?'

'Never more so, my son.'

'We can't'

'Why not? I've got the firepower.'

'We can't just shoot them in cold blood.'

'Why not? Seems like a reasonable idea to me. Rid the streets of some vermin. A public service.'

I couldn't think of an argument against it, not off-hand.

'How?' I said.

'Think about it. We know exactly where they are, regular, one morning a week, after their little night out. Right or wrong?'

He was right. The chaps had settled into a routine. Every Wednesday night, come what may, they got together for a little meet. At first it had been local. Then as they got a few quid in their pockets they thought that an evening up in town would be in order. So they began to head up West or down the King's Road. Always in one car, always law-abiding. They'd start off in a wine bar, then on to an expensive restaurant. They loved to chuck money around and be treated like little gentlemen. After dinner they'd go on to a disco and maybe wind up the night with a little gambling. It became a regular outing. And at six sharp, winter or summer, Dago took them back home, and his mum brought out the bacon and eggs and fried slices so that the boys could have a bit of breakfast before hitting the sack. We'd kept an eye on them but they weren't breaking any laws that we could see. Peter did all the driving and he didn't drink so we couldn't even bust him on a drunk in charge. Anyway, at least one night a week we knew roughly where they were, and that one bunch of villains was out of circulation, if only temporarily.

'They're always there,' Eddie went on, suddenly sober. 'That's the one mistake they make every week. They're like a bunch of old men off to the pub every Sunday for their roast potatoes. You do your arse bandit act. They'll never resist you in your running gear. Look. When they see you coming they'll never guess what you really are. They'll think you're a poof with a skinny little arse. They'll think it's their birthday. Someone easy. Someone to push around with no comebacks. They start performing and I come out shooting.'

'Come out from where?' I asked. It was important. To me at least.

He waved his hand in the air as if it was a minor detail. 'I don't know. We'll think of something.'

'It's a bit thin.'

'It's a million.'

'You're fucking mental.'

'How much more can you take from them?' he said.

'We're coppers. Not vigilantes.'

'We're what we need to be.'

'Then we go down. For ever.'

'Self-defence.'

'Eddie. Don't talk such shit. No jury's going to wear that. You're pissed.'

'Pissed off. How many more little girls do you want to find like we found Sarah? Come on, tell me. How many?'

My mind went back to her broken body, with her

pathetic fingers trying to hide her bloody pubic hair, and the dried blood and come on her thighs. 'Maybe you're right,' I said.

''Course I am. I'm fed up with this shit.' His gesture took in the whole world. 'I don't care what happens to me anymore. I've had this fucking crap up to my fucking eyeballs. Those fuckers are poncing round like they own this town. We're supposed to keep the streets free from scum like that. But all we do is sit around shitholes like this begging drinks off civilians. I want to be a policeman again. I want vengeance. I want revenge. I want justice for all the little Sarahs who get pissed on, and can't do anything about it. If you won't help I'll do it on my own.'

I knew I couldn't leave him to it. We were friends. That was all that mattered.

So the seeds were planted over a table covered with sticky glasses and dead cigarette ends. The seeds that flowered into bloody murder.

It didn't take long to get it together. Once these things start rolling they never do. Eddie showed me the gun I was going to use. A Mossberg Model 500 Persuader ATP8 model. 12 gauge, pump action with an eight-shot capacity and a twenty-inch barrel. Ideal for the conditions. We were down in his gun room.

If the commissioner could have seen Eddie's collection, mostly illegal, he'd have had kittens. Right on the floor in front of us.

'You've used this before,' said Eddie. So I had. Firing at clay pigeons and beer cans. Never human beings. I said as much.

'They're not human,' said Eddie.

He showed me the gun he was going to use too. The pride of his collection. A Colt Model I-3 Python .357 magnum, six-shot, double or single action, with an eight-inch barrel. It was over thirteen inches long and weighed nearly three pounds fully loaded. A hell of a gun.

We worked out a plan together over bottles of lager and the sandwiches Eddie's mother brought in every couple of hours. It was simple. We were going to borrow a truck from the motor pool at the station. We knew exactly which one. A rusty old Ford Transit that looked like shit and went like hell. We knew where Peter parked the car. Right in front of the block where Dago lived. We knew because we watched. I would jog around the corner and catch the boys' attention. Eddie would drive round after me, stop the truck, introduce himself, and between us we'd kill anything that moved. Simple. Then ... Well, we'd worry about then later. Eddie took the truck out on the Wednesday morning, all legit. He stashed it in a council car-park in Rye Lane. The guns were hidden in a canvas bag under the floor in a box that had been built in by our lot when the Transit was new.

So that's how we ended up drinking and snorting cocaine in a scabby bar over a betting shop in Peckham High Street, and finally how I came to be running round the streets of the Elephant at five forty-five on a Thursday morning dressed in lilac running strip. I ask you. There just aren't that many fitness freaks in that part of the world. Not in the Aylesbury for sure. I mean the fucking army wouldn't go in there.

I turned into Stanley Street and there they were. Just a bunch of regular geezers back from a night out. As soon as I saw them I felt the short hairs on my neck and the backs of my arms and legs begin to rise as if it was suddenly cold.

They saw me at about the same time. They were grouped round a big red Mercedes-Benz saloon. I don't know how they did it. After all, these boys were officially trying to exist on their Giros from the DSS.

There they stood, all six of them, cool as a sea breeze, and deadly as a collection of poisonous snakes.

One of their girls was with them. There were two or three who hung out with our heroes. They were passed round the firm like sauce bottles in a cheap café, when nothing better was available. The girls knew what was going on. They weren't debutantes. Sometimes they even took part to a greater or lesser extent. They were gore groupies one and all. This one was called Carla. Carla West. She was a good-looking woman, with white skin and a tumble of thick black hair which was pulled back and knotted in a pony tail. She looked great as long as she kept her mouth shut. When she opened it she could empty an Irish doss house with her gutter language. If she worked, which was rarely, she served behind a succession of bars, or one of her numerous relatives' market stalls. That particular morning she was wearing a bright yellow dress that was just a few hours overdue a visit to the cleaners. It was short and tight, and cut low to show off her extensive cleavage. But in the harsh morning light it was grubby and she'd spilled something on the skirt. Still, she'd do a turn, I guessed. Johnny Crawford had one proprietorial arm around her shoulders when I turned the corner. It must have been his turn for a shake at the bottle.

I kept moving towards them, my head down, but I peered up under my eyelids as I got closer. They fanned out to block the pavement. I checked them out. Between them they had it all together. There was enough sharp flannel and shiny mohair and crumpled silk to stock a Bond Street boutique. I knew for a fact that at least three murders, more robberies than you could decently shake a stick at, and one or two particularly nasty assaults had financed their appearance.

Dago nudged Parker who asked no one in particular, 'Who's this cunt then?'

'You're a nice boy, aren't you?' said Dago, who was wearing a pale grey suit, double breasted, with the jacket undone. The sun caught the silver of his belt buckle and splashed the reflection into my eyes. His light blue shirt was open at the collar and the knot of his multi-coloured tie was pulled down to the second button. On his feet he wore grey leather lace-ups. He was the one I wanted most. He was the one that Sarah had identified by name. He'd been arrested twice previously for rape. Once on an eighty-six-year-old and once on an eleven-year-old girl. Not particularly choosy was our Dago. If it moved, fuck it, was his motto. Both times he'd been released through lack of evidence. The other five had seen to that. They'd let it be known that anyone who was prepared to make a statement should book a single ticket in a black Daimler limo. Dago liked to hurt people. Women especially. I was hoping he liked to hurt homosexuals too, or anyone he thought was homosexual.

I stopped running and tried to look confused, as if I'd been interrupted whilst deep in thought. I looked at them properly for the first time and stepped back as if frightened. To tell you the truth I was, just a bit, but getting less so. Up close they were just a bunch of wankers.

Dago liked that. The fear bit. Cunts like him always do. 'Right pretty, ain't he?' he said. I felt the sweat trickle down from my armpits, and behind me I heard the sound of the Transit's engine as it turned the corner and stopped. They paid it no attention. They were the lords and masters here.

Maggs decided it was his turn to get into the act. He slipped out of his linen Harrington jacket. Underneath he was wearing a pink polo shirt. From the tight sleeves his arms emerged like twin hawsers, ropy with muscle and scarred with old track marks. He scratched at his crotch as he moved round to flank me. I moved back to keep him at arm's length, and get closer to the Transit. Dago lunged at me and I jumped. He laughed. It was a horrible sound. I wondered if he'd laughed like that at Sarah. 'Chicken,' he said, smiling.

All of a sudden Little Jase was at my elbow. I swallowed hard and felt the sun's heat full on my back. The other three and the girl leaned casually up against the Mercedes to enjoy the show. Dago came towards me again. I stepped even further back and my spine connected with a lamppost. I slithered round to get it between me and my three opponents and force them to separate. Dago slipped his hand into his back pocket and produced a gravity knife. Everything went quiet as he released the blade with an oily click. The street was as still as a photograph. I stood with one hand on the cool concrete of the lamppost, keeping it between me and Dago, who was holding the six-inch blade. Even the pigeons seemed to be holding their breath.

The creak from the back doors of the Transit as they opened split the silence like an axe through a ripe melon. Seven pairs of eyes moved round to the battered old truck. Eddie stepped out on to the street dressed in an oily boiler suit over his clothes, and carrying the Mossberg in his right hand with the barrel pointing towards the sky. 'Morning all,' he said.

I kicked out with my foot and it connected cleanly with Dago's right wrist. The knife spun into the air, twinkling in the sun. It fell into the front garden of the block and stuck, handle upwards in the dirt. Dago looked at his empty hand and then at me in surprise. 'Cunt,' he mouthed.

'Language,' I said, and hit him in the throat with the tips of the stiffened fingers of my right hand. He fell to his knees, clawing at his neck and vomited the remains of last night's dinner, and all the expensive wine he's consumed, down the front of his jacket. I kicked him in the head just for badness' sake. The thud of my trainer connecting with his skull galvanized some action. Peter Parker bounced off the bonnet of the Merc as if he'd been goosed up his jacksie. He was probably showing off for the girl. Not a good idea, all things considered. He ran towards Eddie, who smiled a rare smile and transferred the shotgun to his left hand. With his right he produced the Colt from the pocket of his overalls and hit Parker across the face with the barrel. Parker screamed a long, drawn-out animal sound and dropped to his knees. I could see that Eddie's blow had revealed the white of Parker's cheekbone. I told you it was a heavy gun. He held his face together with his fingers and blood began to leak down his sleeve. Eddie bounced the barrel of the gun off the top of his head, and he rolled into the gutter where he lay still. Alan Bird dived over the garden wall and went for the knife. Eddie fired the Python, and the bullet clipped a lump of brick off the top of the wall. I grabbed Little Jase by a handful of his short dreadlocks and mashed his face into the lamppost. I heard his nose break like an elastic band snapping, and twin streams of blood and muscus shot from his nostrils.

'Gun,' shouted Eddie, and threw the Mossberg to me. It arced through the air, casting a long, dark shadow on the pavement like a bird swooping towards its prey. The pump slapped into my left palm and I pulled the butt into my hip with my right. I chambered a shell in one smooth motion, and the chunk-chunk of the action sounded loud in my ears. Dago staggered to his feet and stood unsteadily facing me. He held his throat with one hand and the other crawled slowly across his chest and under his jacket.

That's when I should have declared myself. 'Armed police,' is what I should have said. 'Stand still or I'll shoot,' is what I should have said, and perhaps something of law and order could have been saved. Instead I watched Dago's hand go under his vomit-caked lapel and I simply said, 'This is for Sarah.' And pulled the trigger. In the split second between the words and the deed, before the load of buckshot took him in the chest, I saw realization fill Dago's eyes. For one moment. The last moment of his life, he knew that I knew what he'd done. And he knew what he was paying for. Then the shot knocked him back against the wall and he fell to the pavement. The recoil of the Mossberg cracked me painfully in the hip bone. I pumped the action and crouched down, gently fanning the gun across those that were still standing.

'You've killed him,' whispered Maggs.

Even then, there was still time to regain some semblance of civilized behaviour. I looked over at Eddie. He was grinning crazily. Fuck it, I thought. 'I hope so,' I said to Maggs. 'And you're next, you little cunt.' And I shot him too.

That was when the shit really hit the fan. Suddenly the smooth choreography of Eddie's and my plan turned into chaos. Everything seemed to happen at once. Crawford came alive all of a sudden. He grabbed Carla by her arm and pulled her in front of himself. His other hand snaked towards his jacket pocket, and he produced an automatic pistol.

'He's armed, Eddie. Watch it,' I shouted.

Then Alan Bird popped back over the garden wall with Dago's gravity knife in his fist. I'd forgotten about him. That almost finished it.

I couldn't get a clear shot at Crawford with the girl in the way. Eddie wasn't so chivalrous. He dropped to the ground and snapped off a shot without really taking aim. The bullet went neatly through Carla's throat and up to blow the top of Crawford's head off. I clamped my teeth together to hold back a shout of horror, or a laugh, I didn't know which, as I saw a new orifice created by the bullet in the smooth skin of her neck. Blood fountained down over her breasts and on to the bright material of her dress. She cannoned back into Crawford's body and the pair fell in a tumble of arms and legs and flesh and blood and bone splinters. The automatic hit the pavement with a clatter.

Bird was looking from one body to another. I think it was too much even for a vicious little bastard like him. Then Maggs came back from the dead. He rolled over from where he was lying. His face was a mask and the front of his body was a mass of blood and guts, and his polo shirt was still smoking from the shot I'd fired into him at point blank range. In his hand was the automatic that Crawford had dropped. He aimed it at Eddie and I saw his finger tighten on the trigger, as Alan Bird screamed something I couldn't understand and charged at me, the gravity knife held at arm's length. I fired for a third time directly at the gun that Maggs held. It flew on to the pavement, his hand still attached. Then I fired at Bird, but the shot went high and wide. The load took him in the shoulder and blew meat from bone but he kept coming. I fired again, almost panicking. A direct hit. Eddie was firing at him too, double action, and I could see the bullets ripping at his clothes. But still he came through a mist of his own blood that he breathed out through his open mouth.

He was slowing, but not enough to avoid the inevitable collision. He stumbled, tripped and fell. The knife plunged into my leg just above the knee with a horrible thud. A sound I'll never forget. The pain was like a kick from a steel-tipped boot. I fired down again into Bird's back as he lay half on and half off the pavement. Half in and half out of the gutter. The barrel of the Mossberg was red hot and my eardrums felt as if they had ruptured from the concussions of the explosions.

I reached down and started to pull the blade out of my

leg, but blood began to spurt and I knew that it had cut into an artery so I pushed it back to plug the hole.

The pain was worse. My hand was slippery with my own blood and I knew I didn't have many shells left in the gun. I looked around for more people to shoot. I was beginning to enjoy myself.

Little Jase came up from the ground like a fucking athlete. An Olympic runner. A regular Linford Christie. He was hurt but moved like lightning. But no one could move faster than the muzzle velocity of my trusty old Mossberg. I watched him running down the road. So did Eddie. We fired in unison. Eddie's bullet took him in the side. The shotgun load blew his legs from underneath him, and he skidded along the path on his face to stop in a shower of black plastic garbage sacks.

That's how we both missed Parker at first. He'd crawled back to the Mercedes and pulled his fat body into the driver's seat. The saloon's ignition ground, then caught with a roar. I saw the car lurch as he slammed it into gear, then with a screech of rubber, peel away from the kerb and head directly to where Eddie was standing in the middle of the road. I screamed his name and spun on my heel of my injured leg. The pain hit like a hammer and I felt myself falling towards the pavement. As I watched, time slowed. Eddie fired his pistol at the car. I heard glass smash. The huge vehicle swerved and caught Eddie with its radiator, tossing him into the air like a spastic doll. The car skidded, hit the Transit, bounced off and rolled over Eddie on to its roof which collapsed into itself with a crunch. I felt my head hit the kerb and a blood-red fog swept over my eyes. I fired the shotgun once more in the direction of the smoking car, but only heard faintly the click of the firing pin on the empty chamber, before the red mist went black and I slid into unconsciousness.

So I never got to survey the scene.

The blood on the pavement was thick and turning brown and crawling with flies when the first uniforms arrived. Someone said later that it looked like a butcher's shop window that had exploded. Like I said I never saw it, and I never saw my best friend's body crushed by the weight of the Mercedes-Benz. I never saw any of it. Only in photographs. I never saw it. I did it. That was enough for anyone.

Too Late Blues

This story was originally written as an outline for a proposed episode of the TV series *The Bill*. It was sent to the programme makers and returned with a very snotty letter letting me know in no uncertain terms that a) I wasn't a scriptwriter, a fact I've never disputed, and b) it failed to feature a single member of *The Bill* cast. A fact I thought was a plus after having watched the show go down-hill for years. I later met one of the producers of the show at a Carlton scriptwriter's course I attended that confirmed (a) completely. And I totally burnt my bridges with him by saying I thought that the programme was a sad apology for a corrupt regime. There was supposed to be a second story/episode starring the wonderful DI Burnside, but after he quit the sinking ship it never got written.

I still like it, and the title was pinched from a film starring Bobby Darin and Stella Stevens.

If Ronnie hadn't forgotten his cigarettes it would have been all right.

I don't smoke, and Derek only smokes spliff, so Ronnie couldn't even ponce one off either of us. All the way from his place into town, he was going on about it, and he was beginning to get right on my nerves. When we got close to the centre he said, 'We've got time. Pull over, and I'll get some fags in that shop. I won't be a minute.'

Except it's just past nine in the morning, and the shop's

full of schoolkids, and people buying papers, and Ronnie takes considerably longer, and I'm parked on a bus lane. I never even saw the copper. He must have come through the buildings. First thing I know Derek looks round for Ronnie and says, 'Filth.'

I nearly shit myself. I look round too, and there he is. I can only see his middle through the back window. But I can see well enough to know he's a cozzer, and he's writing in his notebook. Then I see Ronnie behind him, and the next thing is the back door's open and they're both in the car, and Ronnie's torn off the copper's radio and tossed it in the front, and he's got his gun stuck in the copper's face. It was unreal because the copper was just a kid, see. He looked like he didn't even shave yet, and before Ronnie knocked it off I saw that his helmet was too big for him. That made it worse somehow, the fact that his bleeding hat didn't even fit. They should have given him one that did before they let him out on the street.

So now we're on the way to a blag, and we've got a bleeding copper as a passenger. I mean, I ask you. And what's even worse is that the local CID are waiting for us to arrive.

You've got to understand I didn't want to grass. I hate grasses. I'd string the bleeders up if I had my way. But Ronnie and Derek were well mental, always armed. A menace to society, and it was only a matter of time before they were back inside with my help or without it. And I'd been captured pulling a stroke of my own a couple of weeks previous. Nothing serious, but with my form I was for the high jump, and that little sod of a DI who nicked me knew it. I told him that Ronnie and Derek had asked me to drive for them on a little over-the-pavement tickle. But I'd turned them down flat. I mean I hate shooters, worse than grasses, worse than nonces even.

The DI worked out that if I went back to the pair of

them and told them I'd changed my mind, and went out on the job and filled in the DI in plenty of time, all would be sweet. He'd get a result. Ronnie and Derek would get their just deserts and I'd get another chance, and maybe a few quid for my trouble out of the informant's fund.

And now what I've got is some young copper lying on the floor in the back of the Granada and a big load of trouble.

'Drive, for Christ's sake,' says Ronnie. 'Before someone susses us out.'

I remembered what I was supposed to be doing then, and I slaps the motor into gear and takes off smartish. Too smartish, as I nearly take the side off a Telecom van, and get well tooted up and a mouthful of abuse for my trouble. If the fat ponce driving had known we had two guns on board, and two nutters carrying them, he would have kept his gob shut. 'Take it easy,' says Ronnie.

'Do what?' I said to him. 'Don't you tell me to take it easy. You're the one who's kidnapped a copper. What the bloody hell did you do that for?'

'What was I supposed to do, shoot him in the bloody street?'

'You weren't supposed to shoot him at all. You were supposed to take the ticket like a punter, and let him get on with his life.'

'Yeah, and if he'd radioed through for a registration check on the car, what then?'

'The car hasn't even been missed yet,' I said. I knew that for a fact. I'd been checking the railway station car park for a week. The geezer who belonged to the Granada parked it up at 7.30 a.m., and picked it up again at 6 p.m. He was as regular as a cat fed on goose grease.

'But you can't prove it's yours, can you?' said Ronnie.

'But he can't prove it ain't. Look at the state of him, he's just a boy. He'd've given me a form to produce my licence within five days, and we'd've been on our bloody way.'

And then the poxy radio does start performing, and I nearly jump out of my skin, and Derek stamps on it until it's quiet, and in little pieces all over the rubber mat in the front.

'Do you think anyone saw?' I asked.

'No,' said Ronnie. 'It was too quick.'

But how the hell would he know?

'Well, what are we going to do with him now?' I asked.

'I don't know,' says Ronnie. Not a great thinker, Ronnie. A great doer, but not a great thinker.

'Let him go,' I said.

'How can we? He's got the number of the car and we're off to knock over a Securicor truck.'

'He didn't know that, did he?' I said.

'Well he knows now for sure,' said Derek.

'So we can't let him go,' said Ronnie.

I knew what he meant, but I pretended I didn't and said, 'We can't take him with us. Let's forget the whole thing.'

Which wasn't going to please the DI and DS and four DCs waiting outside Barclays in the high street, all tooled up, expecting two armed black men in balaclava helmets to rob the truck delivering cash for the weekend rush.

I was meant to get away in all the excitement. That was the deal.

'Sling him out,' I said. 'And let's go home.'

'Bollocks,' said Ronnie. 'He's clocked us.'

'He'll never recognize you,' I said.

'Why, 'cos we all look the same to you lot?' Ronnie said, and he was right nasty with it.

'You know I don't meant that,' I said. Christ, we'd shared a cell together long enough. When you've heard someone doing a shit in the middle of the night it stops mattering what colour their skin is. What I'd meant was, that as he was wearing the balaclava rolled down to just above his eyes, like a woollen cap, and as the collar of his jacket was turned right up, even his own mother would have had trouble recognizing him. Besides, he didn't even look like Ronnie, not the Ronnie I knew anyway. Not with that excited look in his eyes and his nostrils flared and the pistol in his hand. All I could see was that pistol in his hand, and I was willing to bet that it was all the young copper could see too.

'He'll recognize you, though,' said Derek to me, and he was right.

'So that's it,' said Ronnie. 'He goes.'

'Goes where?' I asked.

'Policeman's heaven,' said Ronnie.

'You can't do that,' I said.

'Shut up, you,' says Ronnie, and I can see he's beginning to lose his rag. 'What are you going to do about it? You're not even carrying, raas. The next time I go away, I go away hard. They'd chuck away the key, just for me having this.' He lifted the gun slightly. 'Conspiracy to rob on top and I'm fucked. I ain't going away again, I'm telling you. I'll kill this bastard first.'

'No,' said the young copper. It was the first time he'd said anything, and it shut the rest of us up for a minute.

'I won't tell,' he went on.

Ronnie and Derek had a right chuckle at that. I didn't think it was all that funny.

'It's my first day,' said the copper.

'Do what?' says Ronnie.

'My first day out on my own.'

'Your bad luck, son,' says Ronnie. 'It's not exactly going to be a long career, is it?' And him and Derek have another good old laugh. 'Drive down by the river,' Ronnie says to me.

'What about the job?' says Derek.

'We'll nish it for now. There's always another week. If it wasn't for you, you bastard,' says Ronnie, and hits the copper with the barrel of the gun, like it was his fault, which in a small way it was.

So I did what I was told and drove down to the river, and we found a bit of waste ground, and Ronnie drags the copper out of the car. He makes him take off his tunic and wrap it round his head. The poor kid was crying by then. I felt sick and could hardly look, and even Derek wasn't happy. But Ronnie didn't care. He's right cold-blooded when he gets started, is Ronnie. If I'd tried to stop him he'd have done for me too. Ronnie takes the copper down by the river and does the business. I hardly heard the shot. Maybe he wrapped something around the pistol too. But even so, the noise frightened a flock of gulls away from whatever they were doing.

I cleared the bits of broken radio out of the front of the car, and put them in the kid's helmet and threw it down a hole, between the foundations of some old building that had been knocked down years ago.

Ronnie came back holding the gun down by his side, but like it wasn't there, or he wished it wasn't, if you know what I mean. He was about as pale as any lemonade was ever going to be. I think even he'd realized he'd gone too far that time.

'He's dead,' he said. 'Let's go. Forget this ever happened, both of you.'

I wish I could. I really do. But pretty soon that bastard of a DI's going to come and find me.

Christ knows what I'm going to do then.

Night Moves

What a commotion as Sharman gets mixed up with some loan sharks. There's a lot of this sort of action round South London, and some of it does end with dirty deeds in seedy pubs, which, as you might have guessed, are among my favourite locations. And, I might add, my favourite haunts. The title is from a Bob Seger song.

I was sitting in a pub in the Elephant and Castle on a cold morning in early January. Early enough so that the Christmas decorations were still up. Not my favourite time of year. Not my favourite part of the world, and not my favourite pub either. But I was meeting a bloke. An old acquaintance. He had some work for me. He owned an electrical goods warehouse in Lee Green, and he was losing a lot of gear. It was positively flying out of the door, he reckoned. He had a staff of about twenty, and he hadn't got a clue which of them was at it. So he asked if I'd have a nose round. I was meeting him in the boozer because he didn't want anyone to know he was hiring me. The idea was that he'd put me in as a relief driver or something. Working undercover. Not the best job I've ever had, but I needed a new set of tyres for the motor, and needs must. He was late, and I was already starting on my second pint of watery lager. At almost two quid a pint it wasn't cheap, and I was bored enough to work out how much tread I could get for the money I'd spent.

The place was morning quiet. A couple of geezers in one

corner working out the black economy price for a bit of
roof work and, sitting at the bar, a big bloke in his early
thirties. He was huge across the shoulders, like someone
who worked out a lot, wearing a mid-blue suit, white shirt
and tie, and knocking back the large Scotches as quickly
as the barmaid could fill his glass. He had a familiar look.
But a lot of geezers who hung around the Elephant had
similar, and I didn't know him.

Anyway, just as the hands of the clock behind the bar
reached high noon, the pub door opened, and two more
faces came in. Both in long navy-blue double-breasted
overcoats. They were a hard pair, but I'd've been willing
to bet the nanny-goats were real cashmere. They looked
like they had a couple of stalls down East Street, a
resprayed Roller on an N or M plate each, bought on the
drip, parked outside the council flats that their brassy
missuses kept like little palaces, while their hubbies were
chasing scrubbers down the Old Kent Road on a Saturday,
when the boozers don't shut till two in the morning.

Now one of these two I *did* know. Definitely. His name
was Chris Tennyson, and we'd gone to the same grammar
school together. Even though it was twenty-five years later,
I'd've known him in a minute. Not that I was about to
chat about the best years of our lives. I didn't see him as a
leading light in the Old Boys' Association, any more than
I was.

He didn't see me, sitting where I was, out of the way
between a fruit machine and the Rock-Ola. The pair of
them just walked over to the ice-cream in the blue suit and
Chris put his hand under his coat and dragged out a short-
barrelled revolver that looked like a .357 magnum from
where I was sitting, and the other geezer let his coat fall
open and pulled up a sawn-off pump-action shotgun on a
piece of electrical cable that was slung over his shoulder.
Chris put the barrel of the pistol under the geezer in the

blue suit's chin and pulled the trigger, and most of his head splashed across the notice-board, where details of the pub's pool, darts and football teams' fixtures, printed on exercise-book paper, were pinned up. Then he stepped back, and the other character pulled the trigger of the pump and blew a great big hole just where the top button of the geezer's mid-blue suit jacket was. Even though the bloke's body was hard, solid and muscular, the shot was so close and so powerful that loops of hot, red blood snaked off his torso and slapped on to the wall behind him, and the front of his suit smoked and burned briefly. This took less time than it takes to tell, and my ears were still ringing from the noise of the gun-shots, and the bar was full of blue smoke and the stink of gunpowder, and worse: the smell of the inside of a human body ripped open and suddenly exposed to the air.

Then it was all over. The bloke in the blue suit had been blown clean off his stool by the shotgun blast, and landed in an untidy heap on the carpet. Chris and his mate started backing towards the main door, keeping the guns they were carrying moving in slow arcs across the empty air in front of them. The barmaid, who I couldn't help noticing had got some of the geezer in the blue suit's brain on the front of her jumper, started screaming. A relentless sound like a car alarm going in the middle of the night, with no one taking a blind bit of notice.

As they reached the door, Chris caught sight of me, and that's when I saw recognition in his eyes. Just for a moment, before he put the gun back under his arm, and his mate let the pump drop back under his coat, which he quickly buttoned up. But I knew he'd recognized me, just as I'd recognized him, and I knew it meant trouble. Big trouble.

They pushed through the door, and I stood up from where I was sitting, picked up the glass I'd been using and walked up to the bar. The geezers who'd been doing a bit of business looked at me before they hit the trail to anonymity, leaving just me and the barmaid, who was still screaming, and the corpse of the guy in the blue suit all alone. There was a drying-up cloth on top of the counter and I used it to wipe my fingerprints off the glass. I looked at the barmaid and she looked at me, and still screaming she reached out her hand towards me. I ignored it. Maybe not the nicest thing I've ever done in my life, and if I hadn't recognized Chris Tennyson, perhaps I'd have acted differently. Maybe I would have answered that keening plea, and taken her hand and comforted her. Instead I started to walk across the carpet towards the door. When I was less than halfway there, a door behind the bar opened and a smallish, moustachioed man in an open-necked shirt, braces and dark-grey suit trousers came through. He stopped on the threshold. Christ knows what he thought had happened.

Above the barmaid's racket I said: 'Call the police. And look after her. She's not hurt.' Then I turned and walked the rest of the way towards the door and out into the street. My car was parked around the corner and I went and got in it and drove off.

I parked it again in a twenty-four-hour NCP in Holborn and started hitting the pubs. When the pubs shut, I went to Gerry's club in Dean Street. When that closed, I went round to see Helen at Troy's off Tottenham Court Road, and when she slung me out of there I walked down to the Piano Bar in Brewer Street, where I got into a conversation with a transvestite who was more attractive than most of the women I'd met lately, and stayed there until they finally shut at three-thirty.

I abandoned the car to the four winds and caught a lobster home. I had the driver drop me at the top of my road, and wandered slowly down, checking out the parked motors as I went. I didn't see anything that struck me as suss in the freezing night air, and I let myself in at the front door of the house and walked up the stairs to my flat on the top floor.

I put the key in the door, opened it and stepped inside. I touched the switch on the wall, and the dim forty-watt bulb I'd put in the centre fixture struggled into life. I hate too much light.

They were sitting waiting for me. Chris Tennyson on the bed, his mate in the armchair. Chris held the .357. His pal, the sawn-off. I froze, still with one hand on the switch, the other on the edge of the door.

Shit, I thought. Why the hell did I have to go into that lousy pub, today of all days?

'You're late,' said Chris conversationally. 'We thought you were never coming. I was just saying you must have gone case with some bird.' He grinned. 'But never mind. You're here now. Come on in, mate. Long time, no see.'

For one split second I thought about turning and running, slamming the door behind me. But I knew the magnum would chop it to pieces and me with it before I got to the top of the stairs. And if the magnum missed, the spread of the shotgun's load would blow a hole in my back big enough to park a car. I'd seen what it had done to the geezer in the pub. So I just stayed where I was.

'Come in and shut the door,' instructed Chris. 'We need to talk.'

I did as I was told, and stood in the middle of the room facing the pair of them. Chris nodded his head, and his mate put the shotgun down next to the chair, got up, and carefully avoiding getting in the line of fire walked round behind me and frisked me through the heavy coat I was wearing against the weather.

'He's clean,' he grunted, and walked back, sat down and picked up the shotgun again.

I was, as a matter of fact. Clean as a whistle. And all of a sudden I wished that I had a little .25 stuck in my sock or somewhere else similar.

'How long has it been?' asked Chris, casually.

I shrugged. 'Years,' I replied. 'I was in 4C, and you were in the sixth form.'

'You've got a good memory.'

I nodded. 'How did you find me?' I asked.

'Easy. You're famous round here.'

'You too, now,' I replied. 'I bet you're on everyone's most wanted list.'

He smiled easily. But then he always had. 'One of those things,' he said. 'Except no one but you knows who did it.'

'What about the barmaid, and the other people in the pub?' I asked.

'They're no problem,' said Chris. 'No problem at all. You're the only fly in the ointment as far as we're concerned. A very large fly. A bluebottle, almost.'

I ignored the comment and the veiled threat that went with it. 'What did the geezer do? The geezer you shot,' I asked.

'He owed us money,' said the other face. He had a deep voice. 'He was taking the piss. We couldn't let him do that. We had to make an example. Otherwise they'd all think they could do it.'

I didn't ask what he owed them money for. Or who he was. That wasn't my main concern.

'So what happens now?' I asked.

'We've been discussing that,' said Chris. 'All day.'

'And?'

'And I'm afraid we've come to only one conclusion.'

'What's that, then?'

'Well, sad as it may seem, you know who I am. We

didn't expect anyone to be in that boozer who'd recognize either of us. It's not where we operate normally, see.'

I didn't say a word or move or anything. But I saw.

'Now me,' he went on, 'I'm all for letting sleeping dogs lie. But Chesney here,' he nodded towards his mate, 'he's of a different persuasion. He hates loose ends. And unfortunately, Nick, you come into the loose end category.'

'So?' I said.

'So we're going to have to make sure that you don't let slip who I am.'

'I suppose there's no point in me saying I didn't see a thing.'

'No point at all,' said Chris. 'Because,' he shook his head sadly, 'we'd always be wondering if . . .' He paused. 'Say something else came up concerning you. You might want to do a deal for what you saw today.'

There was no point in arguing. It was a logical point of view, after all. 'So what happens now?' I asked.

'Now the three of us take a little ride together. Over Epping way, maybe. What do you say, Chesney?'

'The forest's nice this time of year,' Chesney grunted in reply.

'If we're quick we'll be there before it's properly light,' said Chris. 'And then . . .' He didn't bother finishing the sentence. 'I'm really sorry, mate,' he continued.

And do you know, I sincerely believe he was.

The three of us went downstairs and out to the street. It was still dark and even colder than when I had come in, if anything. Or perhaps it was just me. Maybe I was anticipating some far-flung corner of an Epping Forest field that would be forever South London.

'The car's this way,' said Chris, taking my arm and leading me across the pavement. All was silent in the street and I took one last look back up at the window of my flat, and suddenly realized I badly needed to take a piss.

I was just about to mention it. You know how it is –
you should always go before you leave home – when all of
a sudden the street was lit up as bright as day as a whole
bank of searchlights bathed us in their brilliance, like a
trio of actors taking centre stage. Behind the searchlights'
beams I could see the blue flashing lights of maybe half a
dozen police vehicles as they started to rotate, and an
amplified voice said: 'Armed police. The three of you stand
still and raise your arms.'

I couldn't believe it. Not twenty minutes before, the
street had been clean, and now there were dozens of blue-
clad figures moving around behind the lights, and with a
roar of its rotors a police helicopter rose behind the houses
on the opposite side of the street and added its Night Sun,
thirty million candlepower searchlight, to the beams that
transfixed us like insects on a piece of white cardboard.

'You in the middle,' the amplified voice barked. 'Stand
still.' That was me. 'You, on his left, move two paces to
your left. Now.' Chesney did as he was told. 'You on his
right, move two paces to *your* right. Now.' Chris obeyed.
'All three of you, on your knees,' the voice continued,
'keeping your hands in the air.'

We all complied. The pavement was hard, cold and
gritty through the material of my trousers.

When the three of us were kneeling, the voice went on.
'All three of you lie face down, keeping your hands away
from your bodies. Now.'

We all fell forward, breaking the fall with our hands
and ended up lying flat out like three fishes on a slab.

When we had done what the voice commanded, I heard
the noise of rubber-soled boots on the road, and we were
surrounded by armed police officers. They all carried
Heckler & Koch automatic weapons, and as I peered up
from my uncomfortable position on the freezing pavement
I noticed that the guns were all set on full auto with the

safety catches off. I just hoped that no one's finger slipped on the trigger.

The three of us were thoroughly searched, and Chris's revolver, Chesney's shotgun, plus a flick-knife and heavy-duty brass knucks which he was also carrying were taken away. Then we were handcuffed and led to three separate cars. I don't know where the other two went, but I ended up at Streatham police station where the custody officer took my watch, cigarettes, lighter, keys, and what money I still had left, from me. I didn't have a belt, braces or shoelaces, but he took the scarf I was wearing, so that I couldn't hang myself with it, and I was put into a holding cell in the basement and left alone. I wasn't charged, or allowed to make a telephone call, or even given a cup of tea, and no one said much. But at least there was a lidless toilet in the cell so that I could finally relieve my aching bladder.

Without my Rolex I couldn't tell how long I'd been there when a uniformed constable and two plain-clothes coppers came to fetch me and take me to an interview room. But it had to have been a couple of hours, if not more.

Once inside the cheerless room, with only a tin desk fastened to the floor, four chairs and a twin-deck cassette player for furniture, the senior of the two detectives, who introduced himself as DI Graves, gave me my cigarettes and lighter back and sent the constable to get me a cuppa before we settled down with his partner, DS Conroy, for a little chat.

'You're a very lucky man, Sharman,' said Graves, as I took a drag on my third Silk Cut in fifteen minutes and sipped at the plastic cup of hot water that might have been shown a tea bag in a previous life. 'Very lucky indeed.'

I nodded. 'I wouldn't have given a lot for my chances if

you hadn't turned up. How did you know where to find me?' I asked.

'We'll talk about that later. First of all we'd like to talk about the shooting that occurred yesterday morning at the Elephant and Castle.'

'I had nothing to do with that,' I said.

'No one said you did. In fact Christopher Tennyson has made a full statement in which he confesses to the crime and clears you of any involvement. He's told us everything.'

'That's very magnanimous of him, considering I hadn't seen him for twenty-five years until yesterday morning. It was pure coincidence I was there at all. Just my bad luck.'

'Which confirms our feelings on the matter,' said Graves. 'You two were at school together, I understand.'

I nodded. 'But don't get all choked up with sentiment. We weren't exactly bosom buddies. I just knew him in passing. That was all. What I'm more interested in is how you knew who I was? I'm not known in that pub. How come you were waiting for me tonight, or this morning, or whatever time it was? Or had you followed them to my place?'

'No. It was you we were looking for. We've had a car outside your place since yesterday afternoon, waiting for you to get home. When the officers inside the car saw Tennyson and Chesney Himes arrive about two this morning, and they fitted the descriptions we had of the two men who shot and killed Jack O'Connor yesterday, and it looked like they were staying, reinforcements were called. By the time you got home the place was surrounded.'

'I didn't see any sign when I walked down the street.'

'You weren't supposed to. This isn't Amateur Hour, you know.'

'And you waited for me before you went in. How thoughtful.'

'We weren't *entirely* sure that you weren't webbed up with the killing, and we figured that nothing much would happen until you got home. Anyway, it's easier to nick bodies in the street than inside a house full of civilians. We knew you'd have to come out sooner or later.'

'Meanwhile they could have topped me inside my flat while you lot were polishing your guns outside.'

'It was a chance we had to take. A calculated risk.'

'Thanks a lot. If the chance ever comes up again, just remember it's my life you're taking a calculated risk with, not half a quid on the favourite at Sandown Park.'

He grinned, but said nothing.

'But how did you know it was me in the pub in the first place?' I asked for the third time.

He clicked his fingers and his oppo gave him a slim, pink file that he'd been holding. Graves put it flat on the table in front of him and opened it. It contained one sheet of thin white paper.

'You were supposed to be meeting someone called Paul Kennedy yesterday morning? About a job he wants you to do?'

I nodded again. 'That's right,' I said.

But how the hell did he know?

'He was late.' Not a question. A statement.

'That's right,' I said again.

'When our first blokes arrived on the scene, a couple of minutes after you left, in answer to the landlord's 999 call, Paul Kennedy rang the pub to apologize for keeping you waiting. One of the officers took the call. Your name rang lots of bells with him. You have a very interesting past.'

'It's had its moments,' I agreed.

'We got your details out of the computer. That's why we were waiting. To talk to you about what you'd seen. We really didn't think that if you were going to be involved in a hit, you'd have someone ring the boozer five minutes

47

after it went down and ask for you by name. But then you never know.' He shrugged. 'Stranger things have happened.'

Another nod. Good for Paul, I thought. He always was a polite bloke. That was half the reason so much stuff was going missing from his warehouse. He cared too much for his fellow man to get ruthless. I definitely owed him one. More than one in fact.

'I'm glad you were there,' I said. 'I wouldn't have given much for my future health if you hadn't been.'

'We try to oblige occasionally,' he replied. 'Despite what you read in the papers. But you really should have stayed where you were, in the pub. Done the right thing. Acted like a good citizen.'

When I didn't say anything in reply, he went on. 'A favour for old times' sake? For an old school friend? It nearly cost you your health.'

'Who said I was doing Tennyson a favour?' I asked.

'Weren't you?'

'No. Not particularly. I just didn't want to get involved.'

He looked at the ceiling. I wondered how many times he'd heard those words before: 'I just didn't want to get involved.'

'We're all involved,' he said. 'In a manner of speaking.'

'You're right,' I said. 'And who was O'Connor? The bloke who was shot?'

'A local boy. Used to be a handy boxer, so I'm told. But he fell on hard times. His eyes went. He supported his mother, or tried to. Got into debt with Tennyson and Himes. That's their game, by the way. Lending money at exorbitant rates. A right pair of sharks. Anyway, O'Connor couldn't pay the interest on what he'd borrowed, let alone anything off the principal. They shot him as an example to others. One thing's for sure. They won't be missed by the local council estates. They're a couple of pieces of garbage that are well out of the way.'

Until a couple more pieces of garbage pick up the business, I thought, but didn't bother to mention it. 'That's all right, then,' I said instead. 'So I take it you won't be needing me any more today.'

'We'd like a statement before you go, if you don't mind,' said Graves, pushing a statement form and leaky ball-point towards me. 'Otherwise I don't think we'll be needing you at all. Both our friends are trying to outdo each other in the cough stakes. It looks like the whole incident has been cleared up to everyone's satisfaction with the minimum of grief.'

Except to poor old Jack O'Connor and his mum, I thought, as I lit another cigarette, picked up the pen and pulled the statement form in front of me.

Sweetheart of the Rodeo

This story has been anthologized loads of times, mainly because it was shortlisted for a Gold Dagger Award for best short story of the year in 1993. Someone at the CWA must've boobed, and I bet the old Zimmer frames were all of a quiver at seeing my name on the list. Of course it didn't win.

The Sweetheart in question is a real person. Someone I met, fancied, but who didn't fancy me back. Can you believe it? I started writing another story about her, but she went back to America and, as I find that out of sight is out of mind, it never got finished. What fickle people we writers are.

The title comes from a Byrds album.

The ring on my flat doorbell came at about eight o'clock on a hot and sticky Wednesday night in June.

I wasn't working. Just kicking back with a can of cold beer and what passed for entertainment on the terrestrial channels of my TV.

I was dressed in an old cotton shirt, blue jeans that had seen better days a long time previous, and a pair of scuffed Timberland loafers with no socks.

I took the beer downstairs to the front door with me for company.

The woman who stood outside was tall in a pair of high-heeled, two-tone, green-suede-on-green-ostrich-skin cowboy boots, and she was fanning her face with a black straw Stetson that would have added another three or four inches to her height with no problem.

The rest of her outfit consisted of a mid-grey cowgirl outfit that perfectly matched the colour of her eyes. It had all sorts of tassels and stuff hanging down from the shoulders and sleeves. It was a little wrinkled and travel-stained around the edges. But then, as I'm sure I've remarked before, no one's perfect. But she was pretty good.

Her skirt was very short and exposed legs that went on for ever, sheathed in charcoal nylon. Her dark brown, almost waist-length hair was backcombed out *real* big, like the woman in *Dallas*. I was intrigued to say the least. I looked her in the eye and said, 'Yes?'

'Is your name Nick Sharman?' she asked.

She had an accent straight out of the deep south of America.

'Yes,' I replied.

'Do you know a guy called Skinner?'

'Who?'

'Skinner. He's a musician. Plays lead guitar.'

Skinner. Sure. I knew him. To call him a musician was something of an overstatement now. Maybe once upon a time. In the disco days of the seventies, perhaps. But now he was too old. And too short. And too fat. So fat that his trousers didn't fit right. Too fat to be a teenage idol. Mind you, Elton John hadn't done too badly. And he was bald too. But Skinner was no Elton John, and that was a fact.

These days Skinner was up to all sorts. Mostly semi-legal. And that was an understatement. He hung out in East London. Well away from my manor, thank God. I'd met him years ago in a pub in Soho, but I'd seen him around before that. One Saturday afternoon session we'd both been in the boozer, and whoever he was with had bought a drink for the company I was in, or vice versa, and as we'd all combined to form one large group, Skinner and I had ended up next to each other and said hello, as you do. Much later, after chucking-out time, I'd bumped into him again at a hot-dog stand in Charing Cross Road where we were both paying good money to risk salmonella or worse. He was staying in Brixton at the time, and thankfully was without wheels as he was as pissed as a pudding, and we'd shared a cab home. On the way, we decided that a late drink at the Fridge, where he knew one of the doormen, was in order, and I'd woken up the next afternoon in the bath in some stranger's flat, where Skinner was dossing down, and we'd been more or less mates ever since.

Mostly less. And certainly not mates enough for what followed.

'Sure,' I said. 'What about him?'

'I was supposed to be staying at his house. I've just arrived from the States. He said he'd meet me at Heathrow, but he didn't show up.'

I wasn't surprised.

'I went to his place, and got this note he left,' she said.

She took a crumpled piece of paper from a huge handbag that swung from one shoulder and looked like it didn't contain much more than all I owned in the world.

I straightened the paper. It read:

Sweetheart,
*   I've had to go away on a gig.*
*   It came up suddenly, and I couldn't get in touch.*
Your phone's always engaged.
*   Go and see a bloke called Nick Sharman. He'll look after you.*
*   I'll be in touch as soon as I can.*
*   Love,*
*   Skinner*

My home address was scribbled at the bottom of the page.

'And you are?' I asked.

'Sweetheart,' she said. 'That's my name, right there. Pleased to make your acquaintance.' If she was, she wasn't exactly showing it.

I looked at her. 'Sorry,' I said. 'I don't know a thing about this.' As far as I was concerned, she was just another of Skinner's women. Fat and unattractive as he might be, he seemed to pull pretty well. Maybe it was the lemon-yellow Stratocaster slung between his legs.

Her grey eyes changed colour and flashed a dangerous shade of blue. 'Jesus,' she said. 'Where's your British hospitality? I've flown over three thousand miles today. Aren't you even going invite me in?'

I looked at her and made my choice. I should have shut the door straight in her face. 'Sure,' I said, and stepped back in the doorway. You would have done the same.

'My things are in that cab,' she said. 'Suitcases and stuff.' And pointed to a black Metrocab parked opposite with its engine running. 'You'll have to pay him. I haven't got any English money.'

I shook my head. This had to be a piss-take. But I decided to go along with the gag and said, 'Go on up. All the way to the top. The door's open. I'll get your bags. There's a beer in the fridge.'

'Thanks,' she said and brushed past me. I went over to the taxi.

'How much?' I asked.

'Hundred and fifty-two quid,' said the cabbie, dead straight-faced.

'*How much?*' I said.

He repeated the sum. 'And the meter's still running,' he added.

'From Heathrow?' I said. 'Did you go the pretty way, through Huddersfield, or what?'

The cabbie looked at me disgustedly. 'Listen, mate,' he said. 'I picked her up at the airport about four hours ago. First of all we have to go to Harrods so she can do some shopping. Then it's off to Edmonton, where she has a long chat with a couple of dikes at the house where she's gone. Then she decides she wants a drink, but the first three boozers don't suit. Eventually we find one she likes, and she's in there for half an hour. Then it's over the river here. I mean, what do you want from me?'

'Nothing,' I replied shortly. 'Wait here . . . And turn the sodding meter off.' And I went upstairs and got my chequebook.

'Do you know how much the fare is?' I demanded when I got back into my flat and found Sweetheart sitting demurely on the sofa sipping at a Heineken and watching the end of *Coronation Street*.

'No,' she replied. 'I never look at cab meters.'

How convenient, I thought, and found my chequebook and card in the chest of drawers where I keep them, and went back downstairs.

I had to do three cheques. Fifty pounds each, and two quid cash.

When I'd paid him, the driver got Sweetheart's luggage out of the cab. It consisted of four Harrods carrier bags and three huge suitcases made from lizard- or snakeskin. Jesus, I thought, I'd hate to be around her if I was an endangered species.

Little did I know.

When all her stuff was on the pavement, the cabbie said, 'What about my tip?'

'Your tip,' I said. 'Here's your tip. Don't pick up American women with big hair from the airport. That's the only tip you're getting out of me.'

He wasn't best pleased by that. 'I know something you don't,' he said.

'What?'

He rubbed the thumb and forefinger of his right hand together in the age-old gesture.

'Tell me,' I said. 'Don't fuck about.'

He shook his head.

I was tired, and getting fed up with playing games. 'A fiver,' I said. 'And it had better be good.'

'Get away.'

All right, I was interested, and he knew it. When Skinner's involved, you'd better get all the information you can. I'd learnt that long ago. 'A tenner,' I said.

'Ten per cent,' he said.

'Fifteen quid?' I said back. 'Are you kidding?'

'It's the recognized amount for a gratuity.'

'It's the recognized amount for daylight bloody robbery if you ask me.'

He shrugged.

'And for what?'

'Pay up and find out.'

I took three fivers out of my back pocket and he reached out his hand.

I pulled the money back and shook my head. 'Don't be soft,' I said.

'How do I know you'll pay?'

'You don't. Just trust me.'

He thought about it for ten seconds or so, then shrugged again. 'We were followed.'

'What?'

'We were followed,' he repeated. 'Two geezers in a motor.'

'From where?'

'Edmonton. The house where she spoke to them two dikes.'

He had a real way with words.

'Are they still with you?' I asked.

He grinned spitefully. 'Sure. They came to the pubs after us and waited, and if you look down the road there,' his eyes moved in a downhill direction, 'you can see them for youself.'

'What car?' I said.

'Grey Granada.'

I let my eyes follow his. Parked about fifty yards down the street was a gun-metal-grey Ford Granada. The latest model.

'Are you sure?' I asked.

He pulled a face. 'What do you think?' he asked.

I pulled a face back.

'What about my money,' he said.

'One minute,' I said, and picked up two of the suitcases and the carrier bags and walked them across the road and into the doorway of the house.

I walked back, but instead of going to fetch the last case I turned and sprinted in the direction of the Granada.

I heard the starter grind and the car took off with a faint screech from the tyres. I was in the middle of the road, maybe twenty yards from it, and whoever was driving spun the wheel and the car lurched towards me, forcing a serious change of direction on my part and making me almost lose my balance and end up in the gutter. As it was, I felt my bad foot react to the effort with a sharp stab of pain.

The car sped away in the direction of Streatham with a puff of smoke from its twin exhausts.

I limped back to the cab.

'Told you,' said the cabbie, with rather more satisfaction than I appreciated, and held out his hand.

I put the three fivers into it, picked up the other case and went across the road into my house. I collected the rest of her baggage and took it all upstairs.

Sweetheart was still sitting where I'd left her, but she'd discovered *Brookside*, and she was on her third beer.

I put the bags down on the carpet, and she looked up from between her can of lager and the TV set.

'Thanks,' she said. 'I appreciate what you did. Up until then, if today had been a fish, I'd've thrown it back.'

Country style. How quaint, I thought. 'We've got to talk,' I said.

'About?'

'You were followed from Edmonton.'

'Tell me something I don't know.'

'What?'

'I saw those guys. That's why I stopped off at a load of bars. Just to see if they stuck with me.'

'You *knew*?'

'Sure. I come from Texas. They grow them smart down there.'

'*Smart?* You pick up a tail and bring it to my house. And you call that smart?'

'Are they still around?'

'No,' I said.

'You chased them off.'

'You might say that.'

'And I've got a place to stay?'

'Yes.'

'Then I would call that smart. What would you call it?'

The actions of a stupid bitch, I thought. And she knew exactly what I was thinking, and her eyes changed colour again, to emerald green, and her skirt slid another inch or two up her thigh, and I just knew that I was being manipulated in the worst way.

I looked down at her and said, 'Forget it. It's done now.'

She smiled a smile like a cat with cream and said, 'Looks like Skinner sent me to the right guy.'

'Sure.'

'So what do you do, then, Sharman?'

'I'm a private detective. When I work.'

'A private eye. No shit.' She laughed like a drain, and snorted like a pig at the thought.

I stood there straight-faced throughout.

'And what exactly do you do?' I asked.

'I'm in the rock and roll business.'

'*No shit*,' I said.

'What exactly does that mean?'

I shrugged. 'I never would have guessed,' I said. 'I thought you might be a Jehovah's Witness when you arrived at the door.'

'Fuck right off,' she said, and her eyes were suddenly that dangerous shade of blue that I'd seen before.

I kicked the Harrods bag that was nearest to me. 'And if you've got no dough, how the hell could you do a load of shopping on your way here?'

She reached into her handbag that was sitting on the sofa next to her and took out a wallet made from yet more skin off some poor little beast that had never done anything to her personally. She extracted two plastic cards and flicked them dangerously close to my head.

'Credit, pal,' she said. 'Never heard of it?'

The cards hit the wall and fell on to the carpet. One was white. The other, olive green. Harrods store cards. I smiled tightly back. 'OK. Now tell me why persons unknown followed you here.'

She shrugged. 'I don't know.'

'Why were you meeting Skinner?'

She shrugged again.

'Don't fuck with me, Sweetheart, or whatever your name is,' I said. 'Tell the truth and shame the devil.'

'Sweetheart it is,' she replied. 'Sweetheart of the Rodeo. Like the song.'

'I'm impressed,' I said. 'Now tell me, why were you meeting Skinner?'

'We had a business deal going.'

'Oh really? I've come across his business deals before. What he means is, you give him a bunch of money, and at some unspecified future date you'll get it back plus a whole load of interest. Trouble is it never happens.'

'It happens this time. He promised.'

'Is that why he wasn't at the airport to meet you? And why I just paid your cab fare? And almost got run over by a car load of people who followed you here?'

Her eyes went grey again and she said, 'Did they hurt you?'

'Would you care?'

She nodded. 'Sure I would. What do you think I am? I'm here in your house, drinking your beer. Where I come from that means we're friends.'

'Where I come from it means you're probably going to ask to borrow more money.'

'Very funny.'

And then she started to cry. Just like that. Great big tears squeezing out of the corner of her eyes and rolling down her cheeks, where she let them drip on to the material of her outfit, where they soaked into big blobs of darker grey on her breasts.

Shit, I thought. I might have guessed. Hard as nails on top. The kind of woman who lights matches on the skin of her thighs. And underneath all soft and mushy. Just my luck. Right then, if Skinner had walked into the room I'd've kicked him straight in the nuts.

I stood there awkwardly. 'What's the matter?' I asked.

She looked up at me through mascara-smudged eyes, which I must admit were kind of appealing, even though deep down I knew I was being manipulated again. 'It's just that I feel so lousy, what with the journey and all. Could I get some sleep?'

'Sure,' I said.

'Your bed feels kind of comfortable. I just tried it.'

'It is. Guests usually sleep on the sofa bed, though,' I said, choosing not to preface 'guests' with 'uninvited'. And tugged off the cushions and pulled out the bedsprings and mattress. It was made up with two sheets and a blanket, for emergencies.

'Looks kinda short to me,' she said.

'Could be.'

'I'm tall. You know.'

'I know,' I replied. 'So am I.'

She gave me another of her appealing looks, and I knew there was no point in arguing, so instead I said, 'Tell you what. You have the bed for tonight. I'll sleep on the sofa.'

The tears stopped miraculously and she said, 'You're cute.'

'How kind.'

'Now will you . . .'

'What?'

'Let me get my night things out and get changed.'

'I'm not stopping you.'

She looked round. 'This is a nice place,' she said. 'Much better than that dump Skinner lives in, and I'm not complaining. But it's kinda cramped in here.'

Cramped. I ask you. It's a one-room studio conversion with kitchen attached, and separate shower and toilet. What the hell did she expect? Longleat?

'It's perfect for one,' I said.

'But there's two of us here now.'

So I'd noticed, I thought. 'If I'd known you were coming I'd've made alternative arrangements,' I said as sarcastically as possible. But Yanks never get sarcasm.

'There's no need for that.'

'What do you want me to do, then?'

'Could you leave for a few minutes?'

'Can't you use the bathroom?'

'I used it already. There's not room to turn round in there. And I need some space.'

'OK,' I said. 'I'll take a walk. But I'll be back in twenty minutes.'

'That's plenty of time,' and she smiled again, showing a mouthful of perfect teeth.

I went down the pub and didn't get back until almost eleven. When I opened the door to the flat, all the lights were off, except for the small lamp that stood on top of the dead TV. It was still lit, and she'd draped a scarf over the shade so that the light was diffused. There was just enough illumination to see that the place was all messed up. It looked like, as she'd unpacked, she'd simply dropped her stuff on to the carpet where it still lay. The three suitcases and the carrier bags were scattered across the room, and dresses, underwear, papers, tapes, books, and all sorts of other junk were everywhere. And from somewhere had appeared another three pairs of cowboy boots, that now stood with the ones she'd been wearing when she arrived, in a line next to my bed as if guarding her as she slept. I looked at them. One leopard-skin pair, one zebra-skin pair and one black-and-red-leather pair, next to the green ones I'd already seen.

Sweetheart was curled up in bed asleep, snoring softly with a light tick-tick sound like a baby. She'd washed her face clean of make-up, and she frowned slightly as she slept.

I left the place as it was, went to the bathroom, waded back through her stuff, took the pillow from next to the one that her head was resting on, and went to bed. Of course I couldn't sleep. The sofa bed was too short. And she wouldn't stop snoring.

*

The next morning I was up first. I went into the bathroom and shaved and showered. When I came back she was sitting up in bed yawning. She gave me a glimpse of all her teeth again. 'Good *morning*,' she said. 'And how are you today?'

'Lousy,' I replied.

'*Oh*. A grouch in the morning. That won't do.'

'Could you keep the volume down until I've had at least one cup of tea?' I asked. Not impolitely, I thought, under the circumstances.

'Of course, *mate*,' she said with what was possibly one of the worst attempts at a Cockney accent I think I'd ever heard. 'Whatever you say.'

I put the kettle on, and as it boiled I found a pair of mugs in the cupboard. 'Tea? Coffee?' I said.

'Coffee. Milk. No sugar.'

I started to prepare the drinks.

'I'm going to get up and get dressed,' she said.

'If you think I'm going out again, you're right out of luck. And listen. Get this place tidied up. It's like a tip.'

'What's that?'

'A dump. A garbage dump.'

'I think you might have been living alone too long, Mr Sharman.'

'Maybe.'

Not that it was any of her damn business.

She snorted a laugh and pulled the covers back. She jumped out of bed and made a run for the bathroom. The nightie she was wearing was long, but not long enough to hide the fact that she was wearing a pair of grey woollen socks on her feet.

'Socks,' I said. 'How can you wear socks in bed? It's summer for God's sake.'

'Summer! Call this summer? It's like winter in this

goddammed town all year round,' and she slammed the bathroom door behind her.

When she returned, her coffee was ready, and we sat opposite each other at the breakfast bar and drank our drinks. By the time I had finished mine I was feeling a bit more human. I lit a cigarette.

'No more messing,' I said. 'Tell me. What was the deal with Skinner?'

She sighed. 'He called me at home last week and told me that if I sent him five thousand pounds sterling, I could quadruple it by yesterday.'

'And you believed him?'

She shrugged. 'Why not? It seemed like a good deal. I wired him my last ten thousand bucks and bought the first cheap ticket to London I could get.'

'And he was going to meet you?'

She nodded.

'But of course he didn't.'

'He'll have a good reason.'

'Christ. You have more faith in him than I do.'

'By the way you act, I have more faith in *anyone* than you do.'

'That's not hard.'

'So I gathered. What are we going to do?'

'We're going to Skinner's this morning. Try and find out where he is.'

'I've already tried. I told you.'

'I'm a detective. I might have more luck.'

She looked towards the heavens as if to say, 'Fat chance.'

Somehow we both managed to get ready to go, without any more hassle. Sweetheart ended up in some kind of dude ranch ensemble in mostly black and gold. I went for clean Levis and a Wrangler shirt. Roy Rogers and Dale Evans, or what?

We went downstairs together and got into my E-Type – which as far as I could gather was my first possession that Sweetheart approved of, although she would persist in calling it an XKE – and arrived in Edmonton at about eleven. We weren't followed. She gave me Skinner's address and I found the street in the *A–Z*.

'What's with these women you talked to then?' I asked *en route*. 'Are they lesbians, or what?'

'Skinner's fan club,' said Sweetheart. 'They're dikes all right. Chuck and Bo. Skinner named them after his favourite guitarists. The big one's the one to watch. Chuck.'

Chuck and Bo, I thought. Outstanding.

I left Sweetheart leaning on the wing of my car and knocked on the door. A massive woman in dungarees with a short haircut answered. It was one of those times when I just knew that whatever boyish charm I'd managed to hang on to was going to be totally wasted. 'Hi,' I said.

The woman chewed on the side of her mouth and didn't answer.

'You must be Chuck,' I said.

'S'right.'

'I'm looking for Skinner.'

'You and a million others. Including your girlfriend out there.'

As she spoke, another woman appeared behind her. Mousy and frightened looking. But pretty in a beaten-down way. I smiled past Chuck and the other woman smiled nervously back. 'And you're Bo,' I said.

'So you know our names,' said the first woman. 'Is that supposed to fill us with confidence? The poll-tax inspector knows them too.'

I smiled, but I could have kicked her.

'Skinner's away,' I said. 'On tour, I believe.'

Chuck didn't bat an eyelid.

'Look, I'm a friend of his. So is she.' I glanced round at the car. 'It's urgent that we speak to him. Really urgent.'

'I told her last night I didn't know where he was. I gave her the note he left. That's all I'm prepared to do. Now go away, will you. We're busy.' And she slammed the door in my face. The last thing I saw was Bo's frightened look before the wood filled the hole with a bang.

I went back to the car. 'Told you,' said Sweetheart.

Don't you just hate people who are always right?

'Lunch,' I said.

She nodded.

Before we drove off, I dropped one of my business cards with my home number on the back through the letterbox of the house. I didn't expect a response, but you never know.

We ate at some overpriced bistro in the West End, and I got a ticket on the car. Terrific.

So that looked like that. There had been no sign of a tail all day. Maybe we were off the hook, maybe we weren't. Whichever it was, only time would tell.

On the way home I stocked up on booze at the offie and picked up twenty quid's worth of rocky from a pal of mine who runs a second-hand furniture shop in Herne Hill, and we went back to the flat. Sweetheart had two packets of leopard-skin-patterned rolling papers that matched her boots, and we spent the rest of Thursday and Friday hanging out in my place getting righteously wrecked.

She played me some of the tapes she'd brought with her. All country. I particularly liked a couple by a geezer called Guy Clark, and made her keep playing them as I got more and more wasted. Every time I hear those songs now, I think of us together in that little flat on those two, long, hot summer days when the air smelled of her perfume and dope and booze.

Thursday night she had my bed again, and I slept on the sofa. Big surprise.

The call came Friday night. Late. I answered the phone and heard a small, nervous voice on the other end of the line. 'Is that Nick Sharman?'

'Yes,' I replied.

'You're a friend of Skinner's. You came round to our house yesterday. You left your card.'

'That's right.'

'I'm Bo. I saw you at the door.'

Somehow, I hadn't thought it was Chuck. 'I remember,' I said. 'What can I do for you?'

'Some men came round looking for Skinner. They were here before. Horrible men. They said horrible things.'

Horrible men often do, I thought, but said nothing.

'They threatened us. Chuck's terribly upset. I thought I should call you.'

I couldn't get my head round the idea of Chuck with an attack of the vapours, so I let it go. 'Yes, Bo,' I said.

'She told them about you and that American girl.'

'Not a good idea.'

'It was the only way we could get rid of them.'

'How long ago?'

'Just a few minutes. I thought I should warn you.'

'Thank you, Bo.'

'And there's something else.'

'What?'

'Skinner's going to be at the Holiday Inn in Dortmund tonight?'

'Dortmund?'

'In Germany.'

Thanks, Bo, I thought, but I did get my O-level geography.

'I've got the number if you want it,' she said. 'I don't know what room he's in or anything. But he did say he'd be there tonight, before he went away. If we needed to get in touch or anything. He's with a band called Satan's Spawn.'

'Satan's Spawn,' I repeated. 'Great. That's a big help. Really.'

She reeled off the number, and I jotted it down on the back of an envelope.

'I hope we haven't got you into any trouble,' she said.

'No more than usual,' I replied. 'Thanks for calling.' And I hung up.

I told Sweetheart what had happened as I dialled the number that Bo had given me. She came and stood close to me as I did it.

The phone rang twice. A foreign-sounding ring, strange to my ears. Then a male voice said, 'Holiday Inn, Dortm . . .'

I cut in before he could say more. 'Do you speak English?' I asked.

'I certainly should, sir,' replied the voice. 'I come from East Grinstead.'

'Great,' I said. 'Do you have any bands in tonight?'

His voice grew cooler. 'Four, sir. You may choose from Heavy Metal, Grunge, Retro-Punk or Psychobilly.'

'Is one of them called Satan's Spawn?'

'They are staying in the annexe, sir,' said the voice.

'Is it cheaper?'

'No, sir. It's just not so many floors up, when they start throwing television sets out of the windows.'

'That sounds like my man's style. Is there a Skinner checked in with them?'

I heard the sound of a computer keyboard being punched up.

'Is he there?' Sweetheart asked.

As she spoke her hair brushed against my cheek, and I felt her breath tickle my ear.

'Yes, sir,' said the voice after a moment. 'We do have someone of that name registered. Shall I try to locate the gentleman?'

'If you wouldn't mind.'

'He's there,' I said to Sweetheart.

When the receptionist returned, he said, 'There's no answer from the bar. Shall I try his room?'

'Please. And make it quick. I'm calling from London. You know, England. The poor man of Europe.'

'I'm well aware, sir,' said the voice. 'I'll try the room.'

There was another dead silence. Then a voice said 'Yeah?' It wasn't the receptionist.

'Skinner?'

'Who's this?'

'Nick Sharman.'

'And Sweetheart,' shouted Sweetheart.

'Christ. How did you find me?'

'Bo told me.'

'Jesus! I was going to call.'

''Course you were. It's just taken you a few days to get it together.'

'It's this fucking band. They're bloody mental. They're only a bunch of kids. They never sleep. Thank God we've got tonight off so's I can get some rest.'

'How come you've got a gig with them?' I asked.

'I haven't really. The lead guitarist can't play a note. He's always too stoned. I stand behind the speaker stacks and play his lead lines, and he mimes.'

'Jesus Christ, Skinner. When will you ever learn?'

'It's a living. At least for the next six weeks. Till this tour's over.'

'And a good way to get out of the country,' I said. 'Do you know we're being followed?'

'I thought it might be possible.'

'Cheers, Skinner. You're a pal. And what about Sweetheart and this money?'

'It's a long story.'

'Tell it. And make it the seven-inch version. I'm paying for this call all by myself.'

'I met a geezer in a pub.'

'No.'

'Yeah. He was the stoppo for a three-handed firm of blaggers.'

'Are they re-running *The Sweeney* where you are?' I asked. 'Big in Dortmund, is it?'

'No. But you understand what I'm saying?'

'Yeah, of course. The driver for a gang of armed robbers.'

'Quite right. They'd done a big job in Oxford and he'd stashed the money away. The driver wanted out, and told me that for a certain sum he'd sell me the location where the dough was hidden.'

'And you believed him? He didn't have a machine with him that changed fivers into twenties by any chance?'

'I thought you were worried about the price of the call?' Skinner said drily.

'Carry on.'

'I had some dough. I called Sweetheart. She supplied the rest. It was all on the up and up.'

I shook my head in wonderment. Just what were this man's parameters on what wasn't on the up and up then?

'How much was involved?'

'On our side? Fifteen K.'

'And the money from the blag?'

'A hundred thousand.'

'A pretty good deal.'

'I thought so.'

'So what happened? Did he do a runner with the dough you were going to pay him?'

'No. I wish he had. Everything was fine. I went where he'd said the money would be. And it was there. I left a mate of mine. A roadie. Chalky. Remember him? With this bloke and the cash for the deal.'

'If the driver needed cash so bad, why didn't he just go and pick up the blag money himself?'

'You know I never thought of that till after.'

'Till after what?'

'Till after they pulled his body out of a skip in Hoxton. Near the Bass Clef, with his knees nailed together.'

'Christ! Was that him? I remember reading about that.'

'That was him all right.'

'Do you know who might have done it?' I hardly liked to ask.

'I know all right,' said Skinner. 'Why do you think I'm here? I hate fucking Germans. When I heard what had happened to the driver, I made a few enquiries about who the other two blaggers were.'

'And?'

'It was the Beverley Sisters.'

I almost dropped the phone. 'The Beverleys,' I said. 'Christ, Skinner, do you know what you've got yourself involved with? Sweetheart involved with? Me involved with? And you'd better not let them hear you call them the Beverley Sisters. Even for a joke. They don't take to it at all.'

Now, for anyone not familiar with the Beverley Sisters, they were a female British singing trio, very popular in the late fifties and early sixties. There were, and still are, three of them. A pair of twins and an elder sister. All blonde. Now the Beverley *Brothers* are a pair of right nutty villains with black hair. I mean *really* nutty. Crazy. Couldn't give fuck for anything or anyone. People call them the Beverley Sisters for a laugh. But only in close company, out of earshot of strangers. Like I said, they don't take to it at all.

In fact, an extended stay in hospital for the comedian often follows. You might wonder, apart from the play on the name, why there isn't another Beverley to make the joke perfect. Well, there is in a way. The younger of the two brothers, Derek, claims that the embryo of his unborn twin brother lives in the space between his brain and the inside of his skull. Swimming in the gunk there, and sleeping in a tiny space inside the bone over Derek's right eye that he, the twin brother that is, has nibbled over the years with his little embryonic gums. Derek refers to his twin as Kevin.

In short, a right nutter.

But a right nutter or not, Derek is the brains behind the operation. I remember once speaking to someone who went to school with the Beverleys. He told me that the only way to beat them in a fight was to put Derek away early. Then Raymond, the eldest one, would go to pieces, and that was that. Not that many people managed to put Derek away even in those days. Now, no one even tries.

'You've done it now, Skinner,' I said into the hum of the line. 'Right and proper.'

'I know. What can we do?'

'We, is it?'

He didn't reply.

'Tell me where the money is,' I said.

'What?'

'You heard.'

'So that you can get it?'

'No. So that I can give it back to them. I've had dealings with them in the past. Years ago.'

Nothing much. Nothing that could possibly have earned me more than the amputation of one or two fingers at the first knuckle. Nothing at all really. They'd probably forgotten all about me. Fat chance.

'Why should you do that for me?' asked Skinner.

'I'm not. It's for Sweetheart.'

'Oh yeah.'

'Yeah.'

'Why would that be?'

I looked at her. 'None of your fucking business,' I said.

'Like that, is it?'

'No. As a matter of fact it isn't.'

He was silent.

'So tell me,' I said.

'We'll lose all our money.'

'Better than losing all our lives.' I let the words hang.

'OK. But don't . . .' he said after a moment.

'Skinner,' I interrupted. 'Don't fuck about. This call is costing me a fortune. Just tell me where the dough is. I'll take care of it after that. And if the Beverley boys don't take to me, I want Guy Clark played at my funeral.'

'Who?'

'Never mind. You'll find the tape in my stereo.'

So he told me. He was very exact. I like that in a person. It gives me confidence. I didn't write it down. It took a while. When he'd finished, he said, 'There's just one other thing.'

'What?' I replied.

I heard him draw breath down the international line and he said, 'When you find the money, there's . . .'

And the door of my flat burst open and two bodies hurled themselves into the room.

Sweetheart screamed as one of the bodies grabbed her by the hair, forced her down on to the sofa, and stuck an extremely large handgun into the side of her head. The other body placed the barrels of a sawn-off shotgun under my chin. I noticed that both triggers had been messily tied together with silver wire. Twin barrels. One squeeze, and two cartridges loaded with God knows what gauge shot would take my head off. Not a pretty thought, especially as his finger was trembling inside the trigger guard.

The body with the shutgun, who as it happened was Derek Beverley, grabbed the phone and said, 'Hello. Hello,' into the mouthpiece, but got nothing but the click of a receiver being replaced at the other end for his trouble.

'Nick Sharman,' he said. 'I might have known you're webbed up in all this.'

I looked down the length of the gun at him. His head *was* a weird shape. Like he'd been dropped on it a few days after birth, before the bone had set properly. And there *was* a lump over one eye. He was wearing a light mac over a purple-and-blue shellsuit. Fashion terrorist.

I looked over at the other body. Brother Raymond, naturally, who was holding Sweetheart by her hair and grinding his gun into her ear. 'Tell the Neanderthal to ease up, will you,' I said to Derek. 'She won't hurt him.'

Derek glanced round quickly, but never let the gun he was holding on me move a centimetre. 'Ray,' he ordered. 'Cool it.'

Raymond looked up through eyes fogged with generations of interbreeding and abuse, loosened the grip he had on Sweetheart's hair and pulled the gun back a fraction. 'Are you sure?' he asked with his nasty wet little mouth.

'I'm sure,' replied Derek. 'Nick here's not going to give us no trouble. Are you, Nick?'

I held my hands up in surrender. 'Not me, mate,' I said.

'Don't call me mate, you cunt. You're not my mate,' spat Derek.

'Sorry,' I said.

'Who were you talking to on the dog?' he demanded.

'No one special.'

Derek saw the number written on the envelope and

picked it up. 'It was that fucking Skinner, wasn't it?' he said. 'Where the fuck is he?'

Under the circumstances I thought there was no point in denying it. 'Germany,' I said.

'Bastard! He had it away with our dough. That little shit who was driving for us stitched us right up. Where is it?'

'I don't know what you're talking about,' I said, and he hit me round the side of the head with the shotgun. Hard enough for me to see fireworks and have to grab the back of the sofa bed to stop me falling over.

'Don't lie,' he roared. 'We know you know.'

'How do you know?'

'Skinner got drunk the other night. Just before he split. And blabbed it around Soho that some cowgirl was going to make him rich. With our dough as it happens. Then we caught up with the geezer who drove for us on the job and we got the whole story out of him. When we found out where Skinner lived and that he was gone, we waited around in case she showed up. Simple.'

Elementary, in fact.

'Now where is it?' he demanded.

'Why didn't you call by the other night? When you tried to run me down?' I asked conversationally. Although I was feeling anything but conversational. Scared shitless in fact. This had all the ingredients of a night to forget in a hurry.

'Didn't recognize you straight away. It's been a long time. You've let your hair grow. If we'd known it was you, we would have done.'

I put my hand up and ran it through my barnet. 'Yeah,' I said.

Sweetheart, who was now sitting up on the sofa, said, 'Old home week, guys?'

Raymond gave her a backhander and she cried out in pain. 'Shut up, cunt,' he said.

'Don't do that again Raymond,' I said. 'It's not nice.'

'What you going to do about it?' he demanded.

I said nothing. There was nothing to say. Everyone in the room knew that I was going to do nothing about it at all. I just shook my head at Sweetheart, and hoped she took the hint.

'You went round Skinner's house yesterday and left your card,' continued Derek. 'And the two cunts there showed it to us.'

Thanks, Chuck. Thanks, Bo.

'The fat bitch said you said it was urgent. A hundred grand urgent, we reckoned.' He shoved the gun further into my face, it seemed. 'Tell us, Sharman, or I swear I'll get Raymond to stripe the Yank so bad that her own mother won't know her.'

I saw Raymond smile in anticipation.

After that I thought there was no point in screwing around any further. 'I was going to give it back to you,' I said.

Derek seemed amused at the concept.

'But you'll never see a penny of it, if Raymond touches her again,' I said.

'Big talk.'

It was all I had.

'Where is it?' asked Derek, after a moment. Seemingly a little more self-controlled.

'Out of town,' I said. 'Skinner told me where,' and I tapped my head. 'It's all up here.'

'Take us.'

'And if I say no?'

He grabbed me, and spun me round and pushed me in the direction of Sweetheart, and came up close behind me and whispered into my ear. 'Then I'll shoot the tart's arm off,' he said. 'Anyway, what's the problem? You were going to give it back to us, weren't you?'

'On my terms,' I replied.

'Now it's on our terms. So let's go.'

I hesitated, but only for a second. 'It's buried,' I said. 'You'll need a shovel.'

'You got one?' interrupted Raymond.

'I live on the top floor,' I said. 'What do I need a shovel for? My window box?'

Derek dug the barrel of the shotgun into my kidneys. Hard.

They had handcuffs with them, the new, one-piece plastic ones, and they trussed our wrists up tightly. Then took us down to the grey Granada that was parked outside. They pushed us into the back, and Derek climbed into the front passenger seat, looked over the back of it, and said, 'Sit quiet, and say nothing or I'll kill her. Don't think I won't.' Then he said something to Raymond through the window, who vanished, to reappear a few minutes later with a spade that he threw into the boot, and got in behind the steering wheel.

A little spot of petty larceny in the night.

Raymond started the car, put the gear shift into drive, and headed up the hill. 'Where to?' asked Derek.

'Make for Oxford,' I said. 'The scene of the crime. Where we want is off the M40.'

Derek seemed satisfied, and didn't say more, just sat so that he could look into the back of the car, with the shotgun poking over the centre console, just to remind us it was there.

I moved my leg so that it touched Sweetheart's and pressed it gently up against hers. She pressed back, and turned and gave me a weak-looking smile. I was proud of her.

We took the South Circular as far as Clapham, then headed over the river and up to Shepherd's Bush, and picked up the A40 and eventually the motorway. I told Raymond to come off at junction 7, then I directed him to turn off the A329 on to the B4011. I counted three more turnings, saw the pub on the corner that Skinner had told me about, took the next road to the right, over a bridge over a river, then I made Raymond slow right down until we came to a lane that disappeared off into the darkness.

'Up there,' I said. 'And keep the speed down.'

He did as he was told, and we came to a five-barred gate, then the lane widened enough for us to pull the car over without blocking the way. 'This is us,' I said.

The Beverleys helped Sweetheart and me out of the car, Raymond got the shovel out of the boot, and we walked back to the gate, which wasn't padlocked, and opened it. By the light of torches that Derek and Raymond had brought with them, we followed a faint path that ran along the edge of a copse of trees.

Sweetheart and I, still both cuffed up, stumbled along, but the boys refused to untie our wrists.

We walked for maybe a quarter of a mile before I saw what I was looking for. It was the red light on top of a telecommunication mast that stood on a hill about five miles away.

'We're almost there,' I said for something to say.

I kept my eye on the light, until it stood exactly midway between the arches of the railway bridge over the river that gleamed in the moonlight in the valley below us. From where we were standing there wasn't a house light in sight. The driver had picked the perfect place.

I turned and looked up at the dark mass of trees that loomed over the path where we were standing. 'Straight up there,' I said.

We cut across the rough grassland and keeping the red light behind me I found the lightning-scarred tree that Skinner had described. 'It's on the other side,' I said.

We walked round the tree and found ourselves in a tiny clearing. In the centre, the earth was bare, and surrounding it was dry-looking undergrowth. Derek uncuffed me, and I massaged some life back into my hands. Raymond tossed me the spade. 'Get digging,' he ordered.

'Aren't you going to untie her?' I asked.

In the wash of light from their torches, Derek shook his head.

'Then dig it your fucking self,' I said. The chances were that I was only digging our own graves anyway. Why make it easy for them?

Derek shrugged, and unfastened Sweetheart's wrists too, and pushed her in the direction of Raymond. 'Keep an eye on her,' he said. 'Now you dig, Sharman, or she'll suffer.'

'Throw us a torch down here,' I said.

Derek did as I asked. I stuck it in the fork of a branch and let the light shine on the ground in front of me.

I pushed the spade into the dirt and it seemed loose, like it had recently been turned over, which made me think that Skinner had been telling me the truth. It didn't matter if he had or not. We were well fucked either way.

I looked at the three of them standing in front and slightly above me. Derek was on my left, shotgun in both hands. Raymond was next to him, torch in one hand, gun in the other, pointing nowhere in particular. Sweetheart was on his left, and to my right.

I started digging. It was a warm night, but I didn't have a coat, so I didn't start to build up a sweat for a few minutes. When I did, I felt better. Never better in fact. Strange, when I knew that I could be dead at any moment.

I dug a pretty big hole. Big round, I mean. I wasn't in any hurry and none of the others said a word as I worked.

After about fifteen minutes' digging, with the earth piling up around me, the blade of the shovel clunked on something hard, sending a shock up both my arms.

'What's that?' demanded Derek.

'Hold on,' I said. 'Give us a chance.'

I went back to my digging, but I was more careful, and in the light of the torch I saw the edge of a black box emerge from the earth that surrounded it.

'It's a box,' I said.

'Get it out,' ordered Derek.

'All right,' I said. 'Don't be so impatient.'

I dug the earth from around the box with the edge of the spade, then got down on my knees and used my hands.

The box was big, with rope handles, and I dragged it out from the earth where it was anchored and dumped it on the edge of the hole.

'Open it,' ordered Derek.

I did as I was told and flipped back the lid. It only went half-way back, the top being attached to the edges by rope hinges. Lucky for me that Derek and Raymond couldn't see inside, because on top of the piles of neatly banded cash was a revolver. I looked at it and decided that Skinner wasn't as dumb as he pretended. It was a Smith & Wesson Model 27 .357 magnum. A right tasty weapon.

I hoped it was loaded.

There was only one way to find out. I hunkered down on my heels in front of the open box, looked at the gun, then up at the three of them standing over me. 'Come on, don't fuck us about. Is the money there?' said Derek, grinding the words out between his teeth.

'It's here,' I replied, and I saw him grin as he started towards me. It was now or never, but I just needed him off balance a little. 'How is Kevin, by the way?' I asked. 'Doing all right in there, is he?'

Derek's eyes widened, and I thought for a moment they were going to pop out of their sockets, and he moved closer still, the shotgun barrel pointing up into the air. I grabbed at the gun, brought it up, and pulled the trigger. The first bullet hit Derek just above his right eye and blew half his head, his brain and presumably the embryo of little Kevin, if it existed, all to hell and gone. At the moment of impact, as his body crumpled to the ground, Derek pulled the triggers of the shotgun. The noise was deafening and the shot ripped through the tree above us, bringing down a load of leaves. The blast lit up the clearing we were in, just as I fired at Raymond. I shot him three times in the chest, and he fell backwards into the bracken, kicked his heels and was still.

I sat down on the edge of the box, dropped the gun into the dirt and sat for a moment trembling and making funny little noises with my mouth. Sweetheart moved away from the bodies, and leant against a tree making little noises of her own.

She pulled herself together first, and came over and looked down at me. 'Come on, Sharman,' she said. 'Get a grip.'

I looked up at her. 'Jesus,' I said through dry lips. 'Oh, Jesus.'

'Come on,' she repeated. 'We've got to get this mess tidied up.'

'You go back to the car and wait,' I said. 'I'll do it.'

'Be the little woman?' she said. 'Fuck off. My great-great-grandmother took Apache scalps in the Indian wars, and was her own midwife eighteen times.'

'Yeah, I know,' I said. 'They grow 'em tough in Texas.'

'Cor-rect. Anyhow, it'll take two of us to get that box back. It looks heavy. Now let's do it. This place is beginning to give me the creeps.'

Beginning? It had been giving me the creeps ever since we'd arrived.

'Come on,' she said again. 'Let's do it.'

So we did it.

We pulled the box away from the hole, then enlarged it, and together we rolled Derek and Raymond's bodies into it, and covered them with earth, then pieces of bracken and leaves. In the light from the torches it looked OK, and with the place being as remote as it was I doubted that anyone would ever bother even to visit it, let alone be interested enough to dig there. Before I buried Raymond, I went through his pockets and found the cars keys.

Sweetheart was great. A tower of strength. There were a couple of times I'd've called it a day if she hadn't been there, I'm sure. But she kept me at it, until she was satisfied that no one would ever know what happened in that clearing in that wood near Oxford.

She was wearing her zebra-boots, and she took them off in case they got covered in dirt, and worked in stockinged feet.

You don't argue with a woman like that.

As we lugged the box of money and the guns and the spade back to where the car was parked, dawn was breaking on the horizon.

All the time we were there, we never saw or heard another soul, and as far as I can make out no one saw or heard us.

I drove sedately back to London, keeping to the speed limit all the way. Sweetheart didn't say anything until we'd crossed the river and picked up the South Circular again. Eventually she asked, 'What are we going to do with the money?'

'Keep it,' I said.

'Won't someone be looking for it?'

'Without a doubt. Too bad. We've earned it. We'll split it three ways. One-third for you, one-third for me, and one-third for Skinner. That'll keep him quiet. He was prepared to lose every penny last night. I'm sure he'll be happy with over thirty grand.'

'What about those two women at his house?'

'What about them? They don't know the Beverleys actually came to see us, do they? And I think they've been scared enough already for them to be happy that they never have to see the rover boys again. Anyway, Skinner'll sweet talk them when he comes back. They'll be OK.'

She nodded and was silent for a moment, and then said, 'I didn't know you guys in Britain went in for gun-play.'

'You'd be amazed,' I replied.

'I was. It was like Saturday night in downtown Dallas there, for a while.'

'It must have made you feel right at home,' I said as drily as possible.

'It did.' She was silent again, and then she turned in her seat to face me. 'Do you think they *were* going to kill us?'

'Well I don't think our well-being was their major priority, exactly,' I replied.

'But if they did,' she said, 'they'd've had to go back and get Skinner, and maybe even Chuck and Bo.'

'People like that don't think that far into the future,' I said. 'They were nuts. Crazy men. We crossed them and they didn't like that one bit. It was a chance I couldn't afford to take. I had to make a call, and I made it.'

'But won't someone be looking for them?'

'I doubt it. They weren't the most popular pair in London.'

'Won't they be missed?'

'Who's going to miss them? They had no families. Just each other. They were totally self-sufficient. Old Bill ... that's the police,' I said as a look of puzzlement crossed her face, 'might wonder what's become of them. But even they won't care. They'll just be grateful that the crime rate's fallen. No, doll. I doubt that many tears'll be shed about the Beverley Brothers. People'll think they've scarpered to Spain or somewhere. They'll be forgotten in twelve months. Good riddance.'

'I'll never forget them.'

'Nor me.'

She was silent again, and then with a look of utter bewilderment on her face she said, 'And who the hell is Kevin?'

'Don't ask,' I said.

For all my brave talk, I had to stop twice on the way back because I started to shake so hard I couldn't drive. Both times Sweetheart leaned over and held me tight, and I could smell her perfume, and her sweat, and her fear, and a faint tang of earth on her. Each time, after a few minutes or so, I was all right.

It was about five when I reversed the Granada up on to the open space in front of my house. To tell the truth, I was a bit worried about letting it be seen, but I had to take that chance. I went upstairs and got an old blanket and wrapped the guns and the shovel in it, before taking them into the house. After they were safely inside, Sweetheart and I took the box of cash up to my flat and emptied the money on to the carpet in the middle of the room.

'You sort out the money while I dump the motor,' I said.

'What about the box?'

'I'll find a skip and drop it in.' I don't know if they have skips in America, but I imagine she got the concept.

'OK. Don't be long.'

'Just as long as it takes, babe,' I said.

She smiled tiredly at me and started putting the banded stacks of bank notes into three piles.

I left the Granada in Victoria, doors and windows open, key in the ignition. The only other thing I could have done was leave a note under the windscreen saying 'Steal me'. But I thought that was a trifle excessive. I wore gloves and wiped all the places I remembered touching, just in case. I hopped an early morning bus to Tulse Hill and got back to Sweetheart around seven.

Her stuff was all packed away in her unecological suitcases. I was going to miss her shit everywhere. The money had been neatly divided into three, and put into plastic shopping bags she'd found in the kitchen drawer.

'When are you going back?' I asked, when I'd got a cup of tea.

'On Tuesday.'

'So you've still got a few days.'

She nodded.

'But now you've got enough cash to stay five-star.'

She nodded again.

'Anywhere in mind?' I asked.

She nodded yet again.

'Hilton? Intercontinental? Brown's? The Connaught? The Savoy? What?'

She shrugged.

'Well, at least I'll get my bed back.'

Nod number three.

'Want a lift anywhere?'

Shrug number two. Then she said, 'Can I ask you something?'

'What?'

'How come you've never hit on me since I've been here? Aren't I sexy enough for you?' Her eyes were that perfect shade of grey as she spoke.

'Give it a rest,' I said. 'No. I just assumed that you and Skinner had something going together.'

'Is that what he says?'

'No. He's never mentioned you. I just assumed it. Don't you?'

She smiled. 'You might call it that. Once.'

'Once what?' I asked. 'Once, one time only. Or once upon a time.'

84

'Once, once,' she said. 'In Burnley, on some godforsaken tour.'

'Why?' I asked. Thinking about it, Skinner would probably just about come up to her left tit. Still, not a bad job, I suppose.'

'What else do you do on a wet afternoon in Burnley? It was a mistake. One of those things. Nothing happened anyway. I didn't even get my skirt creased. Christ. Just look at the guy, will you? Whoopee-fucking-do. You don't give me much credit for taste, do you, Sharman?'

'Sorry. So where's it to be?' I asked. 'What ivory tower of luxury shall I transport you to?'

She went and sat on my bed. 'I want to stay here,' she said.

'That sofa's breaking my back. And I deserve a good night's sleep,' I said.

'Who said you'd be sleeping on the sofa?'

'You want to swap?'

This time she shook her head.

I looked at her and she patted the bed again. 'Christ, Sharman,' she said. 'Do I have to draw you a map?'

As a matter of fact, she didn't.

Christmas (Baby Please Come Home)

The title of this one says it all. Sharman takes on a simple job during the festive season, which turns out not to be so simple after all. My favourite part is when he visits the squat in King's Cross; it reminds me of my youth. The story also gives me a chance to get him out of South London for a bit and up to the flesh pots of Soho and Shepherd's Market.

The story is named after the best track on 'The Phil Spector Christmas Album', sung by Darlene Love, and is reputedly about being a drug dealer. Work it out for yourselves.

Soho – the capital's centre of vice. Only minutes from the glittering lights of Piccadilly that shine like the jewels in the crown of Great Britain's major city, lies this blot on our nation's conscience.

Blimey, I thought. Where do Channel 4 dig up these funny old short movies to fill the time between the commercial break and *The Oprah Winfrey Show*? And as the pedantic tones of the narrator droned on, the grainy old black and white film switched from a view of Eros, to Old Compton Street, where half a dozen elegant-looking women in high heels, pencil skirts and short fur coats patrolled the deserted pavements. Then to the front of the old Windmill Theatre, and inside, where half a hundred geezers in long macs and trilby hats were watching a tableau of naked girls standing so still on stage that you could almost count the goose bumps on their upper arms.

Back here in the real world it was 5 p.m. four days before Christmas, and rods of almost solid, freezing, black rain beat down on to the window of my office from the dark mass of cloud that seemed to sit only inches above the roof of the boozer opposite, where the warm, golden light that seeped from the front door and the gaps in the curtains seemed to beckon me over.

So that was the deal. An hour of Oprah interviewing a woman who'd hired a killer to shoot her husband, and, after the contract had gone sour, had spent four years in prison, and then returned, reconciled, to hubby's loving arms. After that, an hour in the pub, then off home with a bag of fish and chips for another evening in front of the TV watching the rest of the world get ready for the annual festivities. Me, I wanted none of it. And intended to spend Christmas Day in bed with a good book, a microwavable spaghetti bolognaise and a bottle of Jack Daniel's. No cards. No presents. No funny hats.

The narrator's voice on the soundtrack of the film continued with the story of the Windmill, and just as I was sure he was going to tell us how the place never closed, the door of my office opened to admit a man and a woman, water dripping from their umbrella, and I'd never know. I switched off the TV and looked up at my visitors from the chair I was sitting in.

'Is your name Sharman?' asked the man. He had a northern accent. He was well built with thick, short dark hair.

I nodded.

'Thank goodness,' the woman cut in. 'We thought we'd never find you.' She was blonde and quite nice-looking, though her eyes looked tired. Her accent was northern too. And slightly stronger than the man's.

'I'm usually here,' I said.

'But this is such a big city and we didn't have your proper address,' she went on. She was wearing a red cloth coat, the skirts of which were dark with moisture. The man was dressed in a rich-looking leather jacket and jeans, with a scarf knotted at his throat and leather gloves. They both looked to be about forty.

'What can I do for you?' I asked.

'Find our son,' said the woman. 'He's disappeared.'

'You'd better sit down,' I said, and got up, pulled my two clients' chairs in front of my desk and took her coat. It felt expensive and I noticed that the label was from Lewis's in Manchester, as I hung it up to dry close to one of the two central heating radiators. Underneath she wore a simple dark blue dress and a cardigan.

'My name's Himes,' said the man as I did it. 'Douglas Himes. This is my wife, Mona.'

'Pleased to meet you. Do you want some tea? Coffee?' I said as they sat.

They both asked for coffee and I went out back and put the kettle on. Whilst it was boiling I spooned coffee powder into three mugs and took the sugar bowl and put it on the edge of my desk. 'Milk?' I asked. They both nodded, and I went out back again, splashed milk into the mugs and when the kettle boiled, filled them.

I passed round the drinks and sat back in my own seat and said, 'Tell me about it.'

Douglas Himes started the story.

'Jimmy, that's our son's name, left school last year. He was sixteen, and he'd been wasting his time there for years. He was never very academic. Not that I cared. Neither was I, and I did all right. I offered him a job in my business. I own a firm that wholesales motor spares around Manchester. Business isn't bad. It isn't what it was a couple of years ago, but what business is? But at least we're keeping our heads above water. There aren't many other jobs to be had up there right now. None, in fact. This *damned* recession. But Jimmy didn't want to know.'

'He just lay around the house all day,' interrupted Mona Himes. 'He couldn't get the dole because he wouldn't take a training scheme. So we gave him money.'

'Then one day, just after last Christmas, he told us he was going to London,' Douglas Himes went on. 'Just like that. We tried to stop him, but what could we do? You know what kids are like these days.'

I do as it happens, if only from a distance, and I nodded and took out my cigarettes. 'Do you mind?' I said to Mona. She shook her head and I offered the packet to the pair of them, and Douglas Himes took one. I pushed the ashtray in his direction and flicked my ash into the waste paper basket next to my chair.

When Himes' cigarette was fired up to his satisfaction with a gold lighter he took from the pocket of his jacket, he continued his story.

'We begged and pleaded with him not to go. He knew no one down here, but he wouldn't listen. Eventually I gave him a couple of hundred pounds so that at least he could get somewhere decent to stay, and he left. I told him if he was short to let me know. I couldn't see him down here with no funds. You read such terrible things.'

I nodded. 'And you haven't seen him since?' I asked. You weren't exactly in a rush to find him, I thought.

'Oh yes,' said Mona Himes. 'He kept in touch. Regularly. He'd phone at least once a week. He even came home in the summer for a couple of weeks. He had money to burn then. But . . .'

'But what?' I asked.

'He'd changed. He was always a very private boy, but when he came home he was worse. He wouldn't let me into his room, and even though it was hot, he always wore a long-sleeved shirt. Then one day I walked in on him whilst he was having a wash in the bathroom. I was looking for dirty towels. He went mad. And his arms . . .'

She hesitated. 'What about them?' I asked, although I thought I could guess.

'They were bruised. Badly. And worse than that they were covered in little bloody holes. It was horrible.'

Track marks. Just as I had thought.

'Did he take drugs before he left home?' I asked.

'Not that we knew of,' said Himes. 'Though he might have.'

'And you said he had a lot of money?' I asked.

They both nodded. 'Hundreds,' said Himes. 'He even tried to give us back the money we'd lent him, although we wouldn't take it.'

'He said he had a job in a restaurant as a waiter and got lots of tips,' said his wife.

'Any idea which restaurant?' I asked.

'No. He didn't say.'

'And why are you worried about him now?'

'He said he'd come home for Christmas. He told us he'd come up last weekend. When we hadn't heard from him by Monday we started to get worried. We'd never had a phone number for him. He always called us. We kept asking, but he told us he didn't want us phoning him. He rang us last, last Thursday. Said he'd be up on Sunday at the very latest. That the restaurant was very busy.'

But not so busy that they'd let one of their staff have a protracted Christmas holiday. I thought not.

'Did you have an address for him down here?' I asked.

'Yes,' said Himes. 'He said he had a room at a house in King's Cross. At least he gave us his address. We went round there today but it was awful. Full of the strangest people having a party.'

'A rave, they called it,' said Mona.

'And he wasn't there?'

'We couldn't get any sense out of any of them,' said Himes. 'They were all drugged up.'

'It was a horrible place,' said Mona. 'Filthy. No curtains. No carpets. Nothing. Just a lot of children running wild.'

I nodded again.

'Will you try and find him?' said Mona. 'We've read about you in the papers. They say you always do your best.'

My fame had obviously spread far and wide. 'What about the police?' I asked. 'Have you been to them?'

'They took down his name and that was about all. They suggested we tried the Salvation Army. No. I'm sorry. The police were no use at all.'

'They're busy people,' I said. 'Especially at this time of the year.'

'But he's our son,' said Mona. 'Please say you'll help.'

I didn't want the job. The last thing I wanted to do was schlepp around London during Christmas week looking for some seventeen-year-old junkie. Not with all the once-a-year drinkers out. The half pint and small sherry merchants in their dodgy suits pretending to be full of good cheer. Taking a break from the missus and trying to get some half-pissed secretary to give them a blow job in a back alley. Oh l'amour.

'Please,' she said again, and reached into her handbag for a tissue. I looked into her tear-filled eyes and relented. 'I'll try,' I said. 'Do you have a photograph of him?'

She reached into her handbag again and brought out one of those Kodak paper folders that bulged with photographs. She handled it as if it was a religious object. Maybe it was to her. I know that if my daughter went missing, photos of her would be to me. She opened it and passed me the top photograph.

'That was taken on holiday in Ibiza two years ago when Jimmy was fifteen,' she said. 'It's a very good likeness.'

I put the photo on the desk in front of me and looked at it closely.

It was a study of a boy from the waist upwards dressed in a green vest holding a can of Lucozade. He was handsome, tanned, with shaggy blond hair and looked no more than twelve years old. The flash had reflected in his eyes and gave them a reddish tint.

'Fifteen,' I said. 'He looks younger.'

'He always has,' said his father.

'Can I look at the rest?' I asked.

Mona Himes passed over the packet, somewhat reluctantly, I thought.

I flipped through them. It was a microcosm of Jimmy Himes' life from day one. It was one of the saddest things I'd ever seen, and I've seen some.

I pulled out another couple of more recent pictures and carefully returned the rest to the folder and passed it back.

'I'd like to keep these,' I said. 'For now. I'll make sure you get them back.'

Her sense of relief was almost palpable.

'How much do you charge?' asked Douglas Himes.

'Two hundred a day plus expenses.'

It didn't seem to worry him. The motor spares business must have been better than he'd let on. He pulled a cheque book and pen from inside his leather jacket. 'I'll give you a cheque for five hundred to be going on with,' he said. 'Is that OK?'

I nodded. 'Are you staying in London?' I asked as he wrote.

Mona Himes nodded. 'At Selfridge's Hotel.'

'Have you got a car with you?' It was just something to break the silence really.

She nodded again. 'But we left it parked. We don't know

our way round London. We've been taking buses and cabs. We walked around for hours looking for you. That's why we got so wet.'

'There's a minicab firm next door,' I told her. 'They're all right. They'll get you back up West. How long do you plan on staying?'

'Until we find Jimmy,' said Douglas Himes as he tore the cheque out of the book.

'I'll do my best,' I said. 'Will you write down the address in King's Cross?' and I pushed a notepad in front of him. He scribbled down the information and pushed the notepad back.

That seemed to be about it for then. I helped Mona Himes back into her expensive coat and the pair of them went to get a taxi.

I passed on the pub and took a bottle of white plonk home to drink with my fish and chips. I watched TV for a bit then went to bed. I intended to be up early the next morning to begin my search for Jimmy Himes.

I reached King's Cross at ten. If this place was a squat like I guessed, any earlier would have been a waste of time. Squatters aren't exactly noted for early rising. I was dressed in my battered old leather jacket, jeans, artfully worn at the knees, and a pair of DMs with steel toe caps. Before I'd left home I'd stripped, cleaned and loaded my illegal .38 special Colt Cobra revolver and dropped it into one of my jacket pockets. You never know who you're going to meet in that part of town. Especially if you're asking questions that people don't want to answer. And besides, not everyone in the rave culture was all loved-up. Just the opposite, as I'd discovered before.

In the other pocket, in a white envelope, I put the photos of Jimmy Himes. I didn't want to crease them before I gave them back to his mother. And finally in the back pocket of my jeans I put two hundred and fifty quid in ten-pound notes from a secret stash that I keep at home in case of emergencies. I figured that before the day was out I might have to grease some palms.

The previous night's rain had stopped, but the clouds were still dark and angry and hung over London like they'd never let go.

I parked my E-type on a meter just round the corner from the address that Douglas Himes had given me and finished the journey on foot.

The house I was looking for was a tall, mid-terraced monstrosity round the back of the station. It had seen far better days, but then who hadn't?

The bay window on the ground floor front was half boarded up, and the door that stood at the top of three filthy stone steps was no stranger to blunt instruments. I listened carefully, but there was no sound from inside. Obviously yesterday's rave had reached its logical con-clusion. There was no bell-push by the splintered frame, just two old, bare wires that did nothing when I touched them together. I gave the door a hammer with my fist and felt it give almost an inch in the jamb. There was no answer, and I hammered again. Once again no one paid the slightest bit of attention, so I pulled my credit card case from my pocket and chose one of the cards that was out of date and loided the door. It took less than ten seconds. I slowly eased the door open and peered into the dark and deserted hall. Inside all was serene and I slipped in and pulled the door closed behind me. The hall was freezing and smelt of cat's piss. There was a door on the right. I tried it. The room with the bay window was empty except for about three hundred beer and soft drink cans, cigarette ends, roaches, and two big, battered hi-fi speakers in one corner.

I went further down the hall and came to another door.

I tried that one too and it opened into a bedroom. Hardly the honeymoon suite at the Savoy, but a bedroom nevertheless.

The walls and window were hung with old tapestry curtains, in one corner was a battered chest of drawers that held an ancient black and white TV and a tray covered with loose cigarette papers, shreds of tobacco, stripped cigarettes, small lumps of dope, and minicab firms' advertising cards, some whole, some torn. Beside the tray was a packet of clean hypodermic needles amongst a litter of used spikes, burnt spoons, night light candles, silver foil, and an empty glassine packet with just a trace of golden brown powder sticking to the sides. Against one wall was an old radiogram that looked as if it had come from a skip, and next to it a pile of records. Clothes were scattered everywhere. On a double mattress with no box springs, under a pile of dirty blankets and a stained duvet, two people were asleep.

I went over and looked down at them. On the bare pillows I could just make out that one was male, the other female, although their hair was of equal length. I went to the window and pulled the curtain that covered it across the piece of string that held it up, then went back to the bed and kicked the edge of the mattress hard.

The female opened her eyes and looked up into mine. 'Morning,' I said. 'Full English or continental?'

Her eyes were glazed and I might as well have not bothered. She focused on my face and looked around as if she wasn't sure where she was.

'Who are you?' she said.

I ignored the question. What was the point? She was probably on re-entry from orbit and my name would mean nothing to her. Often it meant nothing to me.

'I'm looking for Jimmy Himes,' I said.

'Who? What the fuck are you doing here?'

I told her again, and she shook the still form next to her until he grunted into life. 'Matt,' she said, 'there's someone here.'

I just knew this day was going to end in tears.

The man sat up, pulling the blankets off his girlfriend's bare breasts. They were thin and long with puckered brown nipples and she didn't try to cover them. I wished that she would. He was about twenty-five, skinny, with tracks on both arms.

'I don't want any trouble,' I said. 'I'm sorry to burst in but the front door was open.'

A white lie. But forgivable under the circumstances, I thought. Although I might as well have saved my breath.

'Are you the filth?' demanded Matt, pushing his hair out of his eyes.

People are always asking me that. 'No,' I said.

'Then what the fuck do you want?' he said.

I repeated myself for the second time.

'Never heard of him,' he said. 'Fuck off.'

I ignored him. He was probably used to it. 'I've got some photos,' I said, and took out the envelope, opened it and pulled one out. I hunkered down on my heels, and showed it to them.

'Don't know him,' said Matt. 'Now fuck off or . . .'

'Don't, Matt,' I said tiredly. 'You're out of your class.' Which was probably the wrong thing to say in front of his inamorata.

'I'll . . .' he said, beginning to push back the covers to get at me.

I didn't want to see any more of his skinny body and shoved him back flat on the mattress. 'I said don't.'

He lay there and I could smell his breath. I've smelled more pleasant things, believe me. I held up the photo again and said, 'Are you sure you haven't seen this boy? His name's Jimmy. Think about it.'

'Maybe,' said the woman.

'That's better,' I said, and eased the pressure off Matt's narrow chest. 'Where? Here?'

'He used to score sometimes.'

'Where?'

'Where we do.'

'Jill,' said Matt, and I increased the pressure on his chest again, until he shut up.

'What does he supply?'

'Everything. Dope. Smack. Coke. Uppers. Downers. Es. Speed. The Lot.'

'Where is he?' I asked.

'How much is it worth?'

Now we were getting there.

'Jill,' said Matt again. 'You don't know who this geezer is.'

'What does it matter?' said Jill. 'That cunt's always shorting us. Serves him right if this bloke does him. How much?' to me again.

'A tenner.'

'Bollocks. Fifty.'

I wasn't going to argue. If she was lying I could always come back. And do what? Shit. It wasn't my money. If she was lying I'd just tell Himes and let him put a bit extra on the price of his spark plugs.

I stood up and took out my money. I wasn't worried about letting them see it. I peeled off five tens and held them up. 'Give,' I said.

'He lives upstairs. Handy, like,' said Jill. 'First floor at the front. His name's Derek. White bloke with dreads. He's probably there now.'

'Thanks, Jill,' I said, and dropped the money on to the bed where she grabbed it and stuffed it under her pillow.

'Don't tell him it was us told you,' said Matt. 'We've got to live here.'

'Fair enough,' I said, and turned to leave.

'You can have this for another fifty,' said Jill, and flipped the covers off her body. She was like something out of Belsen. Emaciated. With tracks up her arms and legs and even in her crotch.

Fifty what? I thought. Pence?

'No thanks, love,' I said. 'Another time maybe.' And I left the room quickly, closing the door behind me. I didn't wait to hear her reply. I've discovered in my little life that saying no to a woman's offer of sex is like asking for credit in a pub. A refusal often offends. I'd leave Matt to catch the flak. I'm sure he was used to that too.

I climbed the stairs to the first floor, found the door of the room at the front and knocked hard. There was no answer, so I tried again and heard a male voice call out, 'Who is it?'

'Jimmy sent me,' I called back.

There was silence again and then from just the other side of the door the voice said, 'Jimmy who?'

'Jimmy Himes.'

'Whaddya want?'

'Guess.'

There was a further pause before I heard the sounds of locks disengaging, and the door opened six inches on a security chain and a white face half hidden by lank blond dreads appeared in the gap. 'Who are you?' the face asked.

'Nick. Are you Derek?'

'Whaddya want?' he said again.

'Can I come in? It's a bit public out here.'

'Bollocks. Whaddya want?'

'I'm looking for Jimmy.'

'He ain't here.'

'Do you know where he is?'

'You Old Bill?' That question again.

'No.'

'Then fuck off.' And the door began to close.

I lashed out with my right foot and the steel toe of my DM slammed into the door, pushing it back to the full extent of the chain, and the face vanished. I slammed my left shoulder against the door, the chain snapped and I was inside. The owner of the voice was on the other side of the room. He turned and I saw he was holding a small baseball bat. A miniature version of a Louisville Slugger, but still plenty weapon enough to crush my skull if he got a good shot in.

I stood inside the doorway as he came at me. He was of medium height and build, but his arms were thick and muscular. He pulled back the bat to give me a good whack and I moved inside his arm and took the blow on my left shoulder, then let him have a good whack of my own with my clenched fist into his solar plexus. He let out his breath with a gasp, all the strength seemed to go out of his body, the baseball bat fell to the uncarpeted floorboards with a clatter and he doubled up. That sort of punch hurts and disorientates. I allowed him to drop to his knees, took hold of his left hand and bent the little finger back until I felt the ligaments at breaking-point and the boy screamed a high-pitched scream. That hurts too. Much worse than a punch in the stomach. A bladder-emptying kind of hurt that fills your whole head with pain.

'You going to be good?' I hissed.

He nodded and looked at me through eyes dulled with agony and I eased the pressure, pulled him to his feet and propelled him across to an unmade bed. I threw him on top, rescued the Slugger and stood over him slapping it into my palm.

'Are you Derek?' I asked.

'What of it?'

'Jimmy Himes,' I said.

'What about him?' I could tell it hurt him to speak.

'You know him?'

A nod.

'He scores off you?'

Another nod.

'Seen him lately?'

A shake of the head.

'How long ago?'

'Last week.'

'Where's he stay?'

Silence.

I slapped my palm again with the bat. Harder.

'Upstairs,' said Derek. 'With Wayne and Duane.'

'Who?'

He repeated the names.

'Where exactly?'

'Top floor.'

'Thanks,' I said, put the bat carefully on the mantelpiece above the dead gas fire and left the room

I went further upstairs. All the way, until I came to yet another door and I wondered what I'd find behind this one. I rapped on it with my knuckles and heard movement, and it was opened by a huge young guy dressed in a white singlet and blue and white checked trousers like the ones chefs wear. Around his head of long dark hair was tied a white bandanna. He had a lot of upper body development, and his skin gleamed with oil.

'Wayne?' I said. 'Duane?'

'Duane. And who might you be?' His voice was surprisingly high for one of his stature.

I got the picture.

'Hi,' I said. 'My name's Nick Sharman. I'm looking for Jimmy Himes.'

'Who isn't? Come right on in. Be my guest.'

He pulled the door back and I went inside. There was a short hall interrupted by three doors, and he pointed me to the one at the end. Inside was another massive young bloke dressed in a white shirt and black trousers. 'Well hello,' he said in a deep, masculine voice. 'Who have we here?'

'Someone looking for Jimmy,' trilled Duane. 'This is Wayne by the way. Wayne, this is Nick.'

'Welcome to our abode,' said Wayne. 'Be it ever so humble.'

I looked round. It was a living room cum gymnasium. One side was furnished with rugs on the floor, curtains at the window, two matching armchairs and a daybed covered with cushions to make a sofa. One wall was lined with shelves holding a TV, video, stereo, albums, cassettes and books. The other side was jammed with what looked like a full Nautilus rig and a whole lot of other weight-lifting shit. Now I knew where Wayne and Duane's muscles came from, and I pulled back my shoulders. The walls of the room that weren't covered with shelves were adorned with posters of gay icons: James Dean in *Giant*; Marlon Brando in *The Wild Ones*; Boy George in full drag; Jimmy Sommerville in nothing much. Par for the course.

'And you're looking for young James,' said Wayne. 'Or just a little romance?'

'Nothing like that,' I replied. 'His mother and father have hired me to find him. I'm a private detective.'

'A private *dick*,' said Duane, with emphasis on the word 'dick', and flexed his biceps at me.

I smiled at him. 'That's right,' I said.

'What if he doesn't want to be found?'

'If I could see him and he tells me that . . .' I shrugged and didn't finish the sentence.

'We'd like to see him too,' said Wayne. 'He owes us some rent.'

'If you know where he is . . .' I said.

'Probably,' said Duane. 'But why should we tell you?'

'To put his mother and father's minds at rest that he's all right. That's all. I don't intend him any harm.'

'Sez you.' Wayne this time. I was getting tired of the double act.

'Anyway,' said Duane 'We can't possibly talk now. We're due at work soon.'

'What do you do?' I asked for something to say.

'We work in a restaurant in Covent Garden. Duane cooks, I serve,' said Wayne.

Jesus. The fucking salmonella sisters, I thought. Perfect.

'So if you'd like to leave,' he went on.

'No,' I said. 'I'd like you to tell me where Jimmy Himes is.'

'Duane,' said Wayne, and Duane flexed his biceps at me again, and moved closer.

I was getting nothing but aggro at this house and I was getting sick of it, and what I did next was probably an over-reaction, but I did it anyway.

I pulled the Colt out of my jacket pocket and stuck the two-inch barrel into Duane's face. On his forehead. Right where his third eye should be if you believe all that mystic bollocks. I cocked it with a loud click. Loud enough to scare the shit out of Duane anyway. 'Relax, Shirley,' I said. 'Don't do anything stupid.' Then to Wayne. 'And as for you, Dorothy. Lie face down on the sofa there and spread your arms. You must be used to that.'

If they thought I was a homophobic fascist, all the better. It wouldn't be the first time. I used to wear a blue uniform, remember.

I didn't want to pull the trigger and splatter Duane's brains all over Marlon Brando, but I hoped he'd think that was exactly what I did want to do, and not get physical and try to be a hero. It worked. He stood stock still while Wayne made a high-pitched sound at the back of his throat, turned, and fell forward on to the mattress of the daybed.

'Right,' I said. 'Now we've got that sorted. How about telling me where Jimmy is? Duane?'

Duane squinted along the length of the gun I was holding, and swallowed. When he spoke his voice was even higher pitched than before. 'He works the meat rack,' he said.

'Do what?'

'The Dilly,' said Wayne, his voice muffled by the mattress he was lying on. 'Piccadilly, Coventry Street, Leicester Square. The cafés and arcades. He's a rent boy. Didn't you know?'

'No,' I said.

'It pays for his habit,' Wayne went on. 'He works there most evenings. We assumed he'd met a rich punter who took him away for a few days.'

'So why didn't you just tell me?' I said disgustedly. 'Instead of giving me the old queen act.'

'We didn't know who you were,' piped Duane. 'You won't hurt me, will you?'

'I shook my head. 'No, Duane. I won't hurt you,' and I put up my gun, and let the hammer down gently. 'I'm off now,' I said. 'Thanks for the information. And next time don't be so aggressive. You never know if it's a pistol in my pocket or if I'm just glad to see you. Have a nice day, girls,' and I backed out into the hall, through the door, down the stairs and outside, back to my car.

I didn't see a soul as I went.

I took the photo of Jimmy and drove up to Piccadilly to try and find him.

103

I parked the Jaguar in the NCP at the back of Leicester Square and started my search. By two that afternoon I'd shown the photo round most of the cafés and arcades in the area, and I think I'd been told to fuck off in fifteen different languages. I went into Gerrard Street and found a pub full of Chinese and bought a pint of lager. At least in that boozer there were no happy Christmas revellers. I was sitting at a table, smoking my second cigarette, when a kid sidled up to me. He was young and looked like he was auditioning for a place in The Jam. He was wearing a skinny two-piece suit of silver tonik mohair, black and white shoes, a pale blue button-down shirt and a narrow black leather tie. He had blond hair cut into a pudding basin, and down his left cheek, from his eye to his chin, he had a nasty-looking thin scar.

'I hear you're looking for someone?' he said.

I nodded. Any port in a storm.

'Jimmy Himes?'

I nodded again.

'I know where he is.'

'Where?'

He grinned. 'Buy us a drink first.'

I was probably being conned, but what the hell. 'What do you want?' I asked.

'Scotch and coke.'

I went up to the bar and bought what he asked for and another pint for myself. When I got back and he had downed half the drink, I said, 'You know Jimmy?'

'I wouldn't be here if I didn't,' he retorted.

'What's your name?'

'Rick. Slick Rick they call me.'

Sure they do, I thought. 'And you know where Jimmy is?'

'I know where he was.'

'Where?'

'It'll cost ya.'

I wasn't exactly amazed at that. 'How much?'

'A ton.'

'How do I know you're telling me the truth?'

'I wouldn't lie, mister.'

'You would say that.'

He looked injured at the thought. 'He's my mate,' he said. 'We work the Dilly together.'

'You're on the rent?'

He nodded and felt the scar.

'A dangerous game,' I said.

'What, this? Not half as dangerous as HIV. You can't get plastic surgery for that.'

I couldn't argue with him on that score.

'So where is he?' I asked.

He held out his hand.

'No, son,' I said. 'You got a drink for your sauce. A hundred nicker and I want some proof.'

'I can't prove it. But it's the truth.'

'Tell me.'

So he did. According to him, Jimmy was with the same old queen who'd given Rick the stripe down his face. Rick would do a lot for money, but not everything, if the everything included grievous bodily harm, which was what the old queen wanted to inflict upon him.

'Has the old queen got a name?' I asked.

'Daddy,' said Rick. 'When I wouldn't do what he wanted, he did this.' He felt the scar again. 'The old cunt.'

'Did you go to the police?'

Rick laughed fit to burst. 'Are you fuckin' joking?' He said. 'They'd bang *me* up if I did.'

He was probably right.

'So where does Daddy hang out?' I asked.

'Shepherd's Market. He's's got a place down there.'

'Let's go.'

105

'Not now. It's too early. He sleeps in. Tonight's favourite.'

'What time?'

'Eight. Meet me outside the Shepherd's pub. Know it?'

I nodded. 'I'll be in my car,' I said. 'A red Jaguar E-Type.'

'It's all right for some. I'll show you his place, then split. OK?'

'OK,' I agreed.

'And bring the dosh.' And with that, Rick swallowed his drink and left.

I was parked where he said just before eight. The rain had started again and was slanting through the light of the street lamps, raising a mist of steam from the long bonnet of the car and obscuring my view through the windscreen like tears. The radio was playing Phil Spector's Christmas album, and a couple of whores were eyeing up the car from the other side of the road.

I was still wearing my leather jacket and jeans, and I could feel the reassuring weight of the Colt in my right pocket. Rick ducked round the corner in front of me as the clock in the car said 8.05. He wasn't wearing a coat and had the thin lapels of his jacket turned up against the weather. I leaned over, slipped the lock on the passenger door, he climbed in, and the whores walked off in disgust.

'Excellent motor,' he said, and he was just a boy again. Not a rent boy.

'It'll do.'

'Take me for a drive one day?'

'One day,' I replied. 'Now where does this bloke Daddy live?'

'Just round the corner. Number seven. Over the pottery shop. There's an entryphone by the door at the side. Got my dough?'

'And he's just going to let me in?'

I saw his face stiffen in the light from the dashboard. 'You promised.'

'Not exactly. You get me in and I find that Jimmy's been there, then you get your hundred.'

'Fuck that.'

'Take it or leave it. You could still be lying. Like I said. If I find Jimmy's been there you get your money.'

'He'll kill me.'

'I'll make sure you're all right.'

'You don't know him.'

'I don't even know that he exists.'

'How do I know you'll pay me?'

I took fifty nicker in tens, rolled up tightly, out of my shirt pocket. 'Half now. Half later. How about that?'

'He *was* there,' said Rick. 'I promise you Jimmy went there.'

'So you've got nothing to worry about.'

'All right. But watch the fat bastard. You don't know him.' And he touched the scar on his face again.

We got out of the car and walked round the corner. Just as Rick had described it, there was a door next to the pottery shop, with an entryphone attached to the frame. I looked up. Dim light escaped from the edges of the curtains at the two windows above us.

Rick pushed the buzzer and waited. After half a minute a voice said, 'Yes.'

Rick looked at me. 'Is that Daddy?' he asked. His voice was softer than the one he used to me, and he put on a slight lisp.

'Yes.'

'My name's Steve. Ronnie sent me. He said I could stay.'

There was silence. Then the voice said, 'Come on up, Steve,' and the entryphone's buzzer sounded and the door clicked open half an inch.

Rick grabbed the roll of notes I was still holding and said. 'See you back at the motor.' And he turned and vanished into the thickening rain. I pushed open the door and was faced by a flight of stairs leading upwards, faintly lit from a bare bulb screwed into a fixture in the ceiling.

I walked slowly up the flight until it dog-legged and I could see an open door with a figure standing in the doorway.

The figure was huge. Bigger than huge. Humungous, in fact. A great fat man in a white shirt and a pair of strides that would have made enough suits to dress a quartet. I stopped about four steps below him and looked up. I didn't like being at a disadvantage, but I didn't want to get close enough for him to aim a kick at my head with the big, black shoes he was wearing.

'Daddy?' I said.

He looked down at me in puzzlement. 'It wasn't you that buzzed, though.'

'No,' I said. 'It was someone I met who told me that Jimmy Himes had been here.'

I saw the fat man's face pale and he licked his lips.

'Who told you that?' he asked.

'It doesn't matter. *Is* Jimmy here?'

'Who are you?'

'Nick Sharman. I'm a detective. Private. I was hired by Jimmy's mum and dad to find him.'

'I don't know any Jimmy . . . What did you say his name was? Himes?'

'That's right. And I've been told different.'

'Then you've been told wrong.'

'Would you mind if I came in and had a look round?'

'I certainly would. You could be anyone. A man alone in my condition . . .'

I wasn't interested in a diagnosis. I took one of my cards

from inside my jacket and climbed the last few stairs until I was on a level with him, and put it in his tiny, fat paw.

He glanced at it and said, 'This means nothing.'

I pulled out the photo I'd been showing around all day. 'This is Jimmy. Are you sure you don't know him?'

Daddy's eyes flicked to the photo, then away. 'Never seen him before in my life.'

I shrugged. 'Fair enough,' I said. 'How would it be if I came back with the police?'

His manner changed and he gave me a smarmy grin, but I saw sweat break out on his forehead like tiny blisters of clear vanish.

'I don't think that will be necessary,' he said.

'Can I come in, then?'

He moved his massive bulk backwards into the flat and admitted me. I pushed the door closed behind me. It was warm, and the hall was freshly decorated, with a thick blue carpet on the floor and a tiny table just inside, underneath the flat's entryphone, with a glass vase of fresh flowers on it. Home sweet home. But the smell of the flowers didn't disguise the sour smell coming from Daddy, and another smell from somewhere inside. Sweet but rank. Faint enough not to be noticeable unless you knew what it was.

I knew. And I was glad I'd brought my gun.

There were five doors leading off the hall. The flat was bigger than it looked from the street. All the doors were closed.

Daddy threw open the first one on the left, reached in and switched on the light. It was the kitchen. It was spartanly neat and the appliances and utensils reflected like mirrors. It was empty.

Next door: bathroom and toilet. Once again everything shone. Once again, it was empty.

End door: a bedroom, simply furnished with a single

divan and a bedside table. The sweet smell was stronger there. The room was in darkness except for the light that entered from outside, between the undrawn curtains at the window that looked on to a bare brick wall opposite. Daddy stepped in and fumbled with the light switch. A dim bulb came on and I saw the door of a cupboard in the far wall. I pushed Daddy towards the divan and went over and yanked the cupboard door open. As I did so, the smell hit me like a muffled hammer. Human decay in its early-to-middling stages. Inside the cupboard, dressed in a puffa jacket and jeans, was the body of Jimmy Himes. His face was bloodless, and his lips were drawn back over yellow teeth, but he was instantly recognizable from the photo I had shown Daddy. There was no visible sign of injury. Jimmy's body was propped up against the back of the cupboard, whether by rigor or because the collar of his jacket has been caught on a hook. I didn't know, and didn't stop to find out.

I looked at the fat man and he grimaced. 'You fucker,' I said.

'There's no need to get personal,' he replied. 'I'm sure we can come to some arrangement.'

'No arrangement,' I said, and drew the Colt from my pocket and pointed it at him.

'And you won't need that either.'

'We'll see. Where's your phone?'

'In the living room,' he said. 'The door opposite the kitchen.'

I backed out of the room, gestured with the revolver, and he followed me. 'Why have you kept him here?' I asked as we went.

'I like him. He doesn't talk back.'

I could have shot the bastard there and then for saying that. I should have. It was all going too easily. I walked backwards into the hallway, Daddy following me all the while, and when he reached the doorway he looked over my shoulder along the length of the hall and said, 'Sonny. Deal with him.'

'Not that old one,' I said. 'You've been watching too much TV.' And then I felt a slight displacement of air by by ear, before the doorway and Daddy exploded in a galaxy of white lights, and I tumbled down into a deep well of blackness where there was no light at all.

I came to for a moment as I was picked up by a pair of strong arms and carried back into the bedroom. I opened my eyes and saw that I was being held by a massive lump of meat in a pale blue, hooded sweatshirt. It had to be Sonny. *Yesterday my life was full of rain.* I was so out of it that I started to hum the tune, and he crashed my head against the door frame as we went, and the black hole opened again and I dropped into its embrace for a second time.

I came to once more lying on the divan with my arms and legs tied tightly and some kind of tape over my mouth. I was on my side, my hands were behind my back, and both they and my feet were numb and cramped, they were bound so tightly. The light had been switched off and the room was dark except for the reflected glow coming through my window, and someone was bending over me. For a second I didn't know where the hell I was, until I was pulled roughly on to my back and I looked up into Rick's face.

Then I remembered.

'And you were going to make sure everything was all right,' he whispered. 'You're fucking useless.' He ripped the tape from my mouth, taking a few square centimetres of skin with it.

'How did you get here?' I said through dry lips, in a voice that I didn't recognize as my own.

'Up the fire escape and through the window. I thought you'd run out on me.'

I shook my head and nearly passed out again.

'Did you find Jimmy?' he asked.

I almost nodded, then thought better of it. 'Yes, I did.'

'Where is he?'

'He's dead. Murdered. In the cupboard over there.'

'*What?*' Rick looked at the cupboard door. 'Christ. I wondered what that stink was.'

'Can you untie me?' I said. 'We can talk about it later.'

'Better than that,' said Rick, and he reached into his jacket pocket and produced a flick-knife. He touched the button on the handle and a six-inch blade popped out, reflecting the dim light in the room.

As he slashed at the cords that bound my wrists we both heard movement in the hall outside the room.

'Quick. It's one of them,' I said, urgently trying to rub some life back into my hands. 'And they've got my gun.'

Rick stood up and went towards the door. 'My legs,' I said desperately, but before he could cut those ropes too we heard the movement get louder as someone approached the room. Rick ran across the carpet, opened the cupboard where Jimmy's body was hidden, slid in, and pulled the door closed behind him. I lay on the bed, put my arms behind me as if they were still tied and squinted at the door through half-closed eyes. It began to open and a shaft of light from the hall crept across the carpet before it was obscured by Daddy's huge bulk. He stood in the doorway, the light behind him, my gun in his hand. I hoped he'd come close enough so's I could grab him because my feet were useless, my hands weren't much better, and I knew I'd only get one chance.

He entered the room slowly and I wondered what was on his mind, when there was a noise from the cupboard and I knew the game was up. Daddy switched on the light, looked at me, then turned in the direction of the cupboard door and raised the gun he was holding. The look on his face was half-puzzlement, half-fear. Slowly the cupboard door began to swing open and Daddy's eyes widened in astonishment. I knew that with my legs tied the way they were I couldn't reach him before he could shoot me, and I knew that Rick and I were done for.

The door opened further. Daddy was frozen to the spot as Jimmy's body appeared in the opening.

Daddy screamed and fired twice at Jimmy. Rick, who was holding the corpse as a shield, let it drop and ran across the carpet, open flick-knife in his hand, and his arm outstretched. Daddy stepped back and Rick plunged the blade upwards into his throat, and blood spouted like a fountain over his gun hand. Daddy fired one more, point blank, into Rick's stomach and the heavy bullet smeared a chunk of his back across the floor.

The fat man fell to his knees like a tower block being demolished, and with much the same racket, one hand clawing at the knife that protruded from his quadruple chins. I threw myself off the bed and crashed to the floor, cursing my useless legs, pulled myself up, using his fat as handholds, tore at the gun he was still clutching, and, hitting at his face and neck with the side of my clenched left fist, hammered the knife further into his flesh. The Colt was sticky with both Rick's and his blood, but I managed to tear it out of his grasp as the door at the far end of the hall opened and Sonny appeared, and ran towards us. I fell flat on the floor and fired upwards, emptying the gun into Sonny's torso as he came. The pale blue of his shirt blossomed red, and he stumbled and fell, and his body slid along the carpet until his head rested in the doorway just a few feet from where I was lying. He opened his mouth and breathed his last with a rattle, and a gout of hot blood.

I looked at the carnage. At Sonny's corpse, at Daddy

bubbling his last around the amateur tracheotomy that Rick had performed on his throat, and at Rick himself, doubled up on the floor, still breathing but with a sound that was anything but healthy.

Fuck me, I thought. How am I going to explain all this?

I managed. Just about.

Rick was still alive, but bleeding badly from the .38 special exit wound in his back, and not so badly from the entrance from his belly. I dropped the Colt, ripped the ropes from around my ankles, took off my jacket, then my shirt, and ripped it in two. I wadded up one half and stuffed it in the hole in his back and covered the hole in his front with the other half. Then I stepped over Daddy's and Sonny's bodies and went to find the phone.

I needn't have bothered. Some concerned citizen had heard the shots and called the police. As I picked up the receiver I heard the scream of a siren in the street outside, followed by the slamming of doors and a buzz from the entryphone. I went into the hall and buzzed back and met the coppers at the flat door with the gun dangling from my left forefinger by its trigger guard. The first copper took the empty Colt gingerly from me, and I told them to call an ambulance. They did.

The first copper went on into the flat while the second put me against the wall and searched me.

The ambulance arrived within minutes, which was a minor miracle, closely followed by a couple of detectives who took me down to West End Central to get my story.

I told it pretty well as it had happened. I just left out one part, and told only one lie.

I left out the part about going to King's Cross that morning, and started my story with my tour of the Dilly where I met Rick. And I said that the gun belonged to Daddy and was at the flat when I arrived, and he'd pulled it on me. Like I said, I'd stripped and cleaned it that morning and I always wear a pair of cotton gloves when I do, so's I leave no prints on the mechanism inside or on the cartridges. My fingerprints were on the outside, but so what? You'd expect them to be if I'd used the gun to shoot Sonny, and there was so much blood on the weapon by the time we'd finished wrestling for it that I doubt if forensics could get decent impressions anyway.

I reckoned the squatters at the house at the Cross wouldn't be big on reading newspapers or watching TV news, and only Wayne and Duane had seen me with it earlier. And if they did tell, it was just my word against theirs.

The police called up Douglas Himes at the hotel and he confirmed hiring me, and Rick lasted long enough in ICU to tell his part of the story, before he died the next day.

The police seemed to be quite happy about getting two chicken hawks off the streets. And as for Jimmy and Rick, there's plenty more like them arriving every day at London's mainline stations for the cops to worry about them overmuch.

Well, I assume I explained everything. It's over three months now since Christmas and everyone seems to have forgotten about the incident.

Almost everyone.

Mona Himes called me up a couple of weeks back to thank me for my help. She was crying before she'd said a dozen words.

While I listened to her sobbing, someone put the phone back on the hook.

I don't think it was her.

Victoria

Until now, this story has only ever been published in America, in a collection called *Royal Crimes*, a title which kind of speaks for itself. In it Sharman gets to meet a member of the royal family who's been a bit of a naughty girl. As some of it almost came true later, I'm glad I didn't name any names. The title is from a Ray Davies tune.

I was standing, looking out of my office window, when he arrived. He was in the back of a gun-metal grey Daimler with military plates. The chauffeuse, all neat in black stockings, jumped out of the front and opened the kerbside rear door. He unfolded himself from inside, then leant back in and collected his brolly. Don't ask me why, as it hadn't rained for weeks. Maybe he felt undressed without it. Maybe he took it to bed with him. I wouldn't like to say.

Of course, then, I didn't know he was coming to see me. And even a few seconds later, when he pushed open my office door, I wasn't certain.

'Mr Nicholas Sharman?' he said, with a question mark attached. Then I knew.

'That's me,' I said, walking around behind my desk in case his accent was infectious. It could have cut glass. At forty feet. You don't get much of that in Tulse Hill. But then you don't get too many like him at all. He was six foot eight if he was an inch. And wafer thin with it. And the fact that he stood as straight as a metal rule made him look even taller if that were possible. I would have put him about sixty, but the skin on his face was pink and smooth and unlined, and shaved to a millimetre of its life, except for the silver bristle of moustache on his top lip. On his head he sported a silk bowler that he wore down over his eyes, guards' fashion. His neck was throttled by a stiff white collar attached to a raspberry-coloured shirt by a gold stud. Above the stud, knotted tightly, was what looked suspiciously like an old Etonian tie. Even on that warm day he wore a double-breasted overcoat of a navy material that by its sheen I took to be cashmere. Under the overcoat a pair of stepped-bottom trousers were visible, creased sharper than a landlady's tongue, that broke over elastic-sided boots with a shine that would shame a mirror. The umbrella he carried had an antique wooden handle and was furled so neatly and tightly I doubted that it had ever got damp. 'I wonder if I could have a word?' he asked.

'Of course,' I said. I was beginning to get intrigued. And polite. Too polite. I'd have to watch that.

He pulled up the hard wooden chair I keep for the customers, removed the bowler to expose a full head of hair that matched the colour of his moustache cut close to his scalp, hooked his brolly over the chairback, opened his overcoat to expose a double-breasted suit jacket, sat down, hiking up the strides as he did so, and crossed his legs. 'May I smoke?' he asked.

'Of course,' I said again.

He extracted a silver cigarette case from the inside pocket of his jacket, opened it, and offered the case to me. I was trying for the four hundred and fourteenth time to give up. Unsuccessfully as it turned out, but even so I refused. He shrugged and placed an untipped cigarette between his lips. From his outside jacket pocket, right-hand side, he took out a matching silver lighter, flicked the wheel, and touched the flame to the tip of the cigarette and inhaled. 'Disgusting habit,' he said by way of apology, though he needn't have bothered. 'But I've been doing it for forty years, and I don't think I'll ever stop.' He coughed discreetly. 'Until they cart me away that is.'

I nodded in agreement. I couldn't think of anything else to do.

'Mr Sharman,' he said. 'Do you remember signing the Official Secrets Act?'

I must have looked surprised at the question.

'When you joined the police,' he explained.

I nodded again.

'It still applies.' He looked round the room. 'Do you have an ashtray?'

'It's a secret,' I said.

It was his turn to look surprised. Then he laughed. A ferocious bark. He sounded like a walrus demanding to be fed. 'Your famous sense of humour,' he said. 'I've been told about it. Now, an ashtray if you don't mind. There's a good fellow.' I got one from on top of the filing cabinet and put it on the edge of the desk in front of him.

'Are you a secret, too?' I asked.

'I'm sorry,' he said.

'Your name.'

'My dear chap, I do apologize.' He stood up and stuck his hand over the top of the desk. 'Cave-Browne-Cave,' he said. 'Browne with an "e".'

I shook the proffered mitten. 'It sounds like a firm of solicitors,' I said.

He barked another laugh. 'Rich. Very rich,' he said. 'I must remember that. But it is my name nevertheless. Peter Piers, to be precise. Major. Ex-Blues and Royals, presently seconded to Buck House.'

'Really?' I asked. If it hadn't been for the car and the chauffeuse, I would have put him down as an absconder

118

from the Maudsley Psychiatric Hospital up the road, given him half a quid, and told him where the bus stop back was.

He let go of my hand and pulled a black leather folder from his overcoat pocket. He flipped it open and held it six inches from my face. Inside were his credentials, complete with a very flattering photograph. Professionally posed, I guessed. I'd seen similar credentials only once before. When I was in the Job. They were carried by the man who carried the briefcase which contained the codes that triggered Great Britain's nuclear strike force. He accompanied the Prime Minister when he or she went walkabout. Never more than a few yards away. They were the kind of credentials that opened any door in the land. Believe me, they don't come inside cornflake packets. I was impressed. More than impressed in fact.

'Really,' he said and returned to his chair. 'Security to HM personally. And I'd like to remind you that breaches of the OSA bear rather serious penalties.' He looked round the room again. 'I'm sure that even this place is preferable to a cell in Wormwood Scrubs.'

'If you're threatening me, Major,' I said, 'perhaps you could tell me why.'

'Threatening you? No, no, no. Just a thought, that's all.'

I wondered if he'd ever come to the point. He must have picked up my thought. 'At present you are engaged in the activity of a self-employed private detective, are you not?' he asked.

Through all the verbiage I picked out the nub of the question. 'That's right,' I replied.

He looked round the room for the third time. 'Has this place been swept recently?' he asked.

'I give it a dust now and then and run the Hoover round on a Saturday morning,' I said.

Again the laugh. 'No. Swept for bugs. Listening devices.'

119

'Here?' I said. 'Who would bother to bug this place?'

'You'd be surprised. I think we'd better continue our conversation in the car. You have no objections, I trust?'

'Whatever,' I said. Anything to get to the point of his visit. He collected his brolly, and we went out to the Daimler. I locked the office door behind us. The chauffeuse opened the car door for us. I smiled at her. She didn't smile back. Once inside the opulent leather interior of the motor, he instructed the driver to take a slow poodle, as he put it, and closed the glass partition between us and her. When the car was safely on the South Circular heading away from town, I asked him, 'Do you need a private detective for something?'

'No.'

'Then why—?'

'I need you,' he interrupted. 'You in particular.'

'Why?'

'Because you know every sleazy little crook in the area,' he said.

'Do I?'

'Oh, yes. I've done my research, asked around. And the consensus of opinion is that, if I need to find one, then you're the man.'

'And *you* need to find one?' I said, allowing a little note of disbelief to enter my voice.

'Exactly. To be precise, a second-storey man. I believe that's what you call them.'

'Not me,' I said. 'George Raft maybe, but not me.'

'What then?'

'Burglar'll do,' I said.

'Yes, you're right,' he agreed. 'A burglar *will* do. One that can crack the combination on a safe.'

'A peterman,' I said. 'Curiouser and curiouser. But why do you need a burglar and a peterman?'

He reminded me about the Official Secrets Act again.

Then he told me. 'A certain member of the royal family,' he began. 'A female member. A married female member, whose marriage is not all it could be. Should be. Recently had an unfortunate dalliance with a young man. A young man she met at an embassy dinner in a foreign country. A foreign country with which on the surface we appear to have good relations. But in fact we don't. The young man took advantage of her and the situation, or she of him. It doesn't really matter. Unfortunately, he was not an honourable young man, I'm afraid. The dalliance was short, but the repercussions could be long-lasting. The young man stole something from her. A ring. A very valuable and singular item. The singularity is the problem, not the value. It is easily recognizable as part of the crown jewels of our sovereign lady.' He stopped and looked out of the window at the passing traffic.

'The ring is now in the hands of another lady.' The way he said 'lady' told me that she was not his idea of one, but he was too polite to mention it. 'She is the wife of the ambassador of that country to the Court of St James. Next week the lady in question intends to wear the ring to a state banquet at Buckingham Palace. It will cause a scandal, and embarrassment to all concerned.' He looked at me. 'I imagine you think that is foolish. But believe me, in the circles we are discussing it is of paramount importance.'

'And?' I said.

'We have a mole in the embassy. The mole has the ear of the ambassador's wife. That is how we know she intends to wear the ring to the banquet.'

'How did the ambassador's wife get the ring?' I asked.

'From the young man who stole it. He had an affair with her also.' His mouth twisted in distaste.

'Couldn't he get it back for you? Couldn't you put pressure on him?'

'Unfortunately not. He died a few months ago. A skiing accident at Klosters. His neck was broken.' He said the last with relish.

'An accident?' I asked.

'That was the verdict of the coroner. Would you question the verdict of a Swiss coroner, Mr Sharman?'

'Illicit sex can be fatal,' I said.

'AIDS?' he asked innocently.

'Or a broken neck,' I said.

He barked his laugh again. 'No comment,' he said. But I knew. I was beginning to think the major was more dangerous an individual than he looked.

'So you want me to arrange a burglary for you?'

He nodded.

'But you have the full resources of the army and the police, not to mention MI5 and 6 to call on. I'm sure there's a few burglars on their strength. In fact, I know there are. Why come to me?'

'This isn't an embassy siege we're talking about. I can't send in the SAS with stun grenades to get the ring back, although God knows I'd like to. If I send someone in and they get caught, the scandal will be twofold. Can you imagine it? It will be a *cause célèbre*. And if the newspapers got hold of it . . .' He shuddered at the thought. 'And I'm sure that the government of that particular country would make sure they did. If not here, then abroad.'

'And if someone I send in gets caught?'

'Then that's his problem. But if you send the right man, he won't, will he? Besides, you're not going to tell him why he's stealing the ring, are you? That's just between the two of us.'

'But if he does get caught?'

'He'll probably be terminated with extreme prejudice.'

'A nice thought,' I said.

'I don't believe in pulling punches. Or sending in troops without all the intelligence I can muster.'

Troops, is it now? I thought. 'And if he does and I go to the newspapers?'

'Official Secrets Act, Mr Sharman. Remember that.'

'But if I did,' I persisted. 'Would I be terminated with extreme prejudice too?'

'Quite frankly, Mr Sharman, I don't think we'd have to bother. You see, even if you did go to the press, who's going to believe you?'

'What? Take the word of a sleazy little South London private detective like me, against a big soldier like you?'

'Exactly.'

'It's nice to know that your informants have such a good opinion of me. So what's in it for the sleazy team?'

'I thought you'd never ask,' he said and reached into the inside pocket of his jacket and took out a thick brown envelope and gave it to me. I opened it. Inside were five plastic packets of bank notes. 'There's a thousand in each packet,' he said. 'Five thousand now. Five thousand more when I receive the ring. You can divvy it up with your man as you see fit. I'm sure you will anyway. Just one other thing. Leave anything else that is in the safe as it is.'

'Why?'

'Because then the ambassador and his wife will know exactly what was wanted and exactly who took it. So get someone you can trust to do the job.'

'Trust,' I said. 'That's a big word round here.'

'It's a big word everywhere. So you'll arrange it?'

'With a pay packet like this, and the charming way you asked, how could I refuse? But I'll need more details.'

'I have the plans of the building in my case,' he said. 'But I doubt you'll need them. We've made things easy for you. Or at least our mole has. There has been unfortunate structural damage to the embassy. Nothing serious. A section of the roof above the ambassador's quarters has sprung a leak. It is going to be repaired on Friday morning. Three days hence. The scaffolding goes up on Thursday afternoon. That night there is to be a reception at the embassy, so the ambassador and his lady wife will be busy between 8 p.m. and 2 a.m. Their apartment will be empty between those hours. Between midnight and 12.30 a.m. the bulb in the light above the balcony doors and the alarm system on those doors will disfunction.' He smiled to himself with satisfaction.

'How come your inside man can do all that, but can't get the ring himself?' I asked.

'The ring is in a safe. A very sophisticated one. He doesn't know the combination, and his talents don't run in the direction of safecracking. So now do you see?'

I nodded. 'They'll know it's an inside job.'

'By that time it won't matter. Now the safe is behind a Constable.'

'A policeman?' I interrupted.

'A picture,' he said drily. I must confess it wasn't one of my best. 'The picture is in the bedroom. The subject is a picnic at harvest time. You can't miss it. Is that clear so far?'

'As crystal,' I said. 'What do I do with the ring when I get it?'

'You'll be contacted.'

'COD?' I asked.

'Of course. Don't worry, there's plenty of money in the public purse. Taxpayer's money. You *do* remember taxes, don't you, Mr Sharman?'

I didn't answer.

'Don't worry,' he said. 'I won't tell.'

I smiled a thin smile at the implied threat. The old bugger *had* been doing his homework.

'So let's get down to cases,' he said and pulled his

briefcase on to his lap and opened it. Inside was a sheaf of papers. He took them out and unfolded the bundle. 'First,' he said. 'The way in.' The top paper was a plan of the embassy and the surrounding streets, complete with a number of photographs of the building. It was located near The Temple, between Fleet Street and Victoria Embankment in the maze of small streets that ran down to the river. It didn't look like much. A modest Georgian house, painted white, set in a tree-filled garden. Mind you, in that part of town, even modesty cost over a million quid an acre. Once again he sensed my thoughts. 'Don't be misled by the photos,' he said. 'The grounds are quite extensive. And pretty wild. And patrolled on a regular basis, night and day. The building is surrounded by a fifteen-foot-high wall with an electric charge going through the razor wire that runs around the top. This serves two purposes. One, to give anyone trying to get in a nasty shock, and two, to trigger the alarm system.' He pulled out photographs of two sets of gates. 'Front.' He tapped one. 'Back.' The other. 'Guarded twenty-four hours a day by armed men. Don't mess with them. They're armed with Heckler & Kochs, as are the guards who patrol the grounds.'

'A piece of piss,' I said. 'Can we borrow a helicopter from the Queen's flight to land on the lawn?'

He laughed again and found another photo stapled to an envelope. 'This,' he said, 'is your access point. It's a small wooden door in the east wall. It hasn't been used for years. It's on the guards' route, but they never check it. It's overgrown with bushes on the inside, and it's more or less been forgotten. Our man has got a copy of the key, and he's even gone so far as to oil the locks and hinges.' He opened the envelope and took out an old-fashioned silver key and gave it to me.

'I hope he hasn't done too good a job,' I said. 'I'd hate

for somebody with an automatic weapon to be waiting on the other side when my man goes in.'

The major shook his head. 'No,' he said. 'He's very discreet.'

'Isn't it wired into the alarm system?' I asked.

'Don't worry. It's all taken care of,' he replied.

I hope so, I thought.

He pulled out another photo. 'This is what you're after,' he said. It was a colour shot of a gold and diamond ring on a blue velvet mount. He touched the photo. 'As you can see, the setting is very distinctive. Get your man to study it closely. I want no mistakes.'

I nodded.

Finally, he turned to a small sheet of paper. 'This is the make, model, year of manufacture, and serial number of the safe. It might come in handy. Forewarned is forearmed. Give that to your man, too. And when you've finished, make sure the whole lot is destroyed. I don't want any evidence left hanging around. Understood?'

'Understood,' I said.

'Good. Now I'm counting on you, Sharman. Don't let me down. Next Friday, 12.30 ack emma. It's all arranged. Be there. It'll be easy.'

Too easy, I thought. 'Yes, Major,' I said.

He tapped on the glass between us and the driver, and she turned off at the first opportunity and headed back in the direction of my office. When we pulled up outside, the major said, 'Until we meet again, Mr Sharman.'

'I can't wait,' I replied and got out and watched as the car did a three-point turn, rolled down to the main road, joined the stream of traffic, and disappeared.

Even though Major Cave-Browne-Cave thought I knew every sleazebag and petty crook on the ground, I didn't. But I knew a few and had one in particular pegged for the job. So I went looking. I found 'Monkey' Mann in Edward G's. Edward G's is a theme bar tagged on to the Slug and Lettuce public house just outside Beckenham. I don't think it had been a great success. Maybe Beckenham just wasn't ready for the concept of a prohibition bar. Maybe it never would be. I know I wasn't. But needs must. And it fitted perfectly with the major's pre-war, Warner Brothers' gangster movie image of villainy in the suburbs.

It was a great barn of a place that had once been the billiards room. It was overheated and underlit. The blowups of Edward G. Robinson that decorated the walls were crooked and dirty. The plastic seating was pockmarked with cigarette burns and ripped and cut so that the foam padding inside burst out like some kind of exotic fungus. In some places it had been repaired with tape, but mostly not. The carpet was spotted with ground-in chewing gum. The sticky cocktails had been replaced with bitter at under a pound a pint during happy hour, which as far as I could make out lasted from opening to closing time, and the juke box had been loaded up with a collection of scratchy Irish favourites. Monkey was sitting next to the pool table. 'Hello, Mr Sharman,' he said, without a trace of surprise in his voice. 'What brings you here?'

'You, Monkey,' I replied. 'Want a drink?'

'I'll have a Blackbushe,' he said. 'Large.'

'Fine,' I replied and went to the bar. The guv'nor was wearing a silver mohair suit, so stiff that he could hardly bend his arms, and white high-heeled winklepickers that laced up the sides. I'd've bet he got them on his last sabbatical in Marbella. 'Large Blackbushe,' I said. 'And a pint of lager.' As the guv'nor was getting the drinks, I peered through the gloom. There were just a few customers in the place, mostly men sitting in the booths that lined the walls. They were mostly alone. It was that kind of boozer.

I collected the drinks, paid, and took them back to Monkey.

Monkey got his name by being able to climb anything, any time. Just what the major ordered. A second-storey man and a safecracker to boot. At fifty-odd, with thinning hair and a love of Irish whiskey, a bit past his prime, maybe. But a real pro.

I put the drinks down and sat opposite him. 'What can I do for you, Mr Sharman?' he asked.

So I told him. Just the bare bones like the major wanted. I showed him the photos and the details of the safe.

When I'd finished, he said, 'How much?'

'Three grand now. Three grand when the job's finished.' I thought that was fair. The rest was a finder's fee. Things hadn't been going too well for me lately.

'Let's see the dough,' he said.

I passed him an envelope I'd prepared earlier. He thumbed the notes. 'All right,' he said, seemingly satisfied. 'When?'

'Thursday night,' I said. 'But there is one thing, Monkey.'

'What?'

'You just take the ring. Nothing else.'

'What else is there?'

I shrugged. 'Don't ask me.'

'How would anyone know?'

'They'd know, believe me. And the people who want this job done. They *never* forget. I doubt if you'd have time to enjoy it. The money's good. Be satisfied.'

'OK, Mr Sharman, whatever you say.'

I believed him; thousands wouldn't. 'I'll take you there,' I said. 'Get you into the grounds and wait. Watch your back. Is that OK?'

'Fine. I prefer to work alone.'

'Right. I'll pick you up here Thursday at about eleven. Don't let me down.'

'I won't.'

'And lay off that stuff.' I pointed at his glass.

He seemed offended. 'I never drink when I'm working,' he said.

'That's what I like to hear. Till Thursday then,' I said, finished my pint, and left.

Monkey was waiting right on time on Thursday night in the car park of the pub. He materialized out of the shadows like a phantom, wearing dark clothes and carrying a small bag. I was wearing black Levis, black soft-soled shoes, a black roll-neck sweater, and a dark leather jacket. Just in case, under the jacket, in a shoulder holster I carried a Colt Commander Light Weight, seven-shot .45 semi-automatic pistol. If the job was going to be as easy as the major had said, fine. If not, well, it pays to be prepared.

We were in town by twelve, and I parked up in the next street to the embassy. Monkey and I padded through the shadows to the embassy wall. I'd made one reconnaissance trip the previous night. I'd found the small door, tried the key, and opened the door. I'd waited ten minutes and no security men had shown up. The major's mole had been right about that at least. A man of many talents, obviously. I hoped he was going to be equally right about the rest.

When we got to the door, I checked for passing cars and pedestrians, but the street was empty, and I was just about to insert the key into the keyhole when Monkey said, 'Mr Sharman.'

'What?'

'There's a slight problem.'

'What?' I said again.

'I don't know how to tell you.'

'Tell me, Monkey,' I said and noticed that his face was slick with sweat.

'You see . . .' he said and hesitated.

'Just tell me, Monkey,' I said. 'Before someone wonders

what the hell we're doing standing here like a pair of prats.'

'It's the climb.'

'What about it?'

'I can't do it.'

'What, you? Monkey Mann, the human fly?'

'I'm sorry, Mr Sharman, but me bottle's gone.'

'Oh no, Monkey,' I said. 'Tell me I'm dreaming.'

'Sorry, Mr S. It's the truth.'

'But, Monkey, there's a scaffold up. It'll be like climbing a ladder.'

'It was a ladder what done me. I fell off painting me sister's ceiling. I can't stand heights since I done it. I can't even go upstairs on a bus.'

'So why did you say you'd do the job?'

'The dough. I'm skint. I can hardly claim redundancy money, can I?'

'Why did you show up tonight, then?'

'I'm a pro, Mr S. I thought it'd be all right once we got started.'

'But it's not?'

'Sorry,' he said again. And I think he really was. He had a code, and he hated to break it. But that didn't help the situation.

'Bloody hell, Monkey,' I said. 'What are we going to do?'

He shrugged.

'You've dropped me right in it, you know that? I suppose you've spent the money.'

'I had some pressing debts.'

'I just bet you did,' I said and made a decision. 'Right, Monkey. I'm coming with you. You're going up to that balcony if I have to carry you. And me with a bad foot.'

'Mr S., please,' he said pathetically.

'Just shut up, Monkey,' I said and checked the street

130

again. No change. I did the business with the key, opened the door, and I pushed him through the gap. I closed the door behind us, but didn't lock it. The overgrown shrubbery inside sheltered us from the house. The scaffolding was straight ahead. 'Get going,' I hissed. 'You first.' We pushed through the undergrowth, snaked between a couple of stunted trees, across a lawn, and there, exactly as promised, was the scaffold attached to the side of the building. I dragged Monkey into its shadow. 'Up you go,' I ordered.

'Mr S.,' he said so plaintively I was almost sorry for him. Almost.

'Monkey, believe me,' I said. 'If you think this climb's frightening, you haven't seen me mad. And the people who supplied that three grand make me look like a sweet little pussycast. Understand?'

'All right, Mr S.,' said Monkey. 'I'm going.'

And he did. Slowly and reluctantly, but he went. Hand over hand, not looking down. It was all so pathetic I almost felt sorry for him again. But not quite.

I followed him up. It was an easy climb. Just as I'd said it would be. Like a ladder. We got to the balcony, which was in darkness, and climbed over the stone balustrade and on to solid concrete. Monkey breathed a sigh of relief, and so did I, to be honest. I've never been mad about heights myself, but I wasn't going to let him know that. I tried the french doors gingerly. They opened without a sound. I pushed through the thick curtains into the apartments, and Monkey followed me. Once inside, I drew them tightly behind us. The room was softly lit by wall-mounted lights, and as I looked round, I realized I was in the presence of sheer luxury. Maybe a bit Imelda Marcos in style, but sheer luxury nevertheless. There were silk drapes and tapestries on the walls. Porcelain statues and vases on every surface. A couple of discreetly placed concealed spotlights picked out paintings that would have made an art expert drool. The furniture was leather or what looked suspiciously like real leopard skin. From somewhere below us I could faintly hear music. The reception, I guessed.

'Nice,' whispered Monkey. It was the way he'd have had his council flat furnished if he could have afforded it.

'Bedroom,' I said and gave him a push.

According to the plan the major had given me, there was a connecting door between the main salon as it had been described on the blueprint, and the master bedroom, ditto. The plan had been correct. Inside the door was more softly lit luxury. At least we weren't going to need torches. A small mercy. On the wall opposite the super king-size waterbed was a four-foot-by-three framed oil painting of a rural picnic, signed 'Constable'. Monkey, who appeared much more like his old self, took over from there. The frame of the painting was attached to the wall by hinges, and he opened it like a cupboard door to reveal the face of a safe set into the wall behind it. He put down his tool bag and opened it. From inside he took out what looked like a digital egg timer.

'What the hell's that?' I whispered.

'You watch,' he said. 'Beats the old stethoscope hands down.'

He touched a switch on the machine, and six zeros popped up on the liquid crystal display on the front. He held it against the door of the safe close to the combination dial, and as he turned the dial gently, he moved the little box across the face of the safe until the display went crazy. 'Gotcha,' he said, reset it, and placed it back on the face of the safe in the same position. Then the hard work started. As he manipulated the dial, the display changed again, but more slowly. 'This could take a while, Mr S. Why don't you sit down and relax,' he said.

I tried, but I found it very hard. I was on hot bricks. Each move of the dial seemed to take hours, and I couldn't even smoke. After about fifteen minutes Monkey said, 'Won't be long now.'

'Thank God,' I said. 'I've got to take a leak. I'm bursting.' I went into the *en suite* bathroom and admired the solid gold fittings as I did just that. As I was finishing, I heard voices from the bedroom. I froze, then went and listened at the door. Definitely voices. Male. One was Monkey's.

Oh shit, I thought and took the pistol from under my arm, let off the safety, and cocked it. I opened the door slowly and silently. Monkey was standing by the safe, which was open. Facing him, with his back to me was another party – average height, black, slicked back hair, and a dinner suit. He must have been a refugee from the reception. He was holding a revolver in his right hand pointed at Monkey's midsection. In his left hand was a large briefcase he tossed to Monkey. 'Fill it up,' he said in a voice that only had a trace of a foreign accent. Monkey must have seen me, but being the pro he was didn't bat an eyelash. He caught the case and stood holding it. I crept over the thick carpet towards the man. 'Come on, quickly,' he said.

I touched the back of his neck between his hairline and his stiff white collar with the barrel of the .45. He stiffened, and I saw his finger tighten on the trigger of the revolver. 'Don't even think about it,' I said. 'Yours is double action. Mine's cocked. You'll be dead before you can shoot.'

He took my word for it. Wise man. And I saw his finger relax. 'Good boy,' I said and reached over and took the gun out of his hand. 'Now turn round.'

He did as I ordered. He was a stranger to me. 'Mr Mole, I presume,' I said.

'Have you seen what's in here?' said Monkey.

I stepped back slightly out of the mole's reach and looked. The safe was packed with bank notes and jewel boxes.

'There must be a quarter of a million quid here at least,' said Monkey. 'In cash. And a load of tom. He wanted the lot.' He sounded quite offended.

'So that was why we were supposed to leave everything but the ring,' I said to the mole. 'Your payoff.'

The man said nothing, just shrugged his shoulders an inch and twisted his mouth in a grimace.

'But you wanted the ring too, didn't you?'

Another shrug, another grimace. Almost a smile that time.

'That would have been a nice little pension for you, wouldn't it? No wonder you made it so easy for us to get inside. But you weren't expecting two of us, were you?'

He opened his arms in gesture of surrender.

'Is the ring there?' I said to Monkey.

He fiddled about inside the safe and opened a couple of ring boxes, then said, 'Here it is.'

'Right. Give it to me, and let's go.'

'What about the rest?'

'We leave it. That was the deal.'

'*Mr S.*'

'That was the deal. Now do you want a foreign government and our own after us for the rest of our lives? I told you these people never forget. Leave it. Give me the ring and let's get out of here.'

'If you say so.'

'I do.'

Monkey walked round to me, being careful not to cross my line of fire, and gave me the ring. It was beautiful and reflected the light like a miniature sun. 'What about him?' asked Monkey.

'I'll lock him in the bedroom,' I said. 'Come on, you.' I

pushed the mole into the room I'd recently vacated, shut the door, and locked it on the outside. I emptied his gun and dropped it and the bullets on the floor, then I holstered mine and we left.

Monkey looked terrified again when we got out on the balcony. 'Go,' I said.

He hung his bag over his shoulder and started down. I followed. Halfway down he froze. Solid. His hands clenched on the scaffolding rails. 'I can't, Mr S.,' he said. 'I can't.'

I banged on his hands with my clenched fists. 'Go, Monkey,' I said. 'You've got to move.'

'No.' As he said the word, I heard shouting from above us and the sound of breaking glass, and the mole stuck his head through a window and started shouting in a guttural language I couldn't understand. It looked like he'd gone double on us and was trying to save his own skin. I knew I should have knocked him out. From the front of the house I heard answering shouts. I leaned right over to loosen Monkey's grip, and the Colt .45 slid out of the holster under my arm and fell to the ground. I made a despairing grab for it, but missed. As it hit the ground it went off, and a bullet spanged against one of the scaffolding supports. The noise of the gunshot and the whine of the bullet as it ricocheted by us galvanized Monkey into action. He let go of the pole he was holding and scuttled down the scaffold like greased lightning. I wasn't far behind him. We dropped the last few feet. There was no sign of the gun, and I didn't have time to stop and look for it because as we hit the ground two men came round the side of the house just a few yards away from us. Both men were carrying machine pistols. I gave Monkey a shove, and we ran towards the gate we'd come in by. We crashed through the undergrowth, the men in pursuit. I pulled open the door, dragged Monkey through after me, slammed it again, and locked it.

He was trembling and pale in the light from the street lamps and breathing hard. We turned in the direction of my car, when another two armed men turned the corner from the direction of the front gate and cut us off. 'This way,' I shouted, grabbed Monkey's arm and headed downhill in the direction of the river.

From behind us I heard the sound of gunfire. Our original two pursuers were shooting the lock off the gate. The odds were getting worse. I touched the ring that nestled in the pocket of my jacket and urged Monkey to go faster. We got to Victoria Embankment, dodged through the traffic heading east, jumped the central reservation and across the other carriageway. Monkey was breathing like an engine. 'I can't, Mr S.,' he gasped. 'Leave me, I'm done for.'

'No,' I said. 'We're together whatever happens.' We reached the pavement by the river, and Monkey fell against the embankment wall. I could see that he was finished. The guards had reached the other side of the road and crossed through a break in the traffic. I looked around for help, but the road was empty except for the cars that rushed past. It was all over for us. I pulled Monkey up to his feet, and we stood watching as our pursuers moved in for the kill. The first one to reach our side of the road pointed his machine-gun at us. No one said anything. As the rest arrived, we were covered by half a dozen weapons. Then the mole came running down the hill, crossed the road, and catching his breath said, 'You have something that belongs to us.'

'No,' I said. 'I have something that belongs to the Queen of England.' Pompous, maybe, but the best I could come up with at short notice.

The mole held out his hand. 'Don't be foolish,' he said. 'Give it to me.'

'And if I don't?'

'Then we kill you and take it anyway.'

I put my hand in my pocket and took out the ring. It shone like ice and fire and picked up the colours from the lights along the embankment and in the houses and offices opposite us. 'No,' I said. 'You can't have it.'

One of the armed guards moved towards me, and I turned and hurled the ring as far as I could across the black water behind me. I didn't even hear a splash. 'Go on, then,' I said to the mole. 'Fetch it, boy.'

He stepped over and slapped me hard across the face. One of the other guards made ready to fire. They were so busy that they didn't hear the sound of the three dark-coloured Ford Granadas pull up at the kerbside a few feet from where we were standing. They didn't hear the doors opening, or the eight khaki-clad men step out. But they did hear the sound of eight automatic weapons being cocked ready to fire. The guards froze, and as the soldiers' weapons were also pointing at Monkey and me, I moved my accomplice out of the line of fire. I was prepared to do a lot for my Queen and country, but dying at the hands of our own security forces was not one of them.

'All of you, weapons on the ground move away, and lie face down. Now,' said one of the soldiers. Then he spoke in that guttural language the mole had used. I imagine he was repeating the order for anyone who didn't speak English. The guards seemed to get the message. One by one they put their guns on the pavement, moved away, and lay face down, arms and legs outstretched. 'Now you two,' said the soldier to me and Monkey. 'The same.'

'Give us a break,' I said. 'We're on your side.'

From one of the cars stepped the major. He was as

immaculate as ever. 'Leave them, Jones,' he said. 'I'll deal with them.'

'Sah,' barked the soldier and lowered his gun and went to help his mates deal with the guards.

'Bit of a cock-up,' said the Major to me.

'Not our cock-up,' I said. 'Your man tried to double-cross us.'

'Did you get the ring?'

''Course we did,' said Monkey. 'Piece of cake.'

The major smiled thinly. 'So where is it?'

I looked at Monkey, then the major. 'I wish you'd got here a couple of minutes earlier.'

'Why?'

'I thought they had us.'

'And?'

'And I wasn't going to give them the ring back.'

'So?'

'So I threw it in the river,' I said. I pointed behind me. 'In that direction. I don't know exactly how far. Sorry.'

'Sorry,' repeated the Major. 'Is that all you can say?'

Needless to say we didn't get *all* the rest of the money promised. But I convinced the major to give Monkey his three grand as arranged. After all, although the ring was lost for ever in the silt of the Thames, at least we'd saved Her Majesty the embarrassment of it being worn to the palace by a foreign diplomat's wife. Also, as I explained, people like Monkey don't understand the subtle nuances of the Official Secrets Act. They just understand cash. I even slung him my original deuce to sweeten the pot. I didn't think that Monkey was going to be shinning up too many drainpipes in future, and it's hell getting on a government retraining scheme at his age. And he had turned up, scared as he was. That had taken a lot of guts, and I admired him for it. So in the end I came out with nixes. But that's the breaks.

I didn't hear from the major for over two months. Autumn had come, and the nights were drawing in. I was in my office again one Friday morning when the phone rang. 'Sharman,' I said.

'Good morning.'

I recognized the glass-cutting tones at once. 'Major.'

'She wants to see you.'

'Who?'

'Who do you think?'

'You mean . . .'

'This is an open line, Sharman,' he interrupted. 'No names, please.'

'Of course. When?'

'Tonight.'

'Where?'

'She's attending a civic function in Croydon.' He said 'Croydon' as if it were a disease. Which I suppose in a way it is.

'What time?'

'I'll pick you up at seven at your office. You do know how to behave, I trust.'

'I was a policeman, remember. It's one of the first things you learn.'

'Capital. Seven o'clock, then.'

'I'll be here.' And we both hung up.

He was right on time. So was I. I wore a navy blue suit, white shirt, subdued tie, and shiny black shoes. I'd shaved twice and had a haircut. He looked me over when I got in the back of the Daimler. 'You'll do,' he said. I took that as a compliment.

We were in Croydon by 7.30, and the chauffeuse steered the car into an underground car park near the town hall.

It was huge and empty except for a Rolls-Royce at the far end. 'Go on, then,' he said. 'Don't keep her waiting.'

'Aren't you . . . ?'

'You're on your own. It's not me she wants to see.'

I stepped out of the Daimler and walked across the car park, my heels clicking on the concrete. As I got closer to the big car, I saw the royal pennant on a tiny gold pole on top of the radiator where the flying lady normally was. As I got closer still, a uniformed chauffeur leapt out of the front and ran round and opened the passenger door closest to me. I walked up to the open door and peered inside. 'Do get in, Mr Sharman,' said a woman's voice – one I recognized from countless radio sound bites and TV news segments. 'It's freezing in here.'

I did as I was told and perched on the edge of the wide leather seat. The chauffeur closed the door after me and stood a few feet away from the car, hands clasped behind his back. I felt I should stand to attention and bow, but it's difficult in the back of a car, even one as large as the Rolls. As my eyes became accustomed to the darkness in the car, I saw her sitting in the far corner. The heater was on and the car smelled of expensive perfume, and was so quiet I heard the rustle of her nylon-clad legs as she moved. 'You wanted to see me, ma'am,' I said. 'Ma'am.' How bad's that?

'I wanted to thank you.'

'It was nothing.'

'I'm sure it was.'

I didn't reply. Modesty forbade it.

'I don't have to tell you the favour you did me,' she continued.

'Anyone could have done it.'

'I doubt that. Unfortunately, there can never be any official recognition of what you did.'

'I didn't expect any,' I said. 'Besides, we were well paid.'

'No, you weren't. You gave yours to your friend. I know all about it. I think that was very honourable of you.'

Honourable, that was a first, but I loved it.

'Anyway money isn't everything,' she went on. 'I know that better than most, believe me. So I wanted to give you this.' She extended her hand, which held a small, battered leather box.

'It's not necessary,' I said.

'It is. This belonged to my great-grandfather. He won it in the First World War. It's one of the few things I actually own myself. So it's very precious to me. That's why I want you to have it.'

'You're very kind.'

'I'm famous for it. Take it, please.'

I reached over and took the box. As I did so, the light from outside caught the stone she was wearing on her finger. I recognized it right away. 'Is that the ring?' I asked.

'Yes,' she said.

'But I threw it in the river. Did someone dive for it?'

'No. It was discussed, but the mud there is three feet deep at least. It would have been impossible.'

'So how come?'

'The one you recovered from the embassy was a copy. A very good copy. There are copies made of all the crown jewels.'

I felt confused. 'So why bother getting us to steal it back?' I asked.

'Because real or not, the very fact that that damned woman was going to wear it to the palace would have caused no end of fuss.'

'So we risked our lives for a piece of paste?'

'No, Mr Sharman, you risked your life for me. Would you have done that if you'd known?'

I looked at her shadowy figure. 'Of course,' I said. And do you know, I would have, too.

141

'Then open the box.'

I did as I was told and turned it into the light to see what was inside. It was a medal – a very old medal with a faded purple ribbon. 'Ypres,' she said.

'I really can't accept this,' I said.

'I insist. It's an order, Mr Sharman. A royal command, if you like. You can't refuse. I could have your head cut off if you tried.'

'Then I'm very proud.'

We sat there for a moment in silence. Then she said, 'I'm afraid I must go. Duty calls. It's a bore. I'd rather sit here with you and talk some more.'

'I'm flattered,' I said. And I was. But I knew when it was time to go. I reached round and opened the door and backed out. 'Good night,' I said.

'Good night.'

I closed the door behind me. The chauffeur ran back to his seat, and the car pulled off. As it went, I saw her pale face looking out of the back window at me. I went back and joined the major. 'What happened?' he asked.

'She gave me this,' I said and showed him the box and its contents. He took out the medal and looked at it.

He was silent for a moment, then said, 'For valour. Stuff and nonsense.'

Then he got his chauffeuse to drive me home.

Don't Fear the Reaper

This story was commissioned by *Arena* magazine for the first in a series of new works of fiction, a commission for which I am truly grateful. Not only for the fee, but also because it told me that I was finally getting a reputation. As a writer, for a change, rather than as a nutter. In fact it's not that authentic because very rarely, if ever, do people get their stolen property back after a burglary.

The title comes from a song by Blue Oyster Cult.

It was the best of times, it was the worst of times.

'It's not the video, Mr Sharman,' she said. 'Or the TV, or the stereo. Or even the money. Not that there was a lot of that. A hundred pounds, maybe. That was all insured. Steve made sure of that. It was the pot.'

'Sorry?' I said. I was looking at the wall. Staring. I find it easier doing that than actually looking at people these days. The best of days, the worst of days.

'The pot,' she repeated. 'A silly thing, really. A present from Skegness. That's where we went on holiday after he came up on the pools.'

'Splashing out,' I said.

'Are you taking the piss?' she asked.

I looked at her properly then, for the first time. She wasn't tall, she wasn't short. She wasn't fat, she wasn't thin. Just average, with bleached blonde hair cropped short, like it had been done with a knife and fork, but had probably set her back fifty nicker or more in some nice salon in Mayfair where Princess Di once went, plenty of sooty-eye make-up and bright red lipstick. She wore big, gold, hooped earrings, and a dark blue nanny goat that hadn't cost less than a monkey, or my name wasn't Nick Sharman.

Under the coat she wore a black dress that was tight enough and short enough to show off her figure and her legs in their black tights. On her feet she had black patent leather shoes with high heels. She wore some other gold tom too. A necklace and bracelet, but she wasn't dripping with the stuff.

She was in her late thirties or early forties, and all in all wasn't a bad package, although her face was just easing into the kind of hardness that some South London women get as they head towards the menopause and everything that follows.

HRT, I thought. She'll get HRT and go on looking like that till she's seventy.

All in all not a bad little package at all.

And her husband, Steve Jackson, came up on the pools a couple of years before he died. She'd told me all about that after she'd walked into my office that chilly October morning without an appointment, to hire me to find a six-inch-high china pot with 'A Present From Skegness' written on the lid.

'Sorry,' I said. 'I didn't mean anything by it. Sometimes my sense of humour isn't all it should be.'

'OK,' she said. 'Sometimes mine isn't either. It's living on your own that does it.'

I could've seconded that. But I was getting used to it. Enjoying it, in fact. Waking up alone in my little flat and hugging the duvet tight and not having to please anyone but myself.

'It's not even the pot really,' she explained. 'It's what's inside it, Mr Sharman.'

'Call me Nick,' I said. 'Everyone else does.' Except for my bank manager and the computer that writes the terse letters about my credit card limit. They still call me Mr Sharman. But everyone else calls me Nick.

'Nick,' she said. 'And you can call me Avril.' Avril. Now that isn't a name you come across much these days.

'So what *is* inside?' I asked, although I had an inkling. You don't do what I do for as long as I've done it without occasionally getting an inkling.

'It's his ashes. Steve's. I didn't know what else to do with them.'

I thought as much. 'His ashes,' I said. 'His final remains. And you kept them on the mantelpiece?'

It was obviously perfectly natural as far as she was concerned. Perhaps everyone she knew had a casket full of a close relative's relics up there next to the gas bill. 'That's right. The pot was on top of the hundred pounds. Like a paperweight.'

'And that's all they took? The TV, video, stereo, a ton in cash and the pot.'

'That's it. They didn't bust anything up, or do what you read about in the papers sometimes.' Her nose wrinkled in disgust.

I imagined she meant shit on the carpet or wank all over the bedclothes.

'How did they get in?' I asked.

'The patio window. They popped the lock. The insurance man's made me get a security gate before the company will insure me again. I hate it. It's like being in prison.'

'It's what living in London's all about,' I said.

She smiled then for the first time, and she was amazingly pretty.

'So where do you live?' I asked.

She gave me her address. It was one of those new private

developments off Streatham High Road. All yellow brick, bullseye glass in the front doors, hanging baskets and satellite dishes.

'We used to live on a council estate on Brixton Hill,' she explained. 'With people we'd been friendly with for years. But when they found out that we'd come on the pools they went the other way. You'd think they'd've been pleased, but they weren't. Bastards. God alone knows how those people get on who come up with twenty million on the lottery.'

'How much *did* you win?' I asked.

'Eight hundred thousand. We bought a car and the house and things for it. And we insured each other for a lot. So when he died . . .' She didn't finish.

'It was like coming up on the pools again.'

She gave me a slitty-eyed look. 'I'm not short, if that's what you mean,' she said. But the way she said it was, and I deserved it.

'Sorry,' I said again. 'I didn't mean . . .'

"Course you didn't. But people . . .'

'You went to the police.'

'*The police.*' And she snorted a bitter laugh. 'I had to. For the insurance.'

'And?'

'And they showed their faces for a minute or two. But a burglary. Round there. The telly, video and stereo. They were probably sold within two minutes. And as for cash . . .'

'But ashes?' I said.

'Not a lot of call for ashes round the pubs, I'll give you that.'

'No fingerprints or anything?'

She shook her head.

'Did the CID show up?'

'Yes. They came and had a cuppa.'

It was my turn to laugh. 'I know what you mean,' I said. 'Did you get a name?'

She nodded and brought out a card. It read DC Conway, and there was a telephone number. It was for the local nick.

'I'll give him a call,' I said.

'She. It was a woman who left her card. The bloke wasn't interested.'

'I'll give *her* a call,' I said. 'If I take the case. But I'm not cheap.'

'Two hundred a day, I heard.'

'That's right. Plus expenses.'

She brought a white envelope out of the black leather handbag resting in her lap. 'There's a grand here in cash. I reckon that if you don't find anything within five days it's a dead loss.'

I wondered if she realized what she'd said.

I thought about it for less than ten seconds. A thousand quid in cash can be very persuasive. 'OK, I'll give it a go,' I said.

'Thanks,' she replied. 'My number's in the envelope with the money.'

'I'll be in touch,' I said, and watched as she left and got into the BMW 325i on last year's plate that was parked at the kerb outside my office.

I put the cash in my wallet, transferred her phone number to my book and took a drive up to the local police station. DC Conway was in situ, and after a ten-minute wait gave me an interview in the deserted CID office. Maybe the rest of the detectives were out catching villains, or maybe they were all taking an early lunch.

Conway was young and attractive in her jeans, trainers and sweat top. She was dark-haired and olive skinned, and I was willing to bet she was the pin-up at the local section house.

147

She was sitting at a desk that almost groaned with paper, and told me she could only spare me a few minutes. I told her why I was there and she said, 'So what do you want?'

'To get Steve Jackson's mortal remains back to his grieving widow,' I replied.

'Can't help you,' she said.

'Come on,' I persisted. 'You must have some idea who did it. The jungle telegraph always has some names in the frame. I used to be in the Job. I know all about it.'

'I know you used to be in the Job,' was her only reply. Once again, my reputation had preceded me.

'And you do have some names.'

'But no proof,' she said.

'I don't need proof. All I need is names.'

'And you think I'm going to point you in the right direction? Just like that?'

'Why not?'

'Because this is not an information bureau, Mr Sharman, it's a police station.' Now there was somebody else who called me Mr Sharman.

'So why don't we play "let's pretend"?'

She observed me coolly for a moment, then said, 'OK. I don't know why I'm doing this, but there are two names that keep coming up.'

I said nothing.

'Brothers. Billy and Terry McDonnell. Nasty pieces of work, both of them. They've been robbing their way round the manor for years.'

'Ever been caught?'

'Sure. They're not very clever. They've both done a little time.'

'And you think it might be them?'

'Billy came out about four months ago and the burglary rate's gone up ever since.'

'You've done them?'

'Like I said, no proof. We've given their place a spin a couple of times but come up empty.'

'Where do I find them?'

'They drink in a pub called the Pale Horseman. Know it?'

'I know it,' I replied. 'And avoid it as a rule.'

'Like most good citizens do.'

'How will I know them?'

'You'll know them all right. They've both got bright red hair. And a bad attitude. I wouldn't mess with them if I were you, Mr Sharman.'

But you're not me, I thought. 'Thanks,' I said.

'The only reason I've told you this is because it's the poor woman's husband's ashes they nicked. Otherwise I wouldn't give you the time of day.'

Of course, by then I was convinced otherwise, gave her what I hoped was a boyish grin and said, 'I don't suppose you'd fancy a drink some night?'

It's always good to have a friend on the force.

She gave me another cool look. 'I don't suppose I would,' she replied, and without another word she dismissed me and went back to the mountain of paperwork on top of the desk in front of her.

So much for my boyish charm.

I drove back to Tulse Hill, had a snack in my local greasy spoon café and made a plan. There's nothing to making a plan. Making plans is easy. Making them work is another matter altogether.

I went home then, changed into a pair of ancient jeans and my leather jacket, and took a stroll through Streatham to the Pale Horseman for a pint or two and anything else that might turn up.

Now, as South London boozers go, the Horseman, as it's known locally, doesn't go very far. It's a scruffy, flat-

149

fronted little back street pub that escaped being tarted up in the eighties and looks like it'll be the next millennium before someone cleans the windows. It was well known locally as the place to score cheap drugs, cheap women and almost anything else from semi-legal to suicidal. At night it's packed to the doors, but just post-lunchtime, as it was then, it was almost deserted. Inside everything was brown. Brown lino floor, brown seats, brown walls, brown ceiling, and an old brown dog cocked one crooked ear at me as I went inside. There were one or two fly-blown advertisements on the walls for soft drinks that hadn't caught on and had been discontinued years before, a dart-board, a juke box that actually held black vinyl singles, and at the lop-sided pool table at the back were two red-headed youths just finishing a game.

Bingo. The McDonnell brothers.

I joined the other two dispirited-looking drinkers at the bar and ordered a pint of lager. The barmaid, a sluttish-looking thirty-something in a white skirt that was late for its date at the dry cleaners, and a see-through blouse over a black bra, who would probably look OK after a bottle and a half of vodka, slopped my drink on to the mat in front of me. I paid, sat on a wobbly stool, lit a cigarette and scoped the end of the pool match.

The larger of the two boys sank the black and looked round triumphantly as the other moaned that he was too skint to buy his brother a pint.

'Get 'em in, Terry,' the other one ordered.

'That's the third game you've won,' the smaller one whined.

'You should learn to play better.'

I turned back to the bar as Terry carefully counted out some silver for a pint of lager top.

'Winner stays on?' I said.

'Do what?'

'I fancy a game, do you mind?'

'Nah. I'm bleedin' broke anyway. But watch out, he's good.'

'I'm not,' I replied. 'Just fancy a game.'

I stood up, took my pint and walked over to where Terry's brother was standing cue in hand. 'Give you a game,' I said.

'For a pint.'

'If you want,' I replied, and hunkered down, inserted my quid and set up the balls.

He wasn't bad and I didn't have to piss about to let him win. 'Lager top, is it?' I asked when he'd sunk the black with a satisfied grin.

'That'll do.'

'My name's Nick, by the way,' I said.

'Bill. That's my bruv, Terence.'

'Terry,' said the other one.

'You want a drink too, Terry?' I asked.

'Sure. Same as 'im,' he said.

I went to the bar, collected three pints, paid and went back. 'Another game?' said Billy to me.

I looked at my watch. 'No, better not,' I said. 'I've got some business.'

'What kind of business?' asked Terry.

'Monkey business. What other kind is there?' I said, and the boys grinned. They knew a crim when they saw one, or thought they did.

'Anything worth a punt?' asked Billy in a lowered voice, although I imagined that anything short of the great train robbery went in the pool bar of the Pale Horseman.

'Just a bit of buying and selling,' I said, offering round the Silk Cuts and lighting them for the boys and myself.

'That's our game too,' said Billy. 'Haven't seen you around before.'

'Norwood, me,' I said. 'Just been paying a flying visit to

a mate's. He's out, but his missus is in if you get my drift. I fancied a pint after and thought I'd pop in. What do you deal in?'

'Anything,' said Billy proudly.

That isn't nailed down, I thought.

'Electronic gear, by any chance?' I asked.

'When it comes to matters electronic, we're your men,' said Billy.

'That's nice to know,' I said. 'Perhaps I could put a few opportunities your way.'

'Such as?'

'Such as let me see what you've got and I could make an offer. I can shift any number of electronic items. 'Specially on the video front.'

'Shit,' said Terry. 'We've just sold a load of gear.'

Billy gave him a dirty look. 'As a matter of fact we're expecting a delivery this afternoon,' he said.

'Local?' I asked.

'Not far.'

'Can I have a shufti?'

'Sure.'

'Where?'

'We'll take you. Can you be back here around five-ish?'

'No problem,' I said.

'See you then,' he replied and tugged his brother out of the boozer.

I popped into the Odeon and saw the new Bruce Willis. I don't care what people say, I think old Bruce is all right, at least now that he's given up mangling old soul tunes, thank God.

There was me and five pensioners in that afternoon.

I came out at five-fifteen and went back to the pub where my two new friends were waiting with half-drunk pints in front of them. In my absence the old brown dog hadn't moved.

I scored a round and Billy said, 'I think we might have some stuff you'd like.'

'Hope so,' I said as I passed the fags round. 'Where is it?'

'In a garage round the corner.'

'Well let's take a squint, then.'

'COD,' said Billy. 'Strictly COD.'

'I've got money,' I said. And I did. Avril's grand was still burning a hole. 'But I've got no motor. It's at home. I can fetch it in fifteen minutes. Let's take a look now and talk business.'

So we did. We drank our drinks, smoked our cigarettes, talked about Crystal Palace's future, which was looking a little dim, then left.

The garage was about five minutes away at the bottom of a tower block. Terry opened up, switched on the ceiling light and closed the door behind us. In the centre of the concrete floor was a big screen TV with stereo speakers, a stereo video and a Sony micro stereo system.

The boys had been busy and had a result.

I looked at the gear and said. 'Got all the remotes?'

Billy nodded.

'Don't suppose you've got the instruction books?'

He shook his head.

'OK. Looks good. How much?'

'Five hundred the lot.'

I laughed out loud. 'No, mate,' I said. 'We're talking second-hand goods here. Second-hand goods without instructions. That's a drag. It means poncing around and getting them. This stuff is so complicated these days it'd take Einstein a month to work them out.'

Both Billy and Terry looked at me blankly. Obviously Einstein hadn't been mentioned when they went to school, if they ever did.

'I'll give you . . .' I pulled out the wodge of notes Avril

Jackson had given me and peeled off six fifty-pound notes.
'. . . Three ton.'

'Bollocks,' said Billy.

'Take it or leave it,' I said. 'But remember. This is regular. Any time you've got gear I've got dough. It'll be a good career move for you.'

As a matter of fact, a good career move for these boys would've been stacking shelves at Sainsbury's. Or getting a squeegee and a bucket and cleaning windscreens at Vauxhall Cross. But I didn't mention that.

I saw greed behind the older one's eyes. 'Three fifty,' he said.

'Done,' I replied, adding another note to the thin pile.

Billy reached out his hand.

'Uh, uh,' I said. 'COD, remember? I'll get my motor and be back in a trice. Where will you be?'

'At Mum's,' said Terry. 'Number thirty-seven upstairs. That's where the remotes are.'

'I'll meet you there in half an hour,' I said. So that was why the boys' place was always clean. They did all their business from their mother's.

And I did just what I said. I thought I'd need wheels so I sloped off home, picked up my car and drove back. I parked it up close to the block and took the lift. When I rang the doorbell of number thirty-seven, a hard-faced bag answered. 'Billy and Terry in?' I asked. 'I'm expected.'

She sniffed through cigarette smoke and gestured for me to enter. I walked down the hall behind her and into a tiny, smoky front room crowded with knick-knacks on every available surface.

Terry and Billy were sitting on the sofa watching *Emmerdale*.

'Hello, boys,' I said.

'Cuppa tea?' said Terry as Mum took the armchair and lit another fag from the stub of the first one.

'No thanks,' I said. 'Let's get down to business.'

Billy stood up and got three remote controls from under the cushion he'd been sitting on and passed them to me. As I slipped them into my jacket pocket I saw, sitting on the window ledge, a six-inch-high pot with 'A Present From Skegness' written in fancy script on the top.

'Where'd you get that?' I asked.

'What?' said Billy.

'The pot. The Skegness pot.'

'It was a present for Mum,' said Terry. 'She collects stuff.'

'So I see,' I said. 'But where'd you get it?'

'None of your business,' said Billy. 'Oi, what're you doing?' he shouted as I walked over and picked it up. It was suspiciously light and I opened the top. Empty.

'You nicked it, didn't you?' I said. 'From a house off the high road.'

'What?' said Billy, and I slapped him hard round his face.

'You heard,' I said.

'Oi,' said Mum, and made as if to get up.

'Sit down, Mother,' I said. 'I don't make a habit of punching women, but I'm prepared to make an exception in your case.'

She did as she was told but Terry unwisely decided to get into the act, jumped up from the sofa and headed towards me. I kicked him hard on the right kneecap with the heel of my boot and he fell over a little table loaded with china cats, crushing them to powder as he went. Then I whacked Billy in the stomach and, as he doubled over, pushed him back on to the seat he'd vacated.

'Now where's what was in this?' I demanded.

No answer, so I grabbed Terry, the weaker of the two, by the hair and pulled his face close to mine. 'Where?' I yelled.

'I flushed it down the toilet. It was only muck.'

'You wanker,' I said, shoving him hard against a side-board which wobbled precariously, depositing several of the ornaments balanced on top on to the carpet. 'Right. I'm taking this,' I said, holding up the pot. 'And if I find you've been back where you nicked it from, I'll come and find you no matter where you go.'

I didn't wait for an answer, just surveyed the wreck of the room and left with the pot in my hand.

I drove straight round to the nick. DC Conway was still on duty. She saw me in one of the small interview rooms. I showed her my prize. 'That was quick,' she said.

'Thanks to you. You were right about the two who did it.'

'And you got a result.'

'Not so's you'd notice. I'm afraid Steve Jackson's remains were flushed down the toilet.'

'Life's a bitch,' she said.

'I agree, but I think I've got the solution.'

'I hope so.'

I nodded, told her where to find the gear and gave her the remotes. 'I reckon it was nicked local this afternoon,' I said. 'And the boys are at Mum's. You do know that address?'

'We know it.'

'If you're quick you'll get them *and* the stuff. They weren't feeling too grand when I left.'

She smiled, went outside and was back within minutes. 'It's all sorted,' she said. 'There's a car on the way. It should be there in two minutes. It was just round the corner.'

'Of course, they may claim that I assaulted them,' I said.

'I don't think that should worry you too much. We can be pretty persuasive when it comes to things like that.'

'Don't tell your inspector. I know him and I don't think

he likes me. He'd probably want to convince them to press charges of attempted murder just to see me banged up downstairs.'

She smiled, and she was amazingly pretty too.

'Well, I'm off,' I said. 'Got a few things to do before I see the widow Jackson.'

She showed me out and at the door she said, 'About that drink.'

'Yeah?'

'Maybe. Call me.'

I looked at her, suspecting a wind-up.

'I mean it,' she said.

'OK,' I replied. 'Next week?'

'I'm on days.'

'Fine. So am I.'

I drove back to my office and went out into the tiny walled garden at the back. There was an old, half-dead tree there, and I broke off some of the petrified branches and made a small fire. The weather forecast promised a fine night and I left it to burn. The next morning I sifted the ashes and filled the pot. I know what dead people's ashes are like. I've seen some. They're not smooth like you might think, but full of lumps, so I tried to make them look as authentic as possible. Then I went round to Avril Jackson's.

'You got it back,' she said delightedly when she answered the door, and saw me clutching the pot. 'You're a marvel.'

'That's me,' I said, wincing slightly as she opened the top.

'God, that's great,' she said, not suspecting a thing. 'Come on in.'

She made me tea and put the pot back on the mantelpiece, centre stage. 'How did you do it?' she asked.

'Long story. And listen, I only worked one day, so I want you to have the balance of your money back.'

'Like hell,' she said. 'You keep it. You earned it.'

I stood there with the money in my hand and looked at her, all neat in a short skirt and sweater and said, 'OK. On one condition.'

'What?'

'You let me spend some of it on buying you dinner tonight.'

She thought about it for a second and said, 'Fine. I'd like that just fine.'

'I'll pick you up at seven. Choose your cuisine.'

'I'll think about it,' she said, and I drank my tea and left.

'See you later,' I said.

'You will,' she said.

It was the worst of times, it was the best of times.

By Hendon Central Station
I Sat Down and Wept

I wrote this one for the 1995 Bouchercon convention book of short stories. The convention was held in Nottingham, which saved on fares to the USA, and you could get a decent cup of tea. Except as it turned out you couldn't, so I stuck to Bourbon and beer and behaved extremely badly. That man Maxim Jakubowski edited the anthology, and it was published by Ringpull.

Nick Sharman's brother was mentioned briefly in *Romeo's Tune*, and a full-length version of this story was going to be the third Sharman novel under the title *The Young Mod's Forgotten Story*. However, the lack of serious violence later ruled that out, and Paolo Hewitt has since gone on to write about the Small Faces under that title on Acid Jazz, and pretty damn good it is too, and the apostrophe's in a different place. But ask my editors: I never was any good at punctuation. So, to avoid further confusion, here's the story, set in 1989, which is so named because I saw a poster for a Broadway show called *By Grand Central Station I sat Down and Wept*. I've always loved that poster.

'The Young Mod's Forgotten Story' is the title of a song by Curtis Mayfield. Or Mods', if you prefer. I lost my copy of the album so I don't know.

It had been twenty-five years since I'd last seen Allie Parker, when I met his train that Monday at Waterloo station.

Then it had been a warm July afternoon in 1965. Now it was a bitterly cold December morning just before a new decade began.

Then I'd been eleven and Allie eighteen, the same age as my brother Bob. Allie and I both grew older, Bob didn't.

Allie and Bob had both been mods. Nineteen-sixties-style freaks, into amphetamines and sweet soul music, part of a loose gang of maybe fifty geezers, known locally as the Streatham Boys.

One night in that long-forgotten summer there'd been a ruck at the Lyceum in the Strand, where the faces gathered to admire the cut of each other's trousers, listen to the latest sounds, pop pills and pull birds. The fight was over a girl from Hendon who Allie fancied, but whose boyfriend didn't appreciate the competition. Some blood was spilled, and the following Sunday a dozen of the Streatham Boys got tooled up and made a sortie up to North London to sort out the aggro.

Bob never came back. In a running battle outside Hendon Central tube station he ended up with a knife in his chest. Allie's print were the only ones found on the murder weapon. He was nicked and tried, pleaded not guilty, but was convicted and sentenced to life. He always maintained his innocence, but refused to identify who did kill Bob. He was doing his time in Strangeways a couple of years later when a fight broke out one lunch-time in the mess hall. Somewhere Allie had got hold of another knife and he stuck a fellow prisoner, killing him immediately. That time he did plead guilty and got another life sentence. Twenty-five years he did in all, and that Monday he had been released from Parkhurst and was coming home.

Although I hadn't seen him he'd sent me letters from day one, and I'd spoken to him on the phone. He called me regularly once prisoners got the privilege and always maintained his innocence, but wouldn't say more. At first

I'd ignored his correspondence and been pretty short with him on the dog. But he persevered, and over the years as I took my GCEs, went to university until I was slung out, joined the police, got into bad company and did bad things and was slung out of the force too; got married, had Judith, then lost her and my wife to a dentist, and became a private investigator down in South London, we got as friendly as it was possible for us to be.

But I hadn't seen him. No. That was out of the question. However much he pleaded he was innocent, I could never be sure.

You see, a murder is like a stone tossed into a still pool. The ripples spread, and keep on spreading, for years.

My mum and dad were never the same after Bob died. Mum went a bit strange, and eventually Dad left and vanished out of our lives for ever. And we weren't the only ones to suffer. Bob had had a girlfriend, Veronica – Ronnie. They'd been together for a couple of years, and there was talk of an engagement. That's how they did things then. Ronnie took it hard when Bob died, and she killed herself a few years later with an overdose of smack. That was two families ruined. Then there was Allie's folks. They nursed a lot of grief too. They ran a little grocer's shop in the Old Kent Road. I went to visit them irregularly, but when the old man died I didn't go to the funeral. Allie was out on day release with an escort, and I still couldn't face seeing him. His mum told me he'd lost a lot of hair but was cheerful.

I was made up.

Mrs Parker's still in the shop every day, although she's close to seventy-five, and she's had a lot of offers for the place. Mostly from the Asian community, but she keeps saying no. She hired some staff and they do most of the work while she keeps an eye on them. She told me she'd keep the business for Allie to come home to.

And eventually he did. All things must pass.

I miss my brother. He was a good bloke. Kind. Let me tag along. I miss my dad as well. And my mum, in a lot of ways. And Ronnie too. Maybe if she and Bob had got married I'd have some nephews and nieces to spoil, and Mum would have more grandchildren.

Maybe if the family had stayed together things would've turned out differently, and I wouldn't be missing my own wife and child, Laura and Judith, so much.

Do all the things you love slip through your fingers?

I even miss Allie in a way. He was a laugh. Underneath it all.

When he got news of his release date he called me up and told me. After twenty-five years a lot of the scars had healed, and when his mum asked me to meet him at the station and bring him home I decided to find out how deep the scar tissue was.

So that's why I was standing at the barrier to platform twelve when the nine-fifteen arrival from Portsmouth came chugging in.

I never would have recognized Allie. By then he was almost completely bald, he'd put on a lot of soft weight, and his face was pale and lined from prison life. But he recognized me and came over. He was wearing a bomber jacket and jeans with trainers, and carrying a nylon holdall.

'Nick,' he said.

I looked into his pale blue eyes. 'Allie,' I said back.

We didn't shake hands.

'I would've known you anywhere,' he said. 'You look just like your old man.' He didn't add 'and Bob', but I could see it in his eyes.

'Is that right? I can hardly remember. He fucked off.'

'I know,' he said. 'Mum told me.'

'It was a long time ago, Allie.'

'Yeah. Everything's changed. Even since I came up for the funeral. Everything's bright.'

'Is that right?' I said again. It wasn't bright at all that day.

'Yeah. There's not much colour inside. It's all grey.'

I almost found out for myself, I thought. 'I've got the motor outside. Your mum's expecting you,' I said.

'Can we get a drink first?'

'At this time?'

He glanced at the cheap Timex on his wrist. 'Sorry. I forgot. Licensing hours don't mean much inside.'

'They wouldn't.'

'Cup of tea, then. I need some time.'

'There's a café on the station.'

'No – outside. There's too many bodies here. I'm getting a bit freaked.'

'All right, Allie. We'll stop on the way.'

I rescued the car from the short-term parking and threw Allie's bag into the boot, then turned the car south. We found a greasy spoon by the Elephant, and I stuck the wheels on a meter and we went in.

It was steamy and warm inside the café, with a bunch of *Sun*-reading individuals tucking into their breakfasts. Allie ordered beans on toast and a mug of tea. I settled for the tea only, and lit a cigarette as we sipped at the boiling brew and waited for his food to come from the kitchen.

'Long time, Nick,' he said.

'Yeah.'

'I'm forty-three now. Don't seem possible.'

'Same age as Bob would've been.'

'Yeah.' He started to roll a needle-thin, jailhouse cigarette. 'I never done it, you know.'

'No, Allie, I don't know. Not for sure.'

'But I never. He was my mate.'

'Then who did?'

163

He regarded me through the smoke, and the steam from his mug. 'I've never told a soul.'

I said nothing.

'But I want to show you. You deserve that at least. That's why I got Mum to get you to meet me.'

'Yeah?'

He nodded, and a middle-aged woman in a white overall called out his order, and he sloped off to get it. 'Fuck me,' he said when he got back. 'Nearly fifteen bob for a few beans and a slice. I don't think I'll ever get used to this new money.'

'It's been going for nearly twenty years, Allie,' I said. 'You'd better. So tell me about Bob.'

'In a bit,' he replied, finishing his snack fast, like the food might be swiped from under his nose if he ate slowly. 'Let's go and see Mum.'

The shop was open, with the two assistants busily serving, Mrs Parker sitting in the back with her eyes on the TV screens that monitored the shop.

'Allie,' she said, with tears in her eyes as she got up to greet us. 'Hello, son. It's good to see you out. Cuppa tea?'

'Hello, Mum,' said Allie awkwardly, as he dropped his bag and clumsily embraced her. 'In a minute, yeah. I've got something I want to show Nick here first.'

'Whatever you like, son,' she said. 'Your room's just as you left it, but I gave it a rub round.'

And it was. I'd been there a couple of times with Bob and Allie, when they let me come along during the school holidays, and it was like stepping back thirty years to a more innocent time.

The room was medium-sized, at the top of the house, looking down at the dreary backyard full of crates of old bottles and other rubbish from the shop. The windows were streaked and dirty, but the curtains were clean, as if Mrs P. had made sure that her boy didn't come back to complete squalor. The bed was freshly made too, with clean sheets, and the place had been dusted, but otherwise it was just as I remembered it from all that long time ago.

One wall was taken up with shelves of LPs and singles, all pristine in their sleeves, as if they'd just come out of the shop. Against another wall was a chest of drawers, on top of which stood a Dansette record-player with an autochange. There was a big wardrobe against the third wall, and Allie opened the door to show off maybe twenty moddy-boy suits and close to a hundred shirts with tab or button-down collars on hangers, plus two overcoats and a mackintosh. Neatly lined up beneath them were a couple of dozen pairs of shoes and boots.

'All me old clobber,' he said proudly. 'But I betcha I couldn't get into them now.' He rubbed his protruding stomach. 'Prison grub. All carbohydrates.'

He went over to the record shelves and riffled through a few albums, then picked up a handful of singles.

'All mint,' he said, tossing them on to the bed. 'Tamla, Sue, Atlantic. Worth a packet now. I kept up inside. I still love this music. It's all crap what they do now.'

'Bob,' I reminded him.

'Sure. Sorry. Give me a hand with this.' He moved over to the chest.

'Do what?'

'Give us a hand. Pull it out from the wall.'

I did as he said, and it slid over the carpet. Behind it the wallpaper had been stripped to the bricks, four of which had been loosened from their cement.

'Coppers never found this,' he said with satisfaction. 'I betcha Mum and the old bloke give 'em a right hard time when they came round.'

He pulled the bricks out of the wall, exposing a gap. 'Bathroom next door,' he said. 'This is where the pipes go.' Then he pulled out a sawn-off shotgun, a box of shells and two big jars. One was full of old banknotes, and in the other were little blue and purple pills.

'This was what it was all about, Nick,' he said, hunkering back on to his heels. 'Our little earner.'

'What?' I said.

'Me, Bob and another geezer, Jimmy Gurney, used to do chemist shops and wholesalers. We nicked uppers and sold them round the clubs. Simple.'

'I never knew,' I said.

'You weren't supposed to, little brother. You worshipped Bob, everyone knew that. He wasn't going to let on that he was a tea leaf on the side.'

He saw my look.

'Christ, Nick, don't look so surprised. We never did any harm. We never hurt no one. A bit of thieving, that was all. We were innocent, mate. Innocent times.'

'But it ended in murder. My brother's murder. And that murder fucked up a lot of people.'

'Tell me about it. What do you think it did to me, and Mum, and the old man?'

'So why didn't you tell them the truth at the time?'

'Because we didn't grass. The rules of the road. Nowadays the little scumbags will turn their best mates over for twenty quid. But we didn't. Innocent, see. And then when I killed the other fella . . . Well, I was up for life on that too, and it didn't seem to make much difference.'

'So who did it?'

'That bastard Gurney. He wanted to make a career of being at it. I didn't care one way or another. Bob wanted to knock it on the head. He had that bird. What was her name?'

'Veronica.'

'That's right, Veronica. They were serious. He didn't want to get caught. Knew it would do your mum and dad up. Whatever happened to the bird?'

'She's dead. She turned into a junkie.'

'For fuck's sake. Ironical, ain't it, Nick?'

He hefted the bottle of pills, then picked up the jar of money. It was all old notes, well out of date. 'You'll have to take those to the Bank of England,' I said, for something to cover my confusion. 'They'll change them for new.'

'Hardly seems worth it,' said Allie. 'I bet there's not more than a couple of ton in here. And at more than a nicker for beans on toast and a cuppa, how far will that get me? A souvenir, Nick, that's what they are.'

'So what now?' I asked.

'Now I go and do for Gurney. That bastard killed my best mate and let me rot inside.' Allie hefted the shotgun.

I picked up the box of shells, opened it and took one out. The cardboard tube of the .12-gauge cartridge was crazed and cracked under my fingers, dropping shot on to the carpet. 'Not with these you won't,' I said. 'They've perished.'

'Shit.'

He knelt again, put his hand back into the hole and brought out a flick-knife and popped the blade. It gleamed in the dull morning light, still sharp after all that time. 'Looks like this'll have to do, then. Poetic justice.'

'You can't just kill him.'

'Why not? Mum'll know where he is. She knows everything. Besides, I've been inside so long, outside is like a prison to me. In there I get three meals a day, don't have to worry about me laundry, and I've made a lot of mates. I don't mind going back.'

He made it sound almost desirable.

'I'm coming with you,' I said.

'Nah.'

'Yeah. Otherwise I'll set the Bill on you.'

'You wouldn't.'

'I was one, don't forget.'

'I always wondered about that.' He looked at me hard, then shrugged. 'All right,' he said. 'It's your funeral.'

He emptied his holdall and put the gun, the cartridges, the knife and the two jars inside.

We went back downstairs. 'Cuppa tea, son?' asked Mrs P., hopefully.

'In a bit, Ma. Me and Nick's got a coupla people to see.'

'Who?'

'Jimmy Gurney. Remember him?'

''Course I do. I ain't lost my marbles yet.'

I had to smile.

''Course you ain't, Ma,' said Allie. 'He's still about, ain't he?'

'Sure he is. Dirty little sluice. Lives down on the Walk Estate with that slut of a wife of his, and all them poor kids.'

Bandit country.

'Know where?'

'Hamlet House. Top floor. Number seventy as I recall.'

'OK, Ma,' said Allie, kissing her on the cheek. 'We'll see you later.'

'Mrs Parker,' I said.

'Nick.'

We went back to my car and I turned in the direction of the Walk Estate. We were silent on the journey, although there were a million questions I wanted answered.

When we got on to the estate I parked on the corner opposite Hamlet House and we got out. A cold wind struck hard and there was snow in the air.

Allie grabbed hold of my arm and said, 'When I was a little kid I used to go round my nan's. She had this kitchen at the back of the house. It had one of those big, old-fashioned stoves. And she did all the cooking on it, and all the boiling and washing and stuff like that. And she had a coal fire too, and she kept it on all the time. It was always hot in there, winter and summer. And in the winter, when there was nobody in the room but me, I used to open the kitchen door and there were three steps that went down into the garden. And it'd be cold outside, and I'd be warm inside. And I felt safe. I haven't felt safe since then. How long is it since you've felt safe, Nick?'

'A long time,' I said. 'Twenty-five years at least.'

He let go of my arm then, and we shuffled through the rubbish that was skinned with grey snow, to the front door of the flats. Miraculously the lift was working and we punched twelve.

When we got to the top floor we found number seventy at the end of the balcony. From next door the thud of over-amplified rap music shook the walls. The bell at the side of the door was broken and the knocker was missing, so Allie hammered on the hardboard that covered where glass had once been.

'Salubrious,' I remarked.

'Jimmy always had style.'

The door was answered by a slatternly looking woman dressed head to toe in cheap catalogue clothes. She was about thirty-five, skinny, with big tits, and could've used a decent bra. She had long, lank greasy hair and pimples on her forehead. She was holding a young kid whose nappy needed changing, and a couple of dirty-faced toddlers clutched at her skirts.

'Mrs Gurney,' said Allie.

'S'right.'

'Jimmy in?'

'You the Old Bill?' she said.

'Hardly,' said Allie. 'I just came out today. Is he in?'

She nodded. 'You'd better come in,' she said. Visits from old lags were obviously no novelty.

'In the kitchen,' she said.

We went through into a stench of old sweat, puke, pizza and piss. Nice ambience, I thought.

I'd probably met Jimmy Gurney twenty-five years before, but even if we'd been old mates I doubt if I'd've recognized the vision we found sitting at the kitchen table.

He had long, stringy, dirty grey hair with a big bald spot at the crown, an earring in the shape of a skull, a hippie moustache, and he was wearing a dirty vest and jeans. He was smoking a spliff and nursing another baby.

Jesus. Home sweet home.

He looked up when we entered. 'I've told you a hundred times I haven't got any money,' he said.

Debt collectors must've been a big feature in the Gurney's lives too.

'No money today, Jimmy,' said Allie. 'We've come round to clear up another debt.'

'Who the fuck are you?' demanded Gurney. The music from next door was so loud that we had to shout.

'Don't you remember, Jim? Think about it,' said Allie.

Gurney looked from one of us to the other, but seemed to have a better handle on me.

'It can't be,' he said, his already pasty skin turning pale.

'Like him, ain't he?' said Allie.

'Bob,' said Gurney.

'Bob's dead, you cunt. You fucking know that,' said Allie. 'That's his little brother all grown up. But the resemblance's there.'

'Allie,' said Gurney, now growing even paler.

'Home from the war,' said Allie. 'Now yours starts. You never visited me, Jim. Shame on you.'

'I . . . I . . . I . . .' the seated man stammered.

'Shut up,' said Allie.

'Listen,' said the woman. 'What's going on?'

'You. Take those kids and go into the next room,' ordered Allie. 'And don't even dream of using the phone.'

'The phone's off,' said Jimmy Gurney dispiritedly.

'Fuck me,' said Allie as the woman took the baby from Gurney. 'I was living better inside.'

When the woman had gone, Allie put the bag on the table and opened it. He took out the jar of pills. 'Remember these, Jim?' he said.

Gurney obviously did. Allie put the pills on the table, then took out the shotgun and said to Gurney, 'I brought this for you, son.'

Gurney cringed in his seat.

'Tell him,' he ordered, nodding at me. 'Tell him what you done.'

'I never done nothing.'

'Liar,' said Allie. 'Black liar.' And he pulled both hammers of the shotgun back for effect, even though it wasn't loaded.

'Don't,' said Gurney, covering his head with his thin arms. 'Please don't. My kids.'

'Then tell him, you little bastard.'

Gurney was nearly in tears. 'I never meant to kill him,' he said. 'Just frighten him into keeping on doing the jobs we were doing. It was good money. But he wouldn't listen. We was away from the fight at the back of the station. I was out of me head on them.' He pointed at the jar. 'I never knew what I was doing.'

'See, Nick,' said Allie. 'Told you.'

'But your prints were on the knife,' I said to Allie.

'It *was* mine. But I lent it to this git when we went up to Hendon that day. And Jimmy here always wore gloves, winter and summer. Thought it was cool. Right, Jim?'

Gurney nodded.

Allie looked round. 'Times have changed. This fucking place stinks like shit. And, Jimmy, you look like shit too.'

'It ain't my fault,' whined Gurney. 'I can't work. Got

agoraphobia and asthma. And the fucking social don't help much.'

'You killed my brother,' I interrupted, and I felt a red rage wash over me.

'I swear it was an accident.'

'But you let Allie go to jail for it.'

Gurney said nothing.

'Shall I top him now, Nick?' said Allie.

'No,' pleaded Gurney. Another minute and the stink of his shit would join the rest in the disgusting kitchen. 'The missus would be all on her own.'

'You'd rather be alive in this hole, with that slag,' said Allie disbelievingly. 'I reckon I'd be doing you a favour, topping you.'

'So do I,' I said. 'So leave him, Allie. That's the worst punishment you could dole out.'

Allie looked around again and grinned. 'I think you're right, Nick.'

So we left Jimmy Gurney there with his wife and children in that slum, in the stink of old sweat, puke, pizza and piss with the music thudding through the walls.

We went for a drink at a pub down by the river. We didn't talk much about what had happened that afternoon in Gurney's horrible kitchen. When it started to get dark and the tide was out, we walked on to the flats. I ruined a good pair of shoes. We threw all the stuff in the bag way out into the water: the gun and the knife and the shells and the pills and the money. I think we'd all got too many souvenirs to want any more by then. When we got back to the shore, Allie said, 'You go on, Nick. I can get back home on my own. I want to take a wander.'

That time we shook hands, and I drove home. We didn't make any arrangements to meet again.

The next day I went to Hendon. I'd avoided going there ever since Bob died. I mean, Hendon wasn't part of my regular manor, and even though the police college is there, where you do your induction into the Met, I'd always managed not to go to Hendon Central itself.

But that day I did.

I got up early, had some breakfast, got into the car and pointed it north. Headed over the river, and after a couple of false starts I found Hendon Central tube.

It had started snowing again.

By the station was a bit of green and a bench that looked like it had been taken over by dossers, but that was empty now, so I used it.

And by Hendon Central station I sat down and wept.

Filth

This is *not* a Sharman story. Although it could be in a parallel universe. But even Sharman has something. The hero of this story has nothing and nobody, except a pick-up truck and a bad conscience.

Ever felt like that?

Part One

But don't try to touch me.
Don't try to touch me
Because that will never happen again.

1

I was sitting in the kitchen of a council flat on the thirteenth floor of a tower block on an estate in Deptford that had seen better days by the third day it was finished, while the chemist checked the gear.

The chemist looked to be about fourteen, dressed in expensive, baggy clothes. He had long, thick hair that I just bet he pulled back in a pony tail when he went to raves to get all loved up. Jesus! Do they still do that? I was kind of out of touch with the younger generation of late. Kind of out of touch with every generation, as it happened. I tended to keep myself to myself as much as possible, but some days, this one included, I had to graft.

There were two other men in the room. The money man was around thirty, thin-faced, dressed all sharp in Armani with a portable phone close to hand. He looked a bit miffed, as if he wished he were in some bar where the beer cost three nicker a throw if you could pronounce its name, with a blonde bimbo wearing her skirt up around her armpits sticking her tongue in his ear. I was a bit sad that I wasn't in one myself. I could've used a bit of love action. It had been a long time.

The third geezer was about six foot tall and built like the proverbial. Hands like shovels and wrists as thick as my ankles. The minder. At first I thought he was wearing a flak jacket under his suit coat, but after a bit I realized it was pure muscle. What *wasn't* muscle was the bulge under his left arm. About .45 calibre, I decided, and he had a look in his eye that made me think he wouldn't mind using it. He was standing by the door, blocking my exit.

All in all, a lovable little crew, who I knew were never going to get on my Christmas card list, even if I had one.

The minder had given me a good frisking when I'd arrived. I was unarmed, not as much as a paper clip. I knew better.

The chemist had the usual kit out on the table and was busily testing a sample from the kilo of pure Peruvian I'd brought with me. I almost licked my lips as I looked at it. It had been a hell of a temptation not to have a dig in on the way. But I'd managed to overcome it. I knew better about that too.

As the chemist dropped some of the flakes into a retort full of viscous liquid, I took out my Silk Cuts and lit one. I didn't offer the pack around. That'd teach 'em.

'Do you mind?' said the chemist. 'It can affect the results.'

I crushed the cigarette out on the filthy lino that was cut and pitted with stiletto heel prints and he said, 'This is my home.'

I looked round the grungy kitchen with a pile of dirty dishes in the sink and the unmistakable odour of takeout curry coming from the overflowing garbage bin, and said, 'When you get Harrods in to give the place a makeover I'll donate.'

The minder made a noise in his throat. It could've been a laugh, it could've been a snarl. I didn't care.

I didn't care about much in those days.

I looked out of the partially open window and the thin clouds were a pearly grey made pink by the setting sun, and an airliner circling over London caught one of the rays and turned suddenly gold, and I felt like crying.

'Grade A,' said the chemist when the liquid in the retort turned blue.

The money man sighed, lifted up a briefcase that he'd had hidden under the table, took out a huge brown envelope and handed it to me. I opened the flap. Inside were big wodges of fifty-pound notes.

'It's all there,' said the money man.

'And I just take your word for it?' I said, and took out the first stack.

'Count the soddin' stuff, then,' said the money man, anxious to get back to real life.

I did. He was right – it was all there, and the money looked good enough to spend. Not my problem if it wasn't.

When I was satisfied I stuffed the money back into the envelope and nodded. Everyone seemed to relax a bit then and the money man said, 'Want a line?'

I nodded again, so hard I felt like one of those little doggies you used to see in the back of cars. Did I want a line? Do swallows fly south in the summer?

He rubbed down the formica top of the table with a grubby teacloth, fetched out his wallet, extracted a gold Amex, the flash bastard, dug it into the plastic bag of coke, pulled out a fair load, dumped it on the table top and cut out a dozen lines with the plastic. Then he rolled up a Nelson from the wallet and did four lines. The chemist took the note and did two, then passed it to me. I snarfed up two of my own. The coke was first class and clean, and I felt an immediate hit and swallowed the metallic-tasting saliva that filled my mouth. The minder didn't get offered.

'Cheers,' I said and stood up. The minder moved away from the door. I went through, across the sticky-looking carpet to the front door, through that, along the corridor and took the stairs down, dodging the smoke-blackened silver foil, the syringes and the other human debris that covered them.

Once outside I took the shortest route out of the estate, knowing that if there was going to be a rip-off this was where it would happen. I didn't entirely trust that portable phone. But I was OK, and I crossed the main road, went down a side street to a plain-looking navy blue Ford Sierra that I happened to know had got a three and a half litre V8 lump shoehorned under the bonnet.

I got in the passenger side and sniffed up the mucus into my sinuses.

'Been sampling the merchandise?' the driver asked.

I shrugged as I passed the envelope to her.

'All there?' she asked.

'Yeah,' I said, and she picked up a radio and whispered into it.

When she'd got a Roger she turned and said, 'We'll bust them now. You did good work.'

'I'll be popular, won't I?' I remarked.

'Your problem,' she said, took two bundles of a thousand pounds each out of the envelope and tossed them into my lap, and a small baggie of the same charlie that I'd sold out of the glove compartment. She held it up in front of me teasingly. 'Want this too?'

I looked at her and nodded. Much more nodding and my head would fall off.

She gave me a pitying look and dropped the bag into my hand. 'Enjoy,' she said.

'I will,' I said as I stuffed the money and drugs into my pocket.

She fired up the Sierra's engine and said over its throaty roar, 'Want a lift?'

'Streatham,' I replied. 'By the Cannon cinema.'

2

It was almost full dark when we got where we were going. The coke was still buzzing round inside my skull like a panicked wasp's nest, and the lights from the pub next to the cinema were warm and fuzzy. She stopped the car and said, 'As a matter of fact, there might be something soon.'

'No peace for the wicked.'

'You're certainly that.'

'So I suppose a quick blow job is out of the question?'

'Fuck off,' she said. 'I'll be in touch.'

I got out of the car and walked up the side of the pub to the car park where my motor was waiting. I saw it as soon as I turned the corner, standing head and shoulders above the rest of the cars. It's a six-litre Chevrolet Silverado pickup truck with huge wheels and tyres, finished with a Baja California paint job in shiny black with a red pinstripe, and black windows all round. It's one of the few paid-for, street-legal things I own. I zapped the alarm gizmo as I got close and the lights blinked three times with audible bleeps. I like that. It talks to me when I get close to it. The only thing in the world that does.

I climbed aboard and got out the bag the driver had given me. I stuck my little finger inside and collected some of the powder on my nail. I snorted up what was there and lay back against the seat with my eyes closed. Bastard stuff. But I loved it.

After a minute I stuck the key in the ignition of the truck, deactivated the cut-out, fired it up, and revved the engine hard. It sounded like an angry behemoth, and for the first time in hours I smiled.

I paid the old guy who ran the parking lot for the day and took off over the unpaved surface with a screech from the tyres and a rattle of stones on the chassis. I pulled out into Streatham High Road and headed for home. It's amazing how many fucking arseholes in Escorts and Cavaliers try to cut me off in the truck. If they knew that the chassis's been boxed in with girders, and most of the body panels strengthened, and that if they hit me I'd be the last thing they ever did hit, they wouldn't be so keen.

I went upstairs to my flat, where the ansaphone was a smashed-up pile of electric junk in one corner, and the telephone, a Mickey Mouse upright, scarred from BB pellet shot, was unplugged. There was a cold, takeout pizza in the fridge, which I ate without much appetite while drinking a bottle of Becks, and I switched on the stereo. I played a tape that the last woman who'd stayed had left behind. She'd been half my age and totally crazy, but beautiful. She stayed as long as I could cope with her, but when it got to the stage where I had to sleep with one eye open in case she hauled out one of the kitchen knives she seemed to love so much and decided to do a Mrs Bobbitt on my privates, she had to go. The tape was pure hardcore shit, 180 BPM. Not really my style, but the rock-steady drum beats filled the holes in my head and it pissed off the neighbours, so it suited me fine.

As the music bounced off the walls I snorted more charlie, found a spliff and a bottle of Remy and sat with my back against the wall in the dark room where the only illumination spilled in from the streetlights outside, smoking, and drinking the brandy straight from the bottle until I started to weep, the money I'd earned that afternoon spread out on the carpet in front of me like a sea of paper.

Wicked, the driver had called me. I'd never been wicked. I'd just done what seemed to be right at the time.

3

The interview started out OK. There were just three of us in the room. The suspect who'd refused counsel, a plain-clothes sergeant who'd been working on the case with me, but wasn't my usual skipper, and me. DI in charge. I put on the tape recorder, read out the date and time and those present and began.

'For the benefit of the record,' I said, 'you're still under caution and can call in a solicitor at any time. Is that understood?'

The suspect nodded and I said, 'Would you please speak for the tape.'

'Yes,' he said after a moment.

'Thank you. This is a serious business,' I went on. 'Now I know that you murdered my colleague.'

The suspect laughed in my face. 'No,' he said.

'Don't give me that, you little shit. And this isn't funny.'

I felt the sergeant looking at me but I ignored him.

'Isn't it?' said the suspect arrogantly. 'You can't prove a thing.'

'Can't I? You'd be surprised.' But I couldn't, and everyone in the room, indeed in the station, knew it. We were taking a flyer arresting the geezer, and I was going to look like a bloody fool if I had to let him go.

I listed out the flimsy evidence, circumstantial at best and supposition at worst, linking our suspect with the shooting and death of my old sergeant. We'd worked together for more than three years and were friends. Sitting together in freezing cold cars at the dead of night keeping obbo on someone's house and pissing into fruit jars made *you like that, or the dead opposite. We were lucky, and during those many nights we'd shared secrets that I doubt anyone else in the world knew. I missed him. I missed working with him and I missed drinking with him. And as I looked at the suspect who I knew deep in my heart was guilty, yet for lack of hard evidence would probably walk away, a great hatred grew inside me, and I knew that I couldn't let that happen, no matter what personal or professional price I had to pay.*

We were nearly at the end of the time allowed to keep the suspect at the station. I looked at my watch and said, 'Fancy a cup of tea?'

The suspect nodded and I switched off the tape after saying what time the interview had been suspended for refreshments.

'Get us three teas, Sergeant,' I said.

'Sir. I'll get a PC to come in.'

'Don't bother,' I said. 'This is almost over.'

'But I should . . .'

'You should do as you're told, Sergeant,' I interrupted. 'Now get going and don't rush back.'

He looked me clean in the eyes and I looked back. And he shrugged and left. I was going to fuck him up too, but right then was when I stopped caring about things like that.

'You bastard,' I said to the suspect when the sergeant had closed the door behind himself. 'I know you did it.'

'You shouldn't question me with the tape off,' the suspect said, looking at the machine.

'Don't tell me what I should and shouldn't do. He was a mate of mine. Did you know that?'

'How sweet,' he said, and I came out of my seat and punched him on the side of the jaw, knocking him off his chair.

'You reckon,' I said. 'How sweet was that, then? Or this?' And I went over and kicked him hard in the ribs.

He scuttled over against the wall and huddled there. 'You're mental,' he said. 'This is police brutality.'

'See that on World in Action, did you?' I said. 'You'll fucking know about police brutality before I'm done with you.'

'I'll sue you.'

'And get legal aid, you bastard. You would too, wouldn't you?' And I kicked him again.

'Come here,' I said through clenched teeth and picked him up by his long hair. 'Walkies.'

I opened the interview room door and shoved him out. The corridor was empty and I pushed him towards the emergency stairs. 'Up,' I said, and we walked up the six flights to the roof.

At the top was a push-barred door on to the flat roof outside, and I slammed it open and propelled him through it by his arm.

'What the fuck are you doing?' he said, and for the first time I saw some fear in his eyes and it made my resolve even stronger.

'You're going to tell me the truth,' I said.

'Bollocks. I'm going to tell you nothing. Whatever I say you can't use anyway.'

'And you're going to sue me.'

He didn't reply.

The sun was hidden by dark, broad-shouldered clouds and the wind was fresh from the east and whipped at our hair and clothes as I pushed him over to the low wall at the edge of the roof. 'I hope you're not frightened of heights,' I said.

'You're mad,' he said.

'A bit pissed off, I'll agree. But mad? Not yet.' And I grabbed his shoulder and forced him over, so that he

looked down into the yard below full of parked police
vehicles.

'Listen,' he said.

'What?'

'If I tell you, what will you do?'

'What can I do? Like you said, I've given you a smack
and there's no witnesses to whatever you say. I'm fucked.
But then so are you.' And I forced him down until he was
sitting awkwardly on the top of the wall half over the edge
of the roof.

'OK, I done it,' he said, tears coming into his eyes. 'I
admit it. I shot him.'

'I knew it.'

'Now stop fucking around, and let me up.'

'What? So's you can call your solicitor and have me
done? I don't think so.'

'What are you going to do, then?' His voice was high
and reedy, and his previous arrogance was gone.

'You killed my friend, you scumbag. Someone you
weren't fit to clean shoes for. And I've just messed up a
promising career. And you expect to walk away laughing,
probably with a few quid compensation in your pocket,
and maybe no one will ever prove what you did. What do
you think I'm going to do?'

And I shoved him over the edge and heard him scream
on the way down until he landed on the top of a squad
car.

I looked over the edge as uniformed and plain clothes
men and women rushed out to see what was happening.

The suspect lay spreadeagled on the dented top of the
car, and even from a distance I could see his blood, and
that he was still.

As still as my friend in his grave.

'Got him, son,' I said aloud to my dead friend, and then
I threw up on to the tarmac top of the roof.

4

The driver phoned me three days later. 'Usual time, usual place,' she said and hung up.

I wasn't in the mood to chat either.

She was waiting in the usual quiet boozer in Camberwell. I'd taken a cab. She was sitting at a corner table with what looked suspiciously like plain orange juice. I bought a lager and joined her.

'What's new?' I asked, looking through the open door at the traffic stuttering by outside.

'Lots. We busted the three at the flat the other night. No bail at present.'

'Good job.'

'We need you again.'

'So soon. I'm flattered.'

'Don't be.'

'What's the deal?'

'Same again. You're the delivery boy, but this time we take them down while you're there.'

'Terrific. Why?'

'They're more slippery than most. We need to know the stuff's on the table when we go in. And they're nasty. The place they operate from is a fortress and we understand there's automatic weapons on the premises. This is a big bust, we're going in behind the tactical firearms boys.

'Lock and load.'

'If you like.'

'I don't. Loaded guns scare me.'

'They'll know who you are.'

'When's that ever stopped them shooting the wrong man?'

'You'll just have to trust us.' She paused. 'Or take the consequences.'

'Where and when?' I said.

'Saturday, noon. The courier's due in from Dublin.'

'Circuitous route.'

'That's the way they planned it.'

'And I take his place.'

She nodded.

'Risky,' I said.

'So's crossing the road.'

'Don't they know this guy?'

'He's a mule. A new boy. That's why we chose him.'

'How much?'

'The usual?'

'This can't go on for ever.'

'For ever's a long time,' she said.

'You mean I'm expendable.'

She didn't bother paying the question the compliment of an answer, just finished her drink, got up and left. 'We'll talk,' she said.

'Can't wait,' I replied and watched her bottom move around under her skirt as she left.

I finished my drink and left too. It was a pretty day and I walked along the Walworth Road to the river, found a bar and had too much to drink. Later on, when the sky was a lavender colour over Blackfriars Bridge, I hailed a cab and went home and got stoned again.

5

The driver was as good as her word and phoned me the next day. 'There's a ticket waiting for you at the BA desk at Heathrow. You fly out to Dublin Friday morning at ten.'

'First class?'

'Be serious. You'll be met at the airport by an Inspector Jones from the Irish Garda. We're working closely with them on this one.'

'How will I know him?'

Stupid question.

'He'll know you.'

'And?'

'Don't worry, you'll be briefed.'

'When's the delivery?'

'Saturday.'

And she hung up. Constantly being hung up on by that bitch was beginning to get on my nerves.

I was at the airport in plenty of time, carrying just a small bag with a change of underwear, a clean shirt, and some toilet gear. I collected the ticket and caught the plane. I was served an unappetizing breakfast, and almost before we'd reached maximum height the plane started its descent.

I disembarked, carrying my bag, and went through immigration and customs without being stopped. When I reached the arrival hall I was immediately buttonholed by a big geezer in a dark suit. He spoke my name in an Irish accent and I nodded and he said, 'Jones.' We didn't shake hands. He probably thought he'd get contaminated.

We went down to the car park and over to a dark-coloured Montego. 'In the back,' said Jones. I opened the door and saw someone sitting on the other side of the rear bench seat and climbed in next to him. Jones got behind the wheel.

Jones turned round in his seat and said, 'Smith, from the Met.'

The bloke I was sitting next to, a sandy-haired individual in his thirties, blimped me hard.

'Smith and Jones,' I said. 'How very original.'

Smith said, 'We like it.' He had a London accent.

'I don't know you, do I?' I said.

'You can't know everyone,' and he grinned nastily.

'Can I see some identification?' I said, looking at the inside of the car door which had no handle, suddenly feeling my bottle going.

Smith and Jones both laughed. 'Identification,' said Jones. 'He wants to see identification.'

'Probably thinks we're hit men for the mob,' said Smith. 'Go on, Jonesey, get going.'

Jones started the engine, pulled out of the car park and drove through Dublin, somewhere I'd never been before.

'Pretty, innit?' said Smith.

'Where are we going?' I asked.

'Wait and see,' said Smith, so I did.

We drove out to the suburbs and turned into the drive of a big old Victorian mansion house and stopped in front of its imposing doors.

'Out you jump,' said Smith, and I did as I was told.

All three of us climbed the steps to the door which was opened by a copper in uniform shirt and trousers. At least they were real Old Bill; I'd been beginning to have my doubts. Smith and Jones had been delighted to put the frighteners on me. You could tell by the looks on their faces.

Jones led me through to a large common room where three plain-clothes men were watching the news on TV. 'Wait here,' he said. 'There's coffee. And we'll need a photo for your man's passport. We've got a studio upstairs. He's booked into a nice hotel in the city centre. You'll check in this evening.'

I nodded, got a coffee and sat on a chair as far away from the three men as possible. A news item about the beating of black teenagers by police in Los Angeles came on. They loved it, shouting out encouragement as the cops put the boot in and giving each other high fives.

It was depressing.

Ten minutes later Jones came back, took me upstairs where I had my photo taken quickly, then he said, 'Come and have a look at him.'

We went down again and into a room where Smith was waiting, a cup of coffee in one hand, a cigarette in the other. A portion of one wall was made out of clear glass with a view of next door. I assumed that it was a one-way mirror. The geezer sitting at a table in the room was roughly my age and build. At least that was something. He was sitting slumped forward, his elbows on his knees, with a look of sheer misery on his face.

I knew how he felt.

'Your man,' said Jones. 'We picked him up this morning.'

I shook my head sadly. 'Supposing the people I have to deliver to know him.'

'He's just a mule,' said Smith. 'A one-off. He's not the milkman who comes every day with your pint of gold top.'

'But just supposing,' I said.

'Then it's too fucking bad,' said Smith, and left the room.

I looked at Jones. 'We've got all his stuff,' he said. 'You'd better come through and have a look at the gear.'

6

We went into another room that contained a table and three chairs. On the table was a medium-sized suitcase. It was closed. Next to it was a pile of neatly folded clothing, a toilet bag and a pile of papers, including an American Airlines ticket folder.

'That's what he was carrying,' said Jones.

'Where's the stuff?' I asked.

'Open the case.'

I did so. It was empty, but I could see that the thread that attached the thin leatherette lining at the bottom of the case to the sides of it had been neatly split open. I lifted up the lining. Under the leatherette was a balsa wood support that kept the bag in shape. The balsa was about half an inch thick, and made of wafer-thin plies. Underneath it was a cavity, extending almost to the perimeter of the piece of wood. Inside the cavity was a quantity of fine white powder, made solid from the pressure it had been subjected to. I broke some of the powder with my finger tip and rubbed the residue over my gums. Instant freeze-out.

I looked again at the amount. Paradise. Oblivion. And for just a second I wondered if I could get away with stealing it and vanishing. But one look at Jones's face told me he knew exactly what I was thinking and there was no chance.

This was the kind of geezer who'd pursue you to the ends of the earth over a parking ticket.

'How much?' I asked.

'Enough. We'll have the case repaired in an hour. No one will ever know we've been inside it.'

'We hope.'

'*You* hope.' His meaning was clear. 'Then you go to the hotel and use that ticket tomorrow morning to go to London. Get a taxi, go to the address we give you and deliver the goods.'

'Then it goes down. Armed coppers, the lot.'

Jones nodded.

'Lovely,' I said. 'Just what I need.'

'You should've been a better boy.'

And he smiled. It was not an attractive smile.

7

It all worked out like Jones had said. By late afternoon I had the mule's passport with my photograph in place of his and the suitcase perfectly repaired, full of his belongings. I left my bag of stuff at the house in the suburbs. I was never particularly fond of the shirt I'd brought with me, and the mule's clothes were roughly my size, so I decided to wear one of his the next day. But I transferred my toilet stuff to his bag. I drew the line at using someone else's toothbrush and razor. At five o'clock, a licensed Dublin taxi driven by one of the coppers who'd cheered on the racist beating dropped me outside the hotel the mule was booked into.

I checked in. There were no messages. I went up to the room I'd been given, hung up a shirt, cleaned my teeth and went down to the bar. I left the suitcase with the dope inside in full view on the stand beside the bed. I could hardly take it with me. And if it got nicked, well, tough shit.

I stayed at the hotel all evening, had dinner and drank rather too much gin before going to bed around eleven. I couldn't sleep, so I raided the mini-bar and drank all the spirits I could find, until finally I fell into a fitful sleep.

The temptation to do a number on the suitcase and get totally out of it was almost too strong to resist, but I managed it. The consequences would've been too heavy to contemplate.

I woke up early, regretting the booze, shaved, showered and went for breakfast which I couldn't eat. My plane was leaving at eleven. I packed the bag again, paid the bill from the copious amount of American dollars that the mule had been carrying in his wallet, getting ripped off on the exchange rate at the desk. I didn't care. It wasn't my money. I got the receptionist to call a cab, and was at the airport with time to spare.

I went through passport control and customs with no trouble and was back in London by noon.

Jones had assured me that I'd be cool going through customs at Heathrow, but my sphincter was working overtime as I went through the green channel.

I caught a black cab at the rank and gave him the address Jones had given me. It was in Handsworth, close to the airport, and thankfully well away from my usual haunts.

I got to the house, a smart, fully detached building on the edge of a private development at around one.

I let the cab go and stood for a moment looking at the high wall dotted with broken glass and razor wire that surrounded the house. A fortress, my friend the driver had said. Terrific. I tried hard not to look for surveillance as I approached the iron gate that was set into the wall and rang the bell for attention.

A deep voice barked out of the speaker mounted on the gatepost and I gave the mule's name. After ten seconds the front door opened and a figure appeared. He was big and black, dressed in a turquoise and white shell suit which bulged with muscle, with enough gold on his body to stock a jeweller's shop. He walked down the drive towards me keeping one hand behind his back, which I've found is always a bad sign. I put down the case and stood with my hands away from my body, palms outwards. A casual observer would have noticed nothing, but we both knew what I was doing.

He stopped on the other side of the gate and gave me a long look and it suddenly occurred to me that the people inside had seen a picture of the mule and it wasn't me. I almost winced at the thought of what might happen next.

But all he did was press a button on his side of the wall and the gate swung open easily. I went inside and the gate closed behind me with a clang and we walked up the drive to the front door. I checked out the hand behind his back. Inside it, almost dwarfed by his huge fist, was a Glock niner cocked and ready to fire.

He took me inside the house to meet the main men. As we went down the hall I noticed a Uzi carbine had been left casually on the table next to the lunchtime post. My stomach knotted painfully.

I was taken into a vast room decorated in dark wood and damask, with double doors in the far wall leading God knows where, and huge French windows at one end with a view of the grounds, all velvet lawns and a pond with a fountain that worked. There were two of them waiting, both Indian or Pakistani, all smart in mohair suits, silk shirts and discreet ties. I didn't see anyone else as we walked down the corridors, but I felt the presence of others inside the house.

The two didn't introduce themselves, just dismissed the muscle, then took the case I was carrying, emptied out its contents and slit around the lining with a scalpel. When they saw the gear they tested it with water and seemed satisfied. I listened for the sound of booted feet on the driveway.

That wasn't the first noise I heard. With a roar of rotors a police helicopter swept across the grounds of the house, hovered, and half a dozen blue overalled figures dropped to the grass on the other side of the French windows.

The two Indians gave me looks that could've blistered paint and headed for the doors in the far wall, leaving the case on the table. I went out the way I'd come in and ran straight into the black geezer, who was now carrying a pump-action Ithaca repeating shotgun, the Glock tucked into the waistband of his shell suit trousers.

He grabbed me by the collar of my jacket hard enough to make the tailor who'd sewn it blanch, and propelled me deeper into the house, the barrel of the shotgun close to my neck.

8

The black geezer propelled me into a smaller room at the side of the house, leaving the door slightly ajar, through which I could hear shouting and the popping of automatic fire. A regular world war.

He turned the shotgun on me, and for at least the second time that day my bottle started to go. 'It was you, you bastard, wasn't it?' he said.

'Not me, pal,' I said, almost pleading.

'Coincidence, was it?' he asked. 'You come in and five minutes later the shit hits the fan.'

'I'm just the delivery boy,' I said. 'Someone must've followed me. Someone grassed.'

'Bollocks,' he said and I saw his finger tighten on the trigger, and I half turned as if to make his potential target smaller. Not that that would've made a difference with the spread of the shot.

Then, just as I thought it was all up, the door burst open and two men appeared. One standing, the other kneeling beside him. They were both wearing baseball caps with check bands around the crown, Kevlar body armour, dark blue coveralls and Doc Marten boots. Around their waists were leather belts supporting holsters, handcuffs and CS gas containers. The one standing in the doorway was carrying a Heckler & Koch MP5 fully automatic machine-gun, the other a Browning 9-millimetre pistol. Consummate professionals both, but quite capable of blowing someone away for waving a water pistol around in his back garden on a hot afternoon in the belief that he was holding his family hostage.

The one with the Browning pointed it at me, the one with the H&K pointed it at the black geezer and barked, 'Armed police, drop your weapon.'

I hoped they knew who the fuck I was, I thought, as I backed up hard against the wall and raised my arms away from my body to show I was unarmed.

Meanwhile, the black geezer had swung round, the shotgun pointed at the floor, his finger still on the trigger.

'Drop it,' ordered the standing officer again, and the other swung the Browning round on the black guy, ignoring me.

The black guy looked over at me, then at the two coppers, and smiled. Then he slowly brought the Ithaca up and pointed it in their direction.

Shit, I thought, here we go. And go we did. Before the black dude could pull the trigger both officers fired. The H&K was on full auto and chopped the black geezer down, as the guy with the Browning held the trigger back and emptied most of the fifteen-shot clip into his torso.

At point-blank range the bullets smashed great chunks of flesh and cloth from the black man's body. Blood sprayed everywhere, up the walls, across the floor and on to the ceiling. As the black guy's huge body toppled like a felled tree he pulled the trigger of his gun by reflex and lumps of wood were torn from the door that the police officers had come through. The sound of the reports in the small room was deafening and the atmosphere was thick with smoke and the smell of gunpowder when the firing stopped.

Some of the blood splashed on to me, and one cube of pink flesh landed on the sleeve of the leather jacket I was wearing. I screamed and pushed it off, and it was warm and greasy like a piece of meat fresh out of the oven.

9

The whole station conspired to keep me out of prison. And don't think it never happens. It does.

The story as it was worked out was that the suspect escaped from my charge while in custody and fell to his death from the roof while trying to get away. Of course I had to pay some personal dues. I resigned from the force, which cost me my job and pension, and then the rest of my life went to hell and gone. But that's another story.

And naturally rumours of what had really happened spread through the Job like wildfire, which is where, much later, the driver and her pals came in. What with one thing and another they made me an offer I couldn't refuse unless I fancied spending my middle age on Rule 43 in some provincial prison with the cooks pissing in my tea and putting ground-up lightbulbs in my morning porridge.

So I took up their offer. But I figured I'd just about paid my debt to society. And what had just happened confirmed it. But of course things are never that simple.

10

After all the excitement died down at the house in Handsworth, the drugs squad arrived in plain clothes, bringing with them paramedics, SOCO, forensics, a film crew and Uncle Tom sodding Cobley and all, for all I knew. Smith and the driver were with them, but there was no sign of Jones. Probably having a quiet pint of Guinness in some pretty little Dublin pub and dreaming of his retirement.

I wasn't so lucky. But luckier than a lot of people in the house that day. The final score was three bad guys dead, four arrested, and a tiny amount of the dope that was flooding the country on the way to the evidence lock-up. One of the Asians who'd tested the gear was a goner, and I watched as the other was put into the back of a plain car to be transported to the local nick. I was slung into a police van myself with a white bloke I'd never seen before and didn't want to see again. During the short drive he spoke not a word but the look in his eyes as he clocked me said that he'd know me the next time.

The uniforms at the police station processed me like a regular bad boy and stuck me in a holding cell. I gave the mule's name as my own. I used the water in the toilet and the blanket to wash as much of the black geezer's blood off me as I could. It wasn't a great success. I cooled my heels for hours before Smith came for a visit. He had the bag I'd left behind in Dublin, a big bag of charlie, and two grand with him.

'You're bailed,' he said. 'Now get lost.'
'Just like that?'
'Just like that.'

'What about the others?'

He shrugged. 'What does it matter?'

I had to agree.

'This is the end,' I said.

'What?'

'No more.'

'No more what?'

I started to get annoyed. 'No more work for you or anyone like you.'

'Don't kid yourself. You like the hokey cokey we give you too much.'

I looked at the blood that had dried on my clothes and remembered the feel of the black man's flesh when I knocked it off my sleeve. 'I mean it,' I said. 'Tell everyone.'

Smith smiled. 'I'll pass the message on,' he said. 'Now fuck off.'

Luckily it was getting dark as I left the station, which hid the state of my clothes some. If it hadn't been, I doubt whether the cruising taxi I caught would have picked me up and taken me back to town. As it was I kept seeing the cabbie's eyes watching me in the mirror as we went, and I could hear his sigh of relief when he dropped me off a mile or so from my flat, and I paid him with two new twenties and told him to keep the change.

11

I walked the rest of the way home, undressed and stood under the shower until the water ran cold, and still I stood there until I began to shake like a shitting dog. I towelled myself dry, put on a T-shirt and boxers and went into the living room. I snorted a fat line of coke, rolled a spliff and smoked it, washed down by a cold bottle of lager, then I had more coke and more dope and more booze. I spent the night just sitting there listening to the silence interspersed with the sound of cars going by outside, and the occasional voice of a passing pedestrian. Later on, as it was getting light, and I was too drunk and stoned to think straight, I picked up the phone and dialled a number I kept in my head. The ringing tone went on and on, but I knew it would never be answered. The phone number was as dead as the person who'd subscribed to it. How long? Too long. But I remembered her as the machine buzzed in my ear and I would have given everything I owned plus more if she could just have answered.

I thought about the more recent past too. When I had another woman's hand to hold and her soft voice to listen to, and her beautiful face to gaze at whenever I wanted. Until she was taken away from me so cruelly too, and I thought about the place in the cold, hard earth where she now lay, and wondered whether her coffin had collapsed, and if the worms and bugs and microbes that pushed their way through the dirt were feasting on her corpse.

I fell asleep then and dreamed of the carnage I'd seen that afternoon, until a flash of lightning and a clap of thunder woke me and I listened as the rods of rain washed the streets clean, and I wished that I could wash my soul as clean so easily.

12

And then, almost immediately, I did meet another woman.

It was in a drinking club I use pretty regularly that's located underneath a hairdresser's in a tiny shopping mall in the middle of nowhere between the Elephant and Castle and Kennington Cross. It's a weird place to have a drinker, but when you check out the clientele you'd not be surprised they wanted somewhere discreet. I went down there a few days after the bust, sat on my usual stool by the bar, nodded at a couple of acquaintances and ordered a beer.

It was cool and dark inside, Sinatra on the CD player, and just me, two men I knew vaguely, and a couple I'd never seen before. The woman, a girl really, was sitting a couple of seats down from me. The bloke next to her was a big geezer in jeans and a leather jacket who looked like he'd over-indulged on the booze at lunchtime. At first they were talking quietly, but as the afternoon wore on their conversation got louder as they started to ruck. I didn't pay much attention. It pays not to in that particular place.

She was little, with a soft Welsh voice that was often drowned out by her boyfriend's strident Cockney. She had long, straight, honey-coloured hair, a pretty, snub-nosed face, clear, milk-white skin and striking green eyes. She was dressed all in black, vaguely hippyish clothes, with bare legs and the prettiest ankles I'd seen for years.

You can see I didn't pay much attention, can't you?

Anyway, after a while the row got more heated and eventually the geezer gives her a hell of a clout round the face and storms out, knocking my elbow as he goes, and sending half my drink over my hands and boots. I made a half-hearted attempt at catching hold of him, but I wasn't right in the mood for a punch-up.

Nobody paid any heed to the ruck, the slap and the bloke's runner. The barman hardly looked up from polishing some already sparkling glasses. The girl looked at me, holding her hand to her face where the marks of the bloke's fingers stood out redly against the porcelain colour of the rest of her skin, and tried to smile without much success as her eyes filled with tears. 'Sorry,' she said in that lovely accent. 'He's had a bad day.'

'Are you all right?' I asked, shaking sticky drops of beer off my hand.

'I'll survive. Can I get you a drink to make up for that?'

'Sure,' I said. 'But I need a wash first.'

I went into the tiny toilet at the side of the bar and washed my hands in cold water, using the sliver of soap kindly left by the management for the patrons' use. The hot air dryer didn't work and I dried myself with toilet paper, using some more to get the beer stains off my boots.

When I got back I expected she'd be gone or the boyfriend would be back, but she was still there alone, and a fresh drink was waiting for me. 'Sorry,' she said again, the palm print on her face beginning to recede.

'Not your fault,' I replied.

She told me her name and I told her mine, and we shook hands solemnly. Hers was tiny and finely boned and fitted into mine as if it had been born to.

'Does he do that often?' I asked.

Her face clouded. 'Just the once,' she replied. 'And that's once too often. I've finished with the bastard.'

'What was it about?'

She looked at me.

'Not my business,' I said.

'It's all right. Same old problem. He wants to own me.'

'And you don't want to be owned.'

'Not unless *I* want to be.'

'But not by him.'

She shook her head and her honey hair covered her face for a moment.

'He wants to get married,' she said.

'And you don't.'

'Not to him for sure. Are you married yourself?'

As she asked, I saw a woman's face in my mind's eye for a split second. 'No,' I said.

'Girlfriend?'

'No,' I said again. 'I'm totally free.'

'Anyway,' she said, 'I've got to go.'

I missed her already.

'Maybe we'll see each other again,' I said.

'I hope so.' She went into her handbag, came out with a piece of paper and a pencil and scribbled down her name and a number. 'Call me,' she said. 'I'm totally free too.'

And she slid off the stool and was gone.

13

I called her two days later. 'I didn't think you'd ring,' she said. 'I don't usually have to wait this long.'

'Is that right?' I said.

'Usually.'

'Do you make a habit of giving strange men in dodgy bars your telephone number, then?'

'No. But as I met the last one at a church picnic I figured I had nothing to lose.'

'That's a joke, right?'

'What?'

'The church picnic.'

'Yes. But it was close.'

'I wondered if you might like to get together. Have a drink or something,' I said.

'If you like.'

'I wouldn't've phoned if I didn't like.'

'Touchy.'

'Sorry. I have bad days too.'

'I understand.'

I loved her voice. 'Would you?' I asked.

'When?'

'Whenever. Soon.'

'Tonight?'

'Sounds good. Where do you live?'

'Putney.'

'Shall I pick you up?'

'You already did.'

'Tonight, I mean.'

'OK.' She gave me an address which I wrote down.

'Round eight.'

'I'll be here.'

We made our farewells and hung up.

I found her address at eight sharp and she was waiting. It was a little basement flat in a converted house in a quiet, tree-lined street. She asked me in while she got her jacket. It was anonymously furnished but cosy. She suggested a drink at the pub at the end of the street. I agreed. I'd laid off the coke. It seemed like a good idea.

It was a decent-looking pub, all polished glass and brass with flowers in hanging baskets outside, and I bought her a gin and tonic and a lager for myself and we went into the tiny garden and found a quiet table for two. 'It's good to see you,' I said.

'Mutual.'

'Seen your boyfriend again?' I asked.

'He called.'

'And?'

'I called him a bastard.'

'So no reconciliation.'

'I don't get hit in the face twice.'

'Very wise.'

'That's enough about him. He's history. What about you?'

'What about me?'

'What do you do?' she asked.

'This and that.'

'Most people in that club do.'

'You've been there before.'

'Places like it.'

'You don't look the type.'

'What type do I look?'

I shrugged. 'I don't know. It was just a figure of speech.'

She smiled. She had the most beautiful smile I'd seen

since ... Well, since someone else who had a beautiful smile.

'What do you do?' I asked.

'Temporary office work. I like the flexible hours. At the moment I'm working for an insurance company. When I can be bothered, that is. I'm sort of on holiday right now.'

'That's why you were in today.'

'That's right.'

We stayed there until closing and I walked her back to her flat. 'Coffee?' she asked.

'Sounds good,' I said. She let us in, switched on the lights, dropped her jacket on to a chair and went into the kitchen. I looked round the place. A few books, a few tapes and a portable machine. Not much for a life.

'You lived here long?' I asked when she came back with two mugs.

'No.'

'I thought not.'

'Why?'

'You don't have much. Sorry. I didn't mean to be personal.'

'Possessions hold you down. I like to move around.'

'Me too. But I always come back.'

'Why?'

'The ties that bind.'

'I thought you said you were totally free.'

'There's more than one kind of tie.'

By then we were sitting on the sofa. 'Do you smoke dope?' she asked.

'Sure.'

'Want some?'

'Why not?'

She pulled out a box of makings and expertly rolled a spliff. We shared it, then kissed. 'Do you want to stay?' she asked.

'I'd like that,' I said. 'But don't expect too much.'

'Why not?'

'I'm getting old.'

'You're not that old.'

'Old enough to be your father, I reckon. But that's not the problem.' I tapped my forehead. 'It's up here.'

'Is that your line?' she asked. 'I went out with a bloke once who tried to get me into bed by telling me he thought he was gay and would I cure him.'

'It's not a line,' I said. 'Anyway, you already asked me to stay.'

'I could've meant on the couch.'

'You could've, but you didn't, did you?' I said.

She smiled her lovely smile again and said, 'No.'

14

We went to bed together, and the same thing happened as happened the last half a dozen times I'd tried. Everything was fine up until the moment when I tried to enter her. Then something in my head went wrong and I couldn't. I kept remembering other times, other women, and with those remembrances came the most acute guilt feelings and I froze. It was hopeless. After a minute I rolled off her, lay on my back and felt for a cigarette on the bedside table. In the flare of the match flame her eyes were as green as a black cat's. 'Sorry,' I said. 'But I did warn you.'

'What's the matter?' she asked, and I listened for anger in her voice but there was none. Which was good, because often with the other women I'd tried to fuck there had been. 'Did I do something wrong?'

'It's not your fault. Entirely mine.'

'What is it?'

'Long story.'

'Tell me.'

'I don't know you well enough.'

'Well enough to come to my bed.'

'Maybe that's the trouble.' But of course, it wasn't.

'What do you mean?'

'Maybe I should've got to know you a bit better before I did.'

'There's not much to know. I'm an open book.'

'I very much doubt that. No one is.'

She was silent for a moment. 'Please tell me,' she said.

'Not tonight. I should go.'

'You've had too much to drink to drive.'

'You're very public spirited. But believe me, that's the least of my worries.'

'No stay. Go to sleep.' She took the cigarette out of my hand, took a puff then stubbed it out. The room was very dark and quiet. She took me in her arms and I put my face into the cloud of hair around her neck and smelt her perfume, and very faintly her sweat.

'Sleep, darling,' she said. 'It'll all be better in the morning.'

But of course it wasn't.

15

She made me toast and coffee for breakfast. 'I'm sorry about last night,' I said as I lit a cigarette after I'd finished the meal.

She gave me an impish smile. 'Don't worry about it. I'm a big girl now. I know what the booze can do to a man's libido.'

'It wasn't that,' I said. 'I wish it were that simple. It was something else. I don't suppose you'll want to see me again.' The question hung over the table like bad news.

'Nonsense. I like you. You're just a bit bruised and battered is all. You'll get over it with some tender loving care.'

Bruised and battered, I thought. More like one of the walking wounded. Or the walking dead. 'I really doubt that,' I said.

'Come to dinner tomorrow,' she said. 'I'll make you my speciality.'

'It won't help.'

'No pressure. You can sleep on the couch if you like.'

'I'd rather sleep with you.'

'Well then, we are getting somewhere, aren't we?'

The meal was great, steak in Worcestershire sauce with new potatoes and peas followed by a homemade fruit pie. There was loads of wine and dope, and I almost mellowed out, but not quite. We went to bed late and I kissed her and stroked her to an orgasm but that was all. Neither of us complained, and we both fell asleep soon after, and when I woke up early and she was snuggled up close in my arms and I watched her sleep for a little while, I realized I was getting fonder of her by the minute, which was dangerous. As dangerous for her as it was for me, if not more so. I disentangled myself, went and made some coffee and drank it looking out on to the tiny garden at the back of her flat, smoking a cigarette and thinking about her.

'I got cold,' she said from behind me. 'Why did you leave me?'

'I didn't want to wake you,' I said. 'You looked so pretty sleeping.'

'Was I snoring?' she asked, coming into my arms for a kiss. She tasted of sex and sleep, and I knew the danger was getting stronger with every moment.

'Just a bit,' I said.

'You sod.'

'Coffee?' I asked.

'Sure.'

I poured what was left from the pot and added milk.

'What are you doing over the weekend?' she asked.

'Nothing much. Why?'

'My mum and dad have a cottage just outside Cardiff. I go there sometimes to get away from it all. I'm going on Saturday. Will you come with me? There must be room for two in that great big beast you drive.'

'There's room for two,' I said.

'Say you'll come. It'll help you relax. No strings. We'll have a laugh.'

I didn't even have to think about it. 'OK,' I said. 'You're on.'

16

I picked her up in the truck on Saturday morning, slung
her bag and a box of supplies under the cover on the pick-
up next to my own bag, and motored slowly through the
suburbs to the M4. I didn't take any coke with me. Since
I'd met the girl and told the coppers I wasn't going to do
any more of their dirty work, I'd found I didn't need it as
much. Which was heartening.

'This is a nice car,' she said after a bit.

'Truck,' I corrected her. 'It's a fine distinction.'

'Truck. Sorry.'

'Don't mention it.'

Once on the motorway I put my foot right down and
stayed in the fast lane all the way to the Severn Bridge with
only one stop for food and fuel along the way.

'Do you ever consider the possibility of speeding tick-
ets?' she asked at one point.

'Never crossed my mind,' I replied.

Once over the bridge, where they charged me commercial rates for the Chevrolet and I couldn't be bothered to
argue the point, we headed for Cardiff and took the second
turn-off after, and hit countryside.

The cottage was down a narrow track just outside a tiny
village and only the sight of a pub at the turn-off made me
feel I hadn't made a big mistake heading out into the
boondocks for three days.

The place itself was small, neat and cosy, decorated in
white and full of chintzy, overstuffed furniture. There was
just one bedroom, which was almost filled with a giant
double bed.

'That's ours,' she said unnecessarily.

'Do you often bring blokes down here?' I asked.

She shook her head. 'No. Just lame ducks.'

She made me laugh and I suggested a drink.

After she'd filled the fridge with the supplies she'd brought, we walked back down the lane to the pub.

It was tiny and scruffy, but comfortable, and an unseasonal wood fire burned in the grate of the saloon bar. I went up and ordered the drinks. She sat down at a table. 'Know them well here, do you?' I asked as I sipped at my lager, which cost about half of what it did in London.

'Not really.'

'With your cottage up the road?'

'I don't come here that often. Besides, they've got a new landlord in.'

'So what's the plan?' I asked.

'No plan. That's the whole point. Just hang around and take it easy.'

'Sounds good.' And it did. All alone with a good-looking woman, miles away from trouble, with no one knowing, or I hoped caring, where the fuck I was. 'Sounds very good.'

We stayed in the pub all afternoon nattering about nothing and getting half pissed for our troubles, until at about six she said, 'Hungry?'

'Could be.'

'Then we'd better get back and eat before I fall over.'

'What's on the menu?'

She smiled lasciviously. 'Whatever you fancy.'

'To eat, I mean.'

'Chicken. And if we don't get back soon it won't be ready till breakfast time.'

So we went.

17

The chicken was good. She cooked it in a cream and tomato sauce with mashed potatoes and onions fried until they were crisp, and fresh peas. There was a Marks and Sparks lemon meringue pie for dessert. She'd also brought beer, wine and brandy, so by the end of the meal I was feeling pretty mellow.

'We'll need some more food and booze tomorrow,' she said. 'I hope we can find a supermarket open on a Sunday.'

'We can eat out,' I suggested. 'And I can always get something from the pub.'

After dinner we took the brandy into the living room and switched on the TV with the sound turned down low. We sat close together on the sofa and she rolled a joint. I watched as she concentrated on her task, her tongue sticking out between her lips, and her hair falling over her face so that she had to keep pushing it back out of the way.

'Thank God for hashish,' she said as she finished the spliff. 'If it didn't exist someone would have to invent it.'

We smoked the joint together, then she said, 'If I told you one of my deepest, darkest secrets, would you tell me one back?'

'If I show you mine, will you show me yours. Is that what you mean?'

'I think we've done that,' and she smiled a smile that almost broke my heart. And I thought I was past all that. 'So will you?' she said.

'I don't think you need to tell your secrets to me.'

'But you need to tell yours to someone. Or what's

hurting you inside. Sometimes you're the saddest man I've ever seen.'

'Am I?'

She nodded.

'Sorry.'

'Don't be.' There was a long pause. 'So tell me.'

'It's a long story.'

'We've got all the time in the world.'

'You really want to hear?'

''Course I do.'

So I told her. I told her about my first wife and the divorce, and my second wife and our child. And how my second wife died giving birth, and that the child lives with its grandparents and how I haven't seen it since the day it was born. I couldn't, I wanted to kill it so bad for killing my wife. I didn't tell her that now I don't blame it at all. Not after what happened since. I didn't tell her about my job and what happened there, or how I'd ended up being used by the police. And I didn't tell her about my third wife at all.

'Is that it?' she said when I'd finished. 'I thought it would be much worse than that. Not that losing your wife is a minor thing.'

'There's lots more,' I said.

'Tell me.'

I shook my head. 'Not tonight,' I said. 'Maybe another time.'

I looked at her face, the light from the silent TV screen flickering across her pale features in the otherwise dark room, and for a moment I thought she was going to press me, but instead she said, 'OK. Want to go to bed?'

Her skin went from dark to light, red to blue to green, and I felt disorientated, the dope and alcohol running through my veins like warm honey. 'It won't help,' I said.

'It might. And if it doesn't, don't worry about it. That's your trouble. You think too much.'

And she was right.

We went up to bed together and she was right about that too. It was better. I could tell. Not better enough, but an improvement. I almost relaxed. Almost but not quite.

The room was pitch black, and silent. As silent as the grave. I was used to streetlights, car engines and the scream of sirens splitting the London night. I lay awake thinking about the girl, knowing that with everything that had happened it couldn't work, but hoping that it might. Eventually I fell asleep cradling her in my arms, and I slept better than I had in years.

18

The next day we just messed around. It was warm but dull, close and muggy. We took the truck down to the seaside. It wasn't far. We parked up next to some beach near a place called Breaksea Point, and at lunchtime we found a pub that served food. On the main road was a shop that was open too, and that sold liquor. So that was all right. We got back to the cottage in the late afternoon and I opened a bottle of wine.

'Shall we eat out tonight?' I asked.

'I bought food.'

'We can eat it tomorrow. Or take it back with us.'

'I don't want to go back,' she said.

'Nor do I.'

'Shall we stay a few extra days?'

'What about your job?'

'Sod it. There's plenty more agencies.'

'Suits me.'

She jumped up and gave me a big hug. 'Shall we go into Cardiff?' she said. 'They've got some great curry houses there.'

'Suits me,' I repeated, hope blossoming in my chest again. 'Suits me fine.'

We drove into the city and found an Indian restaurant straight away. It was big and quiet and we got a table in the corner and the food was great. Or maybe it was the company, and I didn't drink too much for once.

We got back late and went straight to bed. She lit up a joint she'd made before we went out, and we smoked it in the dark, the coal the only illumination in the room, and our faces looking ghostly in the flaring light as we inhaled.

'Do you want to tell me some more?' she asked.

'I'll need a drink for that,' I said.

'I brought up the brandy and two glasses,' she said.

'You think of everything.'

'I try.'

She fumbled around on her side of the bed and the glasses and bottle clinked as she picked them up. She poured a slug of liquor into each glass and passed one to me.

I swallowed some and felt it burn a groove down to my belly. I lay back on the pillow, took a last hit on the spliff and said, 'OK, you asked for it.'

I told her about my work that night. Not that it was any big deal, but I'd ended up on the wrong side of the law, got arrested and got an ultimatum. Either help the police or go away for a long time.

'So you helped them?' she said.

'Yeah.'

'That wouldn't make you very popular.'

'You can say that again.'

'But you still go down that club.'

'I like to live dangerously. Does it worry you?'

'Why should it?'

'Your boyfriend. He wasn't the straightest character I've ever seen. You mix with bent people. I help put them away.'

'It doesn't worry me. Is that all?'

'No. The best is yet to come.' I still hadn't mentioned my third wife.

'Will you tell me?'

'Maybe. Maybe soon.'

'Then I'm glad we're staying.'

'So am I.'

19

The next morning I woke up early, disengaged myself from the girl, went to the bathroom, washed, shaved and went down to start breakfast. When everything was almost ready I heard the sound of movement from upstairs and she came into the kitchen in her dressing-gown, pushing her hair out of her eyes. 'You're always abandoning my bed,' she said. 'I'm beginning to think you don't like me.'

'Just the opposite. I thought I'd get the breakfast ready.'

'I was looking forward to a lie-in.'

'We're up now.'

'What are you frightened of?'

'Just about everything.'

She pulled a face, sat down at the table and I dished out the food, poured coffee and sat opposite. She tasted my cooking gingerly. 'This is good,' she said after a moment, her face splitting into a grin.

'Don't sound so surprised. I've had to fend for myself for a long time.'

'Sorry.'

'Don't be.'

When she'd finished her meal, she sat back and said, 'So if we're not going back to bed, what are we going to do today?'

'Don't know. I'd like to get a paper.'

'Ambitious, aren't you?'

'Don't take the mick.'

When we'd both finished our coffee, she went off to get dressed while I rinsed out the dishes, then we got into the truck and headed for the village, where I picked up some newspapers. That day was warmer and brighter than the previous one, so I turned the Chevrolet inland and we went off looking for adventure.

We didn't find much. Just a decent restaurant for lunch, and a hilltop where we sat and watched the clouds scud across the sky, and for thirty seconds a brief shower of rain on to the next hilltop like a grey veil, until it caught the sunshine from the other side of the sky and formed a perfect rainbow from one valley to the next.

'Pretty,' she said.

'Not as pretty as you,' I replied, and she smiled until dimples popped into her cheeks.

We headed back to the cottage after that, and she grilled some lamb chops which we had with new potatoes, and the last of the booze.

'This is great,' she said, when we were sitting together in the living room, and she rolled up a spliff. 'I could stay here for ever.'

'We've got to go back some time.'

'Not tomorrow. Maybe the next day,' she said.

'Whenever.'

The nights were beginning to draw in and it was soon twilight and we sat in the growing darkness holding hands and sharing the joints she kept rolling.

Eventually, as we sat in the silence that enveloped us, she leant over and said, 'I've done something rather silly.'

'What?'

'Touch my face.'

I felt her cheeks with my fingertips and they were wet with tears.

'What's the matter?' I asked. 'Why are you crying?'

'I told you, I've done something silly.'

'What. Tell me?' I couldn't think what she meant.

After a moment she said softly, 'I've fallen in love with you.'

I said nothing in reply. I didn't know what to say.

'Is that wrong?' she said.

'No,' I replied.

'Is it right, then?'

'I don't know. It's been a long time.'

'Then it's about time it happened again,' she whispered.

'Yes.'

'You don't have to do anything.'

'I don't know *what* to do,' I said.

'Don't do anything except hold me.'

So I did, and after a minute she leaned over and whispered in my ear, 'I love you,' and she kissed me, and disturbed the tears that trembled on her lashes, so that they ran down my face too.

20

And when someone says that to you, you tend to believe them. And then the floodgates open. And that's just what happened on that late summer's evening in that tiny cottage that could've been on another planet it was so remote from real life and everything that had happened to me for years.

'For what it's worth, I think I love you too,' I said.

I sensed her smile and said, 'Wait a minute. Not so fast. I told you there were other things about my life. I think you should know them before we go any further.'

'Tell me, then,' and she lit the roach that sat in the ashtray and I poured the last of the bottle of wine into my glass by the light of the flame she held.

'OK. But you might not like it,' I said.

'Try me.'

'I was married again.'

'*Three* times.'

'Yeah.'

'Where is she?'

I swallowed a mouthful of wine before I could answer. 'She's dead too,' I said.

'What happened?'

'She got sick. Very sick.'

'What was it?'

'Cancer.'

'I'm so sorry,' and she held me tight.

'It kept coming and going. She'd go into remission, then it would come back. Like some fucking recurring nightmare. It was killing her. Literally. But it took a long time.'

'How long?'

'Three years. Three sodding years. In the end it was just a drag for both of us.'

'So what happened?'

I didn't answer for a moment and I sensed she was going to say more, so I said, 'One night I killed her.'

'Oh, God.'

'There is no God.'

'What did you do?'

'I smothered her with a pillow. It didn't take too long. The doctor signed off the death certificate. No post-mortem. It could've happened any time, see. She might've died that night, or it might've dragged on for more years.'

I saw my wife as she was that night as I closed my eyes. She was asleep. The drugs she took four times a day had knocked her out as they always did. I saw the whiteness of the sheets and the pillows. And the whiteness of her skin and the contrasting blackness of her hair that had grown back after the last bout of chemotherapy. She'd always been so proud of her hair and had cried bitterly the day it all fell out because of the treatment she was receiving. I always thought that hurt more than the illness. Then I saw myself pick up the pillow on the other side of the double bed and whisper that I loved her for the last time as I placed it over her face and held it there for what seemed like hours, but had only been a few minutes.

'Then she was buried,' I went on. 'And that was that. Except of course it wasn't.'

The girl said nothing.

'You see,' I said. 'You don't kill the one thing you love in the whole world without paying a certain price.'

'What price?'

'Everything.'

21

She held me tighter then. 'It wasn't your fault,' she said.

'Oh, *please*.'

'It wasn't.'

'Come on now,' I said. 'I made one wife pregnant, and she died as a consequence of it. The other I killed in cold blood. She could've lived for years. They could've found a cure.'

'But they haven't.'

'Not so far as I know.'

'Well then.'

'Are you trying to say I did her a favour?'

'Maybe.'

'No. The only person I did a favour for was me. And I've been paying for it ever since. I can't get it off my mind. I think about it all the time. And her. And how I murdered her.'

'Come to bed with me. I'll make you forget.'

'Nothing could make me forget, I'm afraid. Because that wasn't the first time I'd murdered someone.'

'*What?*'

I told her about the suspect and what I'd done to him.

When I'd finished she said, 'You are an amazing man.'

'Really?'

'Really.'

'Aren't you frightened of me?'

'Why should I be?'

'Because death follows me around like a little black dog. I've killed people. And after the first couple they say it gets easier.'

'I don't think you're going to go all homicidal on me if that's what you mean,' she said.

It was a great relief. 'That's exactly what I mean.'

'But maybe I could make you feel better about yourself.'

'You could try.'

'Come on then, let's go.'

We went upstairs and it worked. Some of the guilt was gone and we made love. Properly. Like real people.

Afterwards we lay there in each other's arms and she said, 'See, it wasn't that difficult, was it?'

'Not with you.'

'So can we have that lie-in tomorrow?'

'Sure.'

I could feel her falling asleep beside me, but I was still wide awake, and after I'd spoken to her and she replied with nothing more than a half-grunt, half-snore, I found a cigarette and lay there smoking, then held her tightly as if she might somehow slip away through my fingers like so many others had done, until I finally fell asleep too.

22

We stayed in bed all the next day fucking, with only a break for food, and when I went down to the pub to stock up on booze and cigarettes.

It was great. I felt ten years younger, and, if not totally guilt-free, at least less guilty. I'd never told anyone what I'd done to my third wife and didn't think I ever would. I'd carried the pain around inside me like a festering boil, but at least by telling the girl about it some of the poison had been lanced.

In the late afternoon with the sunshine lying like gold on the wreck of the bed and our naked bodies she said, 'This has been one of the best days of my life.'

'Me too,' I replied, drinking brandy straight from the bottle and lighting a cigarette.

'We've been pigs.'

'Hogs.'

'But we'll have to go back.'

I felt the room darken even though the sunshine was as strong as ever. 'Don't remind me.' If I never saw London again it would be too soon.

'Tomorrow?' she asked.

'I suppose. If you want.'

'I don't want. But we both have lives.'

'I'm not so sure about me.'

'Will you have to do more . . . ? You know . . . ?'

'I told them that the last time was the last time.'

'Will they accept that?'

'They're going to have to. I've paid my dues. Twice over at least.'

'So what will you do?'

'Christ knows. I've got a little money. Just kick back, I reckon. Look for an opportunity somewhere. I dunno. What about you?'

'Same old thing. Look for some temp work.'

'Looks like we've both got few prospects.'

'We've got each other.'

I nodded and went back to the brandy bottle. I was beginning to feel depressed again. I had a premonition that bad things were going to happen when we left the fragile little world we'd put together in Wales.

'That doesn't seem to mean much,' she said.

'Just got the blues, baby,' I said. 'What looks so good down here might look different in the big city.'

She took the cigarette from between my fingers and stubbed it out. 'Come here,' she said. 'I'll get rid of them for you.'

23

We packed up and left early the next morning. We cleaned up the cottage before we went and as I shut the door behind us it was as if we had never been there. Perhaps we hadn't.

We were back in town by midday and I dropped her at her place before going home myself. Home. Now there's a word.

She rang me an hour later. 'Listen,' she said. 'I've just had a call from the agency. They were as good as gold about me vanishing. They've found me a few days' work.'

'Good.'

'Trouble is, it's up north, with a sales director of a Japanese car firm, and I've got to leave now. This minute. His secretary got sick on the plane, so he needs someone immediately. They're sending a car. I'll be moving round. I don't know if I'll be able to keep in touch.'

My heart sank. Literally. 'When will you be back?'

'Friday night or Saturday morning. He's getting the first flight out. Sorry, but I've got to do it. The money's good. Better than good, and full expenses.'

'Try and call.'

'I will.'

'Otherwise I'll hear from you Saturday at the latest.'

'Count on it. We'll have dinner. Don't worry. I'll be back. Love you. 'Bye.'

And she hung up on me so that my answer was to a dead phone.

24

But she wasn't. I waited to hear from her for the rest of the week to no avail. I couldn't get in touch myself, as I had no idea what agency she worked for, or which car firm she'd been employed by. On Saturday, when eleven o'clock rolled round with no word, I tried her number. I let the phone ring twenty times with no reply. I tried again at eleven thirty, noon, and every half hour after for the rest of the day. Still no reply.

I stayed up late, still calling, then slept for a while and began calling again at eight. At ten I got in the truck and drove to Putney. I went down the steps to the basement. The house was all quiet. I took off my leather jacket, wrapped it round my arm and knocked in one of the glass panels of the door with my elbow. The sound of the glass hitting the floor on the other side sounded to my ears like a symphony orchestra tuning up, but got no response from anyone else.

After a second I reached in and unlatched the door. The flat was silent, warm, smelt faintly of her perfume, but had a deserted air about it. I went down the hall and into the living room. The furniture was still there but everything else was gone. It was the same in the kitchen and bedroom, and the bathroom had been cleared of all her personal stuff.

She was gone. And for good, by the looks of it.

I couldn't understand. I sat on the sofa in the living room and lit a cigarette. There wasn't even an ashtray in the whole place, so I used the fireplace.

I couldn't work it out. What the fuck was going on?

This was no trip up north for a few days' work with an automobile salesman. This was goodbye in the worst way.

But why? What the fuck had made her quit her flat? I searched the place again. Properly this time. There was no sign that she'd ever lived there. Not a piece of paper or even an earring down the back of a chair.

Zip. Nada. Nothing.

I left the place as I found it and went home again. For the rest of the day I tried the number every so often without much hope and less luck. On Monday morning all I got was the unobtainable signal. I tried the operator, who told me the line had been cut off. She wouldn't even tell me the name of the subscriber.

That night I broke open the coke again.

25

I stayed awake all night thinking about the girl and what had happened. Christ, I'd trusted her and this was what I got. I should've known better than to get involved with anyone ever again.

The next morning I needed some supplies and went out to the truck and the driver was waiting, leaning against it.

'What do you want?' I said, disengaging the alarm and opening the door.

'You.'

'Dream on.'

'Smith wants to see you.'

'You know what want did,' I said.

'It's serious.'

'So is cancer.'

'Why did you say that?'

'Why not? It's true, isn't it?'

She nodded, then said, 'You'd better come.'

I looked at her and she looked at me and I said, 'OK. My social life has been rather quiet lately.'

'That's not what I heard.'

I frowned but said nothing, just followed her to her car.

She drove me to Denmark Hill police station, parked the car in the walled lot at the rear of the building, then punched a number into the back door security system and took me to an interview room, where she left me alone.

She returned five minutes later with Smith, who sat opposite me without a word. He was carrying a box file which he set on the table between us. The driver remained standing by the door, arms folded.

Smith regarded me closely. I looked back at him.

'We've got a job for you,' he said.

'Is that why you brought me here?' I replied, half rising from my seat. 'I told you before, I've finished with all that, and you.'

'Sit down,' he said harshly.

'Are you arresting me? Because otherwise I'm off.'

'I might be,' he said.

'It'll be interesting when we get to court,' I said. 'I know some things about you lot.'

'And we know some things about you,' he said, opening the file and taking out a cassette tape. He inserted it into the twin-decked machine beside him and pressed the PLAY button. There was a hiss and I heard myself say, '*She got sick. Very sick.*'

I literally felt my jaw drop.

The tape wound on. '*What was it?*' It was the girl.

'*Cancer.*'

'*I'm so sorry.*'

There was a brief pause with only the sound of bed-clothes rustling.

'*It kept coming and going. She'd go into remission, then it would come back. Like some fucking recurring night-mare. It was killing her. Literally. But it took a long time.*'

'*How long?*'

'*Three years. Three sodding years. In the end it was just a drag for both of us.*'

'*So what happened?*'

Another pause, then I heard my voice. '*One night I killed her.*' And some bastard had tape-looped it. '*One night I killed her,*' I repeated. '*One night I killed her.*' '*One night I killed her.*' On and on ad infinitum.

'Turn it off, for Christ's sake,' said the driver after a minute, and Smith did.

26

I looked at Smith and the driver, and I must've looked as stupid as shit to them, my mouth hanging open and all, and sweat popping out on my forehead.

It all came to me in a flash, like a revelation. Like Saint Paul on the road to sodding Damascus.

'She was a fucking copper,' I said.

Smith smiled, the driver looked serious. Like she didn't like what she was doing, but was doing it anyhow. Bastards.

'Fuck you,' I said.

'Language,' said Smith. He was well in control now. The king of his particular shit heap.

I shook my head sadly and looked at the table top. Fucked again. Literally. 'Mind if I smoke?' I said.

'Help yourself,' said Smith.

'I'd rather you didn't,' said the driver.

I lit up anyway. There was a shoddy little tin ashtray on the shelf next to the tape machine. I put the match in that, blew out a stream of smoke and looked at Smith. 'You fucker,' I said.

'All right. You've had your fun. Now listen to me. We've got the complete transcript of you all lovey dovey with her. We've got it in Putney and we've got it in Wales. Having a little problem getting it up, were you? Still, you came good in the end.'

I looked at the driver. She was still looking disgusted, although whether it was the story Smith was telling, Smith himself, me, or my cigarette that was bothering her, I didn't know.

He took one of the files from the box. 'Been checking on your third old lady's ... er ... demise,' he said. 'Sad story.'

I said nothing. There was nothing to say.

'You're very good at getting away with murder,' he said. 'But I reckon that tape could just about put you away where you belong.'

'Are you going to do me?' I interrupted.

He shook his head and pursed his lips. 'Not if you help us,' he said.

And I knew I was his for as long as he wanted me.

27

'So what's the deal?' I asked.

'All in good time,' said Smith.

'This is never going to end, is it?'

'You're too good at your job for it to end.'

'What now, then?'

'You go home. We'll be in touch.'

'When?'

'Like I said, all in good time.'

I shook my head and got up.

I went out of the room first, the driver followed, then Smith carrying the box file. The driver turned left, then left again out of my sight. Smith took my arm with his free hand and turned me right, then led the way along the corridor, up some steps, then along another corridor towards a set of double doors with brass handles. It was a long corridor and dimly lit, and a woman was walking towards us, then turned sharply through another door. I saw Smith hesitate as she vanished out of our sight, and I recognized her. I'd recognize her anywhere. That hair colour, although now it was pinned up, with just a few long, honey-coloured strands hanging down to her shoulders. And the shape of her ankle, even though now it was sheathed in dark nylon, and her figure dressed even as it was in a white shirt and uniform skirt. But I didn't let on, just followed Smith as he walked towards the double doors, past the ladies' room that she'd dived into to avoid us.

It was the girl.

As we came up to the doors, the corridor was deserted except for the pair of us, and hanging on the wall just this side of the door was a fire hose with a brass nozzle, wrapped round a metal wheel.

Smith hit one of the doors and I hit him in the back, hard, knocking him through the doors and on to the ground. I let the door swing back, grabbed the nozzle of the hose, unravelled a couple of yards of it and pushed it through the double handles, looping it round tight to keep the doors jammed shut.

Then I went back to the ladies' room, fast.

As I pushed through the door I heard the panic alarm start its raucous screech and someone hit the double doors behind me. I ignored both sounds.

The main part of the toilet was empty, but one of the three cubicle doors was shut and I could hear the sound of water on water. I kicked the cubicle door open hard so that it hit the wall and bounced back. She was sitting on the lavatory taking a piss, her skirt up around her waist and her tights and knickers around her knees so that I could just see the shadow of her pubic hair.

She looked up at me, fear on her face, and I said, 'Hello again. Fancy meeting you here.'

I grabbed her by the hair and pulled her up into a standing position, then dragged her out of the cubicle towards the big mirror over the wash basins. I stood beside her and forced her head round until she could see both our reflections. 'You cunt,' I said. 'I trusted you.'

She still didn't speak and I began to smash her face against the mirror until her nose and the glass broke and blood sprayed across the glass.

Outside I could still hear the panic alarm screaming and suddenly the door of the ladies' burst open and Smith was standing there, a whole bunch of uniformed officers behind him.

I let go of the girl's hair and she fell to her knees and I said to him, 'You gonna nick me now?'

28

But he didn't. Instead, half an hour later I was out on the street heading home. Simple as that. The uniformed coppers had picked up the girl, a WPC had adjusted her dress, cleaned up her face a bit and given me a look that could boil water and someone had called an ambulance. Smith had bundled me out of the ladies' toilet and slung me out of the back door without a word. When I asked him again if he was going to nick me, he just smiled grimly. I imagined that whatever I did right then, up to and including murder, would just see me out on the street heading home again. Murder, shit ... that was easy. Whatever Smith wanted me for had to be more important than even murder. And extremely dangerous.

I went home and thought about the girl and whether I'd done her any permanent damage, and if I really cared if I had or not. She'd taken me for a mug. Correction. I'd taken myself for a mug. I should've known better than to tell anyone the secret I'd carried around inside me for so long.

Jesus, but I'd been a fool. I'd believed what she'd said and trusted her. Just for a few fucks. However old I got I knew I'd never learn.

So I just sat there snorting cocaine and drinking hard liquor, and waited for Smith to make his move. And waited, and waited.

Part Two

Right now it doesn't look good.
Right now it'll never happen again.

29

It took two weeks, and then they came at night, just before the dawn when it was still dark and I was asleep.

I came awake with a start as light hit my eyes and I heard the sound of shells being pumped into the breeches of automatic pistols. I moved one hand to clear the sleep out of my eyes but it was slapped aside. There were at least four of them, all with high-powered torches which they shone in my face to blind me. I didn't know if they were good guys or bad guys. But right then it seemed there wasn't much difference.

Most of the time, in fact.

'Get dressed,' said a voice from behind one of the torch beams.

'Who are you?' I asked groggily sitting up in bed.

'Never you mind. Just get dressed.'

I got out of bed. I was wearing shorts and a T-shirt. I found my jeans, yesterday's shirt and socks and pulled them on. I slipped my feet into a pair of loafers, ran my fingers through my hair and I was ready. Maybe not immaculate, but as ready as I was going to be.

There were two cars parked outside with a driver at each wheel and the lights off. I heard the birds begin to sing as we left the house, and a faint grey, false dawn tinged the sky behind the houses to the east.

I was put in the back of the first car with one of my captors beside me and another in the front passenger seat half turned to watch me and to let me see the gun he still carried in one hand. The others got in the car behind. It seemed like a big fishing party for a small fish.

The bloke next to me was dark haired and wearing a suit and a stringy-looking tie. The one in front was redheaded and dressed casually. The driver wore a donkey jacket and a woollen cap.

'Who are you?' I asked again as the driver started the engine and switched on the headlamps.

The bloke next to me looked out of the window as the car took off, and the one in the passenger seat put his gun away but didn't say a word.

We drove through Streatham and on to the South Circular, over the river and into the wilds of West London and on to some kind of industrial estate and drew up in front of a beaten-up factory with a lopsided For Sale sign outside. The driver got out and opened a set of sliding doors and both cars went inside then stopped.

The place was dirty and bedraggled with bits of machinery strewn across the filthy floor as if the recession had hit hard and someone had just shut down the place and forgotten about it. Which is probably just what had happened.

The driver of the second car shut the doors behind us and we were left in darkness except for the car headlights. The guy next to me got out of the motor and dragged me out after him. He pushed me towards the only other light in the place, an office made of glass and plywood that had been built in one corner of the factory.

Now I'd find out if they were good guys or bad guys.

30

The office was cleaner than the factory outside, but not much. It contained a desk, two straight-backed chairs, a ratty old sofa and a fridge. Only the redhead and the geezer who'd sat next to me in the back of the car came inside with me. The rest vanished into the darkness of the factory on missions of their own.

The redhead opened the fridge and took out a bottle of water, opened it and took a mouthful. He offered it to the other one who shook his head. He didn't offer me anything.

The redhead sat on one of the straight chairs, the other on the sofa. He gestured for me to sit in the chair opposite him. I did. 'So,' I said. 'Give me a clue.'

He sniggered. 'Think he'll do?' he asked his friend.

The dark-haired one looked at me. 'Needs must.'

'Who the fuck are you?' I asked for the third time that night. 'This is kidnap and false arrest.'

'Crikey,' said the redhead. 'That sounds serious. Looks like a job for the police.'

'And that's me,' said the dark-haired bloke. 'So you're all right. Robbery Squad. My friend here is Special Branch. Smith sent us.'

Neither of them showed ID, but I believed them.

'Special Branch,' I said. 'Political.'

'Very good,' said the redhead. 'Top of the class, in fact.'

'You've got the wrong man here,' I said. 'I'm not interested in politics.'

'That won't be your problem,' said the dark-headed bloke.

Bought and paid for. I felt like a lot in a Dutch auction. 'So this is it?' I said.

'This is indeed it,' said the redhead. 'And you have just won our star prize.'

'Which is?'

Red took another hit at the water bottle and said, 'I'm going to tell you a little story now. Listen carefully. It concerns you and your future wellbeing.' He paused, put down the bottle of water, took a packet of cigarettes from his pocket, and without offering them lit one. He dropped the match on the floor. When he was happy with the way it was lit he continued. 'We have some very good friends in Saudi Arabia. By we, I mean our sovereign majesty's government. Twice a year they pop over to London mob-handed for a week or so to do some shopping. And I don't mean a trip down to Marks for a couple of pairs of new knickers. I mean serious shopping. Lots of money. Oil money. Very good for our economy. And I might add the future of our relationships in that part of the world. They take over a discreet hotel at the back of Harrods and shop till they drop. They bring wives and mothers, kids, the works. And a whole bunch of bodyguards. Heavy bastards who do what they're paid for.' He paused.

'Which is?' I asked.

'To protect their charges up to and including laying down their own lives to save the people they're protecting. And they carry the sort of firepower commensurate with the job.'

Commensurate, I thought. They must be recruiting SB from Oxbridge these days.

'They're due in a few weeks' time,' Red went on. 'And this time they're buying not only the contents of every shop in London, but a great lump of the city too. An expensive lump. Something in the region of a billion dollars' worth. And they're paying for it with negotiable bearer bonds. They don't look like much and they'll fit into a small document case. But believe me they're worth every penny of their face value to anyone who knows how to shift them quickly.'

'And?' I interrupted, tiring of the story. I could see the punch line coming a mile off.

'And someone intends to take them away from their rightful owners, plus loot every penny in cash and jewels that this particular family are so proud of. Someone intends to take over the hotel for a brief period one day and liberate everything.'

'Good plan. Where do I come in?'

'Can't you guess?'

I shook my head, although I could guess very well.

Red grinned. 'You're going to be part of the team that's going to knock over the hotel.'

'Just like that. How do I get the job? Go down the labour exchange?'

'Not quite. We've got to force an opening for you.'

'And how will you do that?' I went along with them. I had no choice.

'One of the gofers, a gunnie just along to put the frighteners on, is due for a tug. He was involved in some nasty business earlier this year at a club in Hackney. He was working the door. A thug in a tux. A bloke got a bit larey and ended up in ICU. Then in the morgue. We can pull this bloke in any time. Then there's going to be a vacancy.'

'So why would they take me on?'

'You've got a friend in the camp.'

My heart sank. 'Who?'

Red mentioned a name and my heart sank further. 'Christ,' I said. 'He's a nutter.'

'That's what's needed.'

'And I'm not exactly Mr Popular lately with the criminal fraternity. I've helped put some bad people away.'

'And your name's never come up. You're fireproof. Our bosses have made sure of that.'

'Oh yeah,' I said. 'Sure.'

'It's a fact. Anyhow that's the risk you've got to take.'

'Amongst others. Gunnies you're talking about. So there's the potential for a lot of bloodshed.'

''Fraid so. I told you, these bodyguards are carrying big time. But the plan is that not a shot will be fired.'

'Optimistic.'

'It's a big team.'

'And you've already got someone on the inside. That's obvious. Why do you need me?'

'Not on the inside exactly, but close. We need you there to relay fresh intelligence and to be there on the day.'

'And if I refuse?'

'I have a warrant for your arrest for the murder of your wife,' said the dark-haired geezer. 'Want me to process it?'

I shook my head after a moment.

'There you go,' said the Redhead. 'You're in.'

I went along again. Once more I had no choice.

'When?' I asked.

'We're going to nick our punter' – he looked at his watch – 'in about forty minutes' time. Word will be round by noon. By one they'll be looking for a body to fill the hole. You'll meet your old pal at around five, all being well.' He mentioned the man's name again and I shivered despite myself.

'Where?'

'A bar he hangs out in in Camden Town. He's there most nights. Even with what's going to happen today I'll be willing to bet he'll be in some time this evening.'

'I just walk up and ask for the job, I suppose, like it was advertised in the *Standard*.'

'No,' said the dark-headed bloke. 'But we'll make sure you get his attention.'

31

They told me what was going to happen, then the driver who'd brought us and one of the other blokes gave me a lift home. After I'd gone in they stayed in the car, parked up outside.

Before I went Red said, 'Don't think about doing a runner. Someone will be watching your place front and back all day. You're in this whether you like it or not. Otherwise you'll be inside. You'll get used to it.'

And I knew he was right.

As I went he said, 'Be ready late afternoon. We'll pick you up.'

When I got in I showered, shaved, had some food and went back to bed but couldn't sleep. I thought about the girl, but that was a waste of sodding time. Eventually I got up, watched TV, and waited for Red and his mate to come back.

They were on the doorstep just after four. I got in their car with them. On the journey Red reiterated what he'd told me earlier.

It took us half an hour to get to Camden and the car dropped me round the corner from a bar called Richardson's. I went in and sat at the corner of the counter facing inwards and ordered a beer. The bloke I was waiting for came in about half an hour later. He didn't see me. He was with a flashy young blonde with a skirt so short you could almost see her knickers, and carrying a shoulder bag. He was exactly the same as I remembered him. Short, squat, suited up in at least a grand's worth of Mile End Road tailoring with what hair he had left shaved to the bone, and looking as dangerous as a Black Mamba. He snapped his fingers at the barman and headed for a table at the back. He sat down on the inside and the blonde sat next to him. As they took their seats a young black kid with baby dreads went to the gents', which was further down towards the end of the place. A minute or so later he came out and as he walked past their table he grabbed the blonde's bag and took off like a sprinter. I saw my man struggling to get out from behind the table as the kid hurdled past the barman who was carrying a bottle of wine and two glasses on a tray. When he got close I stuck out my foot and caught the kid on the shin. He hit the wooden floor of the bar hard and skidded on his front for a yard or so, the bag sliding away from him. I willed him to get up and go before my man caught up with him, when another hand reached out from a shadowy alcove and grabbed the kid by his locks. Whoever it was holding them lifted up the kid's head and slammed it down hard. It reminded me of what I'd done to the girl and I winced as I heard bone splinter. Then my man was on him too, kicking him hard in his side until I heard ribs crack. He picked up the kid, punched him in the stomach and threw him out into the street. What happened to him then I don't know.

My man picked up the fallen bag, turned and said in his rusty voice to whoever was sitting in the alcove, 'Thanks, Des.'

'Pleasure,' said a voice.

Then he came up to me and said, 'Cheers.'

'Well I never,' I said, using his name. 'How's it going?'

He looked at me hard, then recognition filled his eyes. 'Christ,' he said. 'What the fuck are you doing here?'

'Slumming. You?'

'My local. Fuck me, I might've known. Come on, have a drink. Meet the wife. Eddie,' he said to the barman, 'bring another glass.'

32

Whatever she was she wasn't a wife. Not his or anybody's else's. Her ring finger was bare. She was also a lot older and harder-faced close up. And she was pretty shaken. 'Bastard black face,' she said. 'Cheek of 'im.'

'Not to worry, love,' said my man. 'A couple of old mates of mine dealt with it.' He introduced me, she simpered and put my name and face in her mental card file for future business.

'So what are you doing?' he asked me as the barman poured our wine.

I shrugged. 'Not a lot. You?'

'I got something going . . .' He paused for thought. 'You eaten?'

I shook my head.

'I owe you a dinner,' he said. 'The way you took that nigger out. That bag's Gucci. Cost me plenty.'

The woman looked at me again.

'Some other time,' I said. 'I can see you're busy.'

'No. I might have something for you.' He turned to the woman. 'Babe. Why don't you go home? I'll catch you later. Something's come up. Remember, I told you. I want to talk to my friend here.'

She took the hint. 'I think I might,' she said. 'That coon gimme a scare.'

He took a couple of tenners from his pocket. 'Get a cab,' he said. 'Save them lovely legs of yours.'

'Thanks, love,' she said. 'I'll see you later.' And with that and another smile in my direction she left.

'Come on,' he said. 'Let's get a real drink.'

We sat there for maybe an hour drinking Scotch and he

didn't say a word about what I was wanting to hear until he emptied his glass with a swallow and said. 'Chinese do you?'

'Suits me,' I said.

'There's a place just down the road. You got a car?'

'No. I was just wandering tonight. Thought I'd go down West. I didn't want to keep looking for parking spaces so I got a cab.'

He nodded sagely. 'Come on, then, we'll walk.'

We strolled in the direction of Euston until we came to a grubby-looking Chinese café. 'This is the place,' he said. 'Don't look like much, but the food is the best in London.'

And he wasn't far wrong, although I had little appetite. But he more than made up for me, going through the menu so that when the food was delivered it covered the cloth on the table for four we'd taken in one corner, two dishes deep.

'Dig in,' he said, piling up his plate.

I took a little of several dishes and watched as he stuffed food into his mouth.

When he'd washed some of it down with beer he said quietly, 'You still in the same line?'

I nodded.

'Got anything on?'

I shook my head.

'Jesus, this is lucky. Like I said, I've got a little something going and someone's dropped out. Interested?'

'Depends. What's the deal?'

'Just for now, something like a cool million for a morning's work.'

'You're joking.'

He gave me the kind of look that reminded me I was eating with a wild animal. 'I don't joke about money,' he said. 'Might be more.'

'I'm interested,' I said.

'Thought you would be. Come and see me tomorrow. I'll tell you some of the details.'

33

Before we split up he gave me his address on a card from the restaurant. 'Tomorrow morning at ten,' he said. 'Don't be late.'

I caught a cab home and after it had dropped me off and I was looking for my key, Red appeared out of the shadows. 'Got any beer in the fridge?' he said.

I led the way upstairs and found him what he wanted whilst I made some tea. I'd had enough to drink and if I was going for a meet with the bad guys the next morning I wanted my head to be straight.

'So?' asked Red.

'He bought it.'

'Told you.'

'It was too easy. He'll start to think about that.'

'You're old mates.'

'Nobody's old mates with him. If he thought his own mother was telling tales out of school he'd spike her feet to the floor. You can imagine what he'd do to me.'

'Want some advice?'

'What?'

'Don't get caught.'

'I'll try.'

I told Red what had happened at the bar and afterwards at the restaurant and he looked well pleased. When he'd finished his beer he got up to leave.

'What happened to the kid?' I asked.

'What kid?'

'The black kid who put on the show of stealing the bag. I assume he was one of yours.'

Red nodded. 'A couple of broken ribs, some bruising to the kidneys and a busted nose.'

'You train 'em hard.'

'That's my job,' he said. And he was gone.

34

His place turned out to be a small, neat, newly built, end of terrace, two up two down in a mews off Haverstock Hill.

I was dead on time and my man met me at the door wearing suit trousers and an open-necked white shirt.

He led me through to a room that was part living room and part office.

He sat me down in an armchair and took a leather executive's chair at a desk by a window that looked over the tiny back garden. 'Lucky coincidence you turning up yesterday,' he said. I felt a coldness in my guts. 'Dead lucky,' he emphasized.

Christ, he's sussed me, I thought. That's torn it. 'Right time, right place,' I said as nonchalantly as possible.

'How long has it been?' he asked.

'A year.'

'Longer. Two.'

I shrugged.

'Anyhow. Like I said, I've got this job on.'

I looked interested though my mouth was dry. Being anywhere near this bloke scared the shit out of me.

He told me about it. Pretty well what Red had told me earlier.

'How many going in?' I asked when he'd finished.

'Eleven. Plus a couple of reserves on the outside.'

'Big team.'

'Big prize. There's plenty to go round.'

'Top heavy,' I said.

'Not the way I operate.'

'But you've lost one already.'

'That's the breaks.'

'How?' As if I didn't know.

'He got nicked by the filth.'

'Serious?'

'Murder.'

'No chance he's blowing the whistle?'

'He knows better. I can reach him wherever he is.'

'But if he does a deal – murder's serious. He might put you in the frame for a reduction.'

'There ain't a deal could save his skin. Or *anyone* who grassed on me or mine.'

That's what I was afraid of.

'So are you in?' he asked.

'And I'm just there as muscle?'

'That's it. Muscle with a shotgun. An enforcer to make sure everyone stays calm.'

'And a million, you say.'

'That's right.'

'Then I'm in.'

He turned the chair he was sitting in on its swivel base and opened one of the drawers in the desk. He pulled out a snub-nosed .357 magnum revolver, cocked it and put the barrel in the soft spot under my jaw bone so that the sight dug painfully into my skin. By squinting down I could clearly see the noses of the bullets as they snuggled in their cylinders. 'And the same goes for you,' he said. 'If you're in you're in. And even if you're out you're in. You mention one word about the job or me or anything and I'll blow your fucking head off. Understand?'

I understood.

35

When he was sure he'd had my full attention, he let down the hammer of the gun, tossed it back in the drawer and pushed it shut. Right up until then I'd been convinced that he *did* know what I was up to and he was going to finish me off there and then, despite the damage it might do to his soft furnishings.

'Mind if I smoke?' I asked.

'Sure.'

I lit a cigarette and my hands were trembling.

'Nervous?' he asked.

'No. Just thinking about your health. The last person who did that ended up in an all-over body cast.'

'Stop it, you'll get me all excited,' he said drily. 'Now then, we meet tomorrow. You'd better come here so I can take you down and introduce you.'

'Sure.'

'And we don't use real names. You'll be Hurst.'

'Why?'

'You'll find out.'

'And what's your name?'

'Banks.'

I couldn't work it out.

'Nine o'clock,' he said. 'You'll be out all morning.'

And then, as polite as any middle-class homeowner, he showed me to the front door.

36

I made the slog up from South London again the next morning. He was waiting at the door dressed in a Burberry over a suit. I was wearing my usual jeans and leather jacket. I hadn't thought that sartorial splendour was part of the job description. When we left he fetched with him a big, flat, black canvas bag with a fold-over top and brass locks like the ones artists use to carry their work.

We took his car, a silver Jag, and he headed east until we got to Walthamstow, where he parked up a blind turning. 'We'll walk the rest,' he said.

We crossed a couple of terraced streets on to a main road and into the car park of a pub. We went round the back through an open door that was guarded by two heavy-looking geezers in T-shirts and tracksuit bottoms who nodded at him, and up two flights of steps, passing a notice that read: TOP BAR CLOSED FOR PRIVATE FUNCTION.

He pushed open a door and we were in a small bar. The air was smoky and a crowd of people, nine in all, six white geezers, two black blokes, and a blonde woman, were standing around nattering, or sitting on a collection of chairs that had been pushed into rough rows in the centre of the room. Although it was early all of them seemed to have a drink in their hands.

They looked round at our entrance, more closely at me, and then at one another as their conversations ceased.

'Morning,' said my man.

There was a desultory ripple of sound from one or two of them but not much else.

'I called this meeting today because we had a bit of

trouble the day before yesterday. Our friend Hurst was nicked for murder.'

That got a bit more than a ripple going.

My man held up his hand for silence, which he got immediately. He's that kind of man.

'But, as luck would have it, I ran into an old friend recently and I've signed him up. Meet the new Hurst.'

A big bloke leaning on the counter with a glass half full of what looked like neat Scotch and wearing a purple shell suit came up with the same scenario as I had. 'What happens if he puts us in the frame?'

'He's dead and he knows it,' said my man.

'I don't like it,' the same bloke said.

'Then fuck off,' said my man. 'And that goes for any of the rest of you that wants out. We've still got time to recruit a new team. But remember what we're here for, and remember that anyone who leaves this room will be on my shit list.'

That got the point home. I've never met anyone who wanted to be on this particular individual's shit list.

'Who is this geezer?' said a little man at the back who looked like a bookie's runner in some kind of forties-style suit, a trilby and a pony tail.

'A mate,' said my man. 'An old mate. He's kosher.'

Which was patently untrue.

'Now. Are you in or out? You – ' he said to the big bloke. 'Or any of you.' He swung his mean eyes round the room. 'These things happen. We've got to be flexible.'

No one moved.

'Right,' he said. 'Sit down, and let's get started.'

The group did as it was told, apart from me and him. 'Good,' he said. 'Now I'll introduce you.'

There were four men in the front row, including one of the black blokes. My man introduced them left to right. 'Wilson, Cohen, Moore and Stiles,' he said. Wilson was the big bloke in the shell suit. Cohen was the black bloke. One of my man's little jokes, I imagined.

The woman and the other black man were in the second row. 'Hunt and JC,' he said. JC was the other spade.

Then the three in the back row including the bookie. 'Peters, Ball, BC.' The bookie was Peters. 'Recognise us?'

'Sounds familiar,' I said. And it did.

'1966. England won the world cup. Ring any bells now?'

''Course. Our team.'

'Right.'

'Two Charltons.'

'BC and JC. Got it now?'

I nodded again. 'Right,' said my man. 'Get yourself a drink, sit down and I'll go through the plan. You've got some catching up to do.'

Chapter Thirty-seven

There was a blackboard and easel propped up in one corner, and while I went behind the bar, found some bottles of beer floating in iced water, helped myself to one and opened it before joining the blonde and the spade in the middle row, Banks pulled it in front of us, opened the bag he had brought with him, took out a big artist's pad which he hooked over the blackboard and flipped open to the first page.

On it was a hand-drawn map marked 'GROUND FLOOR AND STREET'.

'Now,' he said, fixing his gaze on me. 'There's one other person you've got to meet. The man who found out the details of this job and put it together, and has bankrolled us up to now. Mr Alf Ramsey.'

I didn't think all this had been entirely Banks's idea. Especially the football part. His idea of sport was a dogfight on a wharf in Bermondsey.

As he finished speaking and dead on cue, the door behind him opened and a tanned, fiftysomething bloke with grey hair just beginning to thin out, dressed in an expensive-looking tweed coat, came into the room. Banks sat down in the middle row on the other side of the spade and the blonde.

The bloke walked up to the blackboard and picked up a pointer that was balanced in the chalk tray.

'Thank you, Mr Banks. Good morning, everyone.' Then to me. 'Mr Hurst. Welcome. You come highly recommended. I trust Mr Banks's judgement implicitly.'

Not a good idea.

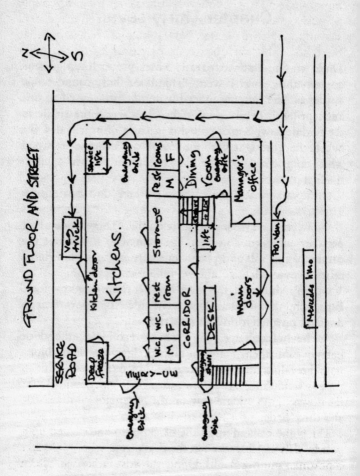

'I am going through the plan for you in particular,' he went on, 'and for everyone else's benefit in general. It bears repeating. And it will be several times over the next couple of weeks, even though it's a very simple one. But I always say, the simpler the better. Now, you must remember that there are only two open exits or entrances to the hotel while the Saudis stay there. The front doors leading to the foyer and reception and the back door that opens into the kitchens. The four doors at the sides of the building will be kept permanently shut, locked and shuttered for security purposes. This is of course strictly against the rules, but when the guests are as free-spending as our friends, the management will accommodate almost any whim.'

He put the pointer on the oblong marked MERCEDES LIMO. 'At eight forty-five on the morning in question, Mr Hurst, BC, Miss Hunt and Mr Banks will be waiting in this car opposite the front of the hotel. The three men will be carrying semi-automatic pump-action shotguns plus any personal weapons they choose to bring to the party. Miss Hunt will have a nine-millimetre automatic in her handbag. Mr Peters, all dolled up in a chauffeur's cap, will be behind the wheel. That way if a traffic warden or copper comes along while you're inside he can chat them up. They're used to that in that area. He will also be carrying a pistol in case anything does go wrong.'

'Where does the limo come from?' I asked.

'I nick it,' said Peters from behind me. 'The night before. That's my game. I know a hire place that's wide open. I did some driving for them a while back. That's what I do. Nicking and driving cars.'

'Mr Wilson,' Ramsey went on, 'wearing what looks like a postman's uniform and driving the Post Office van which Mr Peters has also stolen, from a depot in Hounslow, I believe . . .'

I heard a mumble of assent from behind me again.

'... goes in with some envelopes and a parcel all
wrapped up in brown paper. Normal morning delivery.
No problem. Inside the parcel is another shotgun. When
he gets to the front desk he holds up everyone in the foyer.
Now of course we can't be sure who will be there, but we
do know that one armed guard has always been stationed
there on previous visits, plus the receptionist behind the
desk. There may be more, there certainly won't be less. We
will all carry radios. Each one of you has been designated
a number. Mr Hurst, you are number eight. Strict radio
silence is to be observed apart from orders and urgent
messages. When Mr Wilson has secured the foyer he gives
the word and the four passengers in the limo go in to join
him, deal quietly with the guard and the receptionist and
anyone else there. At roughly the same time, there's a
regular daily veg delivery round the back, in the service
road, by a truck that's distinctively marked with the name
of the supplier.' He touched the pointer to the oblong
marked VEGETABLE TRUCK. 'That day the delivery, or
should I say the collection, is going to be done by us. Mr
Cohen driving, armed with an automatic, JC, Mr Ball, Mr
Stiles and Mr Moore hidden in the back, once again
carrying shotguns. I've discovered they are the most effec-
tive weapon for gaining people's attention in a hurry.
We've watched the van's route for weeks. The usual driver,
who by the way is black—'

'And they all look the same to you white guys,' said
Cohen from his seat beside me, to general amusement.

Ramsey, smiling, let the laughter die down, then said,
'The usual driver is always at the previous call between
eight thirty and eight forty. Delivery takes five minutes,
then he's off. That's when the vegetable team pull him. It
won't be difficult. The delivery is done in the courtyard of
another hotel. There are no windows overlooking, and it's
a busy time in the kitchen doing breakfast, so there're no

cooks or waiters skiving off for a smoke. When the driver comes out he's alone. In the worst-case scenario, the drive between that hotel and the target hotel takes less than ten minutes, so you should all be at the target by nine on the dot, maybe a minute or two earlier. It's not a problem. The limo will be waiting. The Post Office van and the vegetable truck team, in another stolen car that Mr Peters has picked up some time earlier, changed its identification and hidden it at our base, go to the previous hotel in tandem. Then when the vegetable truck's ours, Mr Cohen follows Mr Wilson to the target. That way you're all there together. Mr Cohen drives straight into the service road, he gets out, opens the back and fiddles around until he hears that the foyer is ours. Then he goes to the kitchen door, which is also covered by an armed guard, and as soon as he is inside secures that exit with the gun he has hidden in the broccoli or whatever. He then gives the word to the men in the truck and they go inside also, locking up the staff and the guard in the big freezer' – another tap with the pointer – 'take the service lift to the top floor, then come down, taking prisoners and emptying the place of valuables and cash as they go. Simple as that. The hotel does not have rooms, only suites. The Saudis always breakfast in their own suites so that the ground floor dining room is empty. That saves us the job of securing it, although, BC, you will check that no stragglers are eating their cornflakes or enjoying a fried egg sunny side up, as soon as the team at the front have taken care of the guard and the receptionist. At the same time, Miss Hunt takes over the desk. She is aware of the telephone system they use there and has made herself familiar with it. She will run the hotel until we are finished. All extensions will be engaged if anyone calls in, and no one will be able to phone out. Miss Hunt has had some experience of that particular task, which is why she is with us.'

'Mobile phones?' I found myself asking. I was getting well into the plan.

'There are some very new and very sophisticated devices on the market,' Ramsey replied. 'Mostly built by students in America and Japan. They have terribly devious minds. One such will block the satellite signals from mobile phones over a small area. And at great expense I have obtained one. It will be in the back of the Post Office van and will be activated by Mr Wilson when he collects the parcel he is to deliver to the hotel.'

'Sounds good,' I said.

Ramsey gave me a thin-lipped smile. 'If I may continue,' he said. 'After the foyer is captured, that team breaches the manager's office, where there will be yet another armed guard, and convinces the manager that it is in his best interest to open the safe there, where the Saudis will have left the bearer bonds for safe keeping.'

'How do you know they will?' I asked.

'Because that is their custom. There are ten bodyguards at least in the building, one at all times by the safe, and they think that is the most secure way.'

'What happens if someone comes into the hotel while this is all going on? Hunt can't man the desk and take prisoners at the same time,' I said. This was the first time I'd heard the plan and I was looking for loopholes.

Everyone else had obviously heard the objections before.

'That's your job,' Ramsey said to me. 'You're in the foyer with Hunt. Anyone comes in, you take care of them. With minimum fuss. There's plenty of places to put them to keep them quiet along with the receptionist and the guard. But there shouldn't be many callers, if any. The place has been entirely taken over by the Saudis. They don't encourage visitors. It should be quiet. And the whole deal shouldn't take more than fifteen, twenty minutes from start to finish.'

'And afterwards?' I asked.

'You take off in the three vehicles you came in. Peters will have stashed another three cars close by – '

'I'm going to be a busy boy,' croaked Peters from the back.

' – you change motors and meet up at our base and we split any cash, and there should be plenty, and I take the jewellery and the paper back to where it can be changed into cash,' Ramsey concluded.

And we just trust you, I thought.

'You mentioned a million each,' I said. 'There's no way there'll be that sort of cash on the premises. How long do we have to wait for payday?'

'For the tom, a couple of days,' Banks said.

'*And* I have to go to South Africa', Ramsey continued, 'to change the bearer bonds into a banker's draft, which I deposit in a Swiss bank on the way back, and after that one million sterling gets transferred to accounts that have been opened for all of you under a variety of other names. That money can be moved into any British bank account on the mention of a number and a simple password. You, however, are responsible for your own tax.' He smiled again.

'Complicated,' I said.

'Not particularly. Not under the circumstances.' said Banks. 'Anyway, we've been through all this before. Think about it, and you'll know it's the best way.'

'I don't like the stuff leaving the country,' I said. 'It puts temptation too much in Mr Ramsey's way. No offence meant,' I said to Ramsey.

'No offence taken,' said Ramsey 'But South Africa is the only place that can get one hundred cents on the dollar on the hurry-up.'

I looked at the other members of the group. They were

pokerfaced. 'OK,' I said. 'If everyone else agrees, I suppose it's all right by me.'

'Good, Mr Hurst,' said Ramsey sarcastically. 'I'm so pleased that you're happy with the plan. Now, the finer points shouldn't concern you as long as you get paid, which you will. I'll just show you the make-up of the rest of the floors.'

He flipped over to the next page of the pad which was marked 1ST FLOOR.

'The whole place is a sodding maze inside,' he said. 'We must all be careful not to get in one another's way. The rest of the floors are residential and identical . . .' Another flip, another plan labelled UPPER FLOORS.

'How many?' I asked.

'Three,' came the reply.

There were four suites per floor, a dozen in all, and a load of corridors, but as I had no business there I hardly took it in.

'And finally,' he concluded, reaching into the bag that Banks had brought with us. 'This gentleman is our main target. The hotel manager.' He brought out an eight-by-ten glossy photograph and passed it to me. It showed a pleasant-looking dark-haired bloke of about forty. 'Remember him,' Ramsey said to me. 'He holds the combination of the safe. We don't want him hurt or vanishing. OK?'

I nodded.

'Right,' said Ramsey. 'Let's break this up, have a bevvy and split. I've got things to do.'

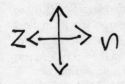

1ST FLOOR

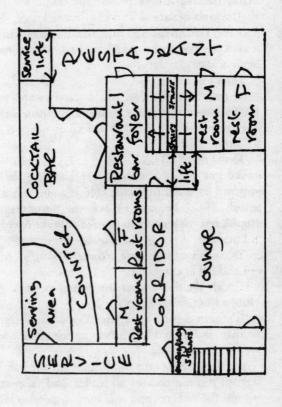

RESTAURANT

Service lift

COCKTAIL BAR

Serving Area

COUNTER

SERVICE

M Rest rooms

F Rest rooms

CORRIDOR

Restaurant bar foyer

Stairs

lift

Rest room M

Rest room F

Emergency stairs

lounge

38

Everyone seemed to relax and the blonde sitting next to me turned and stuck out her hand. 'I'm Hunt,' she said. 'That bastard Banks picked the name for me. And no rhyming-slang jokes.'

'I don't make jokes,' I said, shaking her hand briefly.

'Looks like we're going to be working together,' she said. 'Closely.'

'Looks like it.'

'A nice thought.' She was attractive, and showing out, but I was in no mood for women right then. Or ever again.

I smiled politely and that was all.

'Drink?' she asked.

'Don't mind if I do.'

We got up and went to the bar. On the way I was waylaid by a hard-looking face in a single-breasted mackintosh. 'BC,' he said by way of introduction. 'Fuckin' stupid, but what can you do. We're in the Merc together.'

I nodded.

'Done this sort of thing before?'

I nodded again.

'Good. We don't want any virgins around.' And he gave Hunt a long, sardonic look.

'It's been a long time since I've been a virgin,' said the woman and patted him gently on the cheek. 'So don't you worry about a thing.'

She swished by him and headed for the bar. Peters, who seemed to be a jack of all trades, had taken up residence behind the counter and was busy dispensing drinks to one and all.

As we were waiting, Ramsey grabbed me by the arm. 'You've got a lot of questions,' he said.

'I'm not noted for taking things at face value,' I replied. 'This could get heavy, and I want to be sure my back's covered.'

'Fair enough. I can understand that. Banks was adamant you were the man for the job, and I'm happy to trust his judgement.'

I wasn't sure he was telling the truth. 'It's always nice to get a good reference,' I said.

Hunt turned as I spoke and said, 'What's yours?'

'Scotch,' I replied. 'Large.'

She made the order and Ramsey said, 'Listen, I've got to go. Anything you need, see Banks,' and he slipped away towards the door.

'Don't I know you?' said a voice from behind me as Ramsey left the room.

I hope not, I thought as I turned towards whoever had spoken. It was one of the men who had been sitting in the front row, a slim bloke of about my age with a rapidly retreating hairline. 'Call me Stiles,' he said. 'Now, where was it we met?'

'I think you're mistaken,' I said, although there was something vaguely familiar about him that I couldn't place.

'Never forget a face.'

'I've got a pretty forgettable one.'

'I wouldn't say that,' said Hunt as she turned and gave me my drink. 'It looks all right to me.'

'Thanks,' I said and raised my glass in a salute.

'Three years ago,' said Stiles. 'A bank job in Southampton.'

I relaxed slightly. That definitely wasn't me. 'Not me,' I said. 'I've only been there once to catch a ferry to France.'

'Shit,' he said. 'If you say so. But I'm damn sure—'

'And you know we're not supposed to pry,' said Hunt. 'So why don't you just leave him alone—'

She was turning out to be my saviour. All I needed was some nosy bastard to start digging.

'—or I'll tell Banks, and you know what a stickler he is for keeping to the rules.'

Stiles shrugged. 'Sorry,' he said to me. 'But I'm sure we've met. It'll come back to me.' And he wandered off.

'We're not supposed to fraternize,' said Hunt. 'But I'll make an exception for you.' She was drinking something as pale and interesting as herself.

'I don't think so,' I said. 'I've just come out of a bad relationship.'

'What other kind is there?' she asked. 'Never mind. Think about it.'

'I will,' I said. 'Now I've got to talk to Banks. Thanks for getting me a drink.'

'That's my job. Total submission.' And she winked at me.

I went over to my man and said, 'Two questions?'

'What? I thought you'd had enough during the meeting.'

'Just checking. First. Who the hell's this Ramsey character? And secondly, where's this base he kept talking about?'

'He's someone I met,' replied Banks. 'You don't need to know. Apart from that he knows what goes on at that hotel, and he's got enough money to bankroll us. The base is in Wandsworth. I'm going to take you there now. So drink up and we'll get going.'

'OK,' I said. 'But I'm still not mad keen on him taking the bonds out of the country.' I thought I might as well keep my bit of the charade going. After all, I was the only one kidding. As far as I knew.

'Trust me,' said Banks with a mean smile that gave me cold shivers. 'It'll be fine.'

39

Their base was an old garage, another piece of flotsam washed up by the recession, just on the north side of Wandsworth Bridge before you got to the posh part of Hurlingham.

It was behind a cheesy-looking furniture warehouse with special offer flyers peeling off the windows, and a general air of doom and gloom all around.

'Salubrious,' I said.

'It does for us. They think we're refurbishing the place.'

'I bet that's cheered them up.'

We parked the Jag down the side of the garage, and he let us in through a door that was chained and padlocked from the outside.

Inside, it looked like some attempt had been made to clean the place up and he took me through into the back which was stacked with new-looking pine boxes, and cardboard cartons.

'The ordnance,' he said.

'I hope you never get a break-in.'

'It's got to be somewhere, and there's guards here at night.'

'I hope they don't collect car numbers.'

'It wouldn't get them far if they did. That Jag out there is perfectly legit. Registration and engine numbers match. The only thing is it's registered to a company in the Cayman islands. See how long it would take Old Bill to track that one down. I'll be shot of it after the job.'

'Lost at sea, huh?'

'Well, Docklands,' he said. 'Want to see what you'll be carrying?'

He opened one of the pine boxes to reveal a neat stack of Winchester Model 1200 Police issue pump-action shotguns with pistol grips and no stocks, wrapped in thick plastic.

'Buying in bulk?' I asked as I took one out, slid it from its packaging, hefted it for weight and worked the action. It was as smooth as the satin chrome the gun was finished in.

'Stolen in bulk,' he said sardonically.

'That's my boy.'

'You're familiar with the gun.'

'I was trained on them. Or something similar. It wasn't quite so flashy.'

'That was all we could get.' He opened another box to show me a collection of 9mm Browning 1935 model, Hi-Power semi-automatic pistols. 'Spare magazines for these, and ammunition for both in the smaller cartons,' he said. 'We're using high-explosive flechette cartridges for the shotguns. That'll make a mess of anyone who gets in our way.'

The man was obviously mad. 'Good deal,' I said. What else could I do, although my insides curdled at the thought. That sort of ammunition could cut a man or woman in half.

'The best. We're all going to get rich out of this.'

40

When we'd packed everything away again, he said. 'I've got to be off. Want a lift anywhere?'

'No,' I replied. 'I'll get a cab.'

He locked up behind us, rescued his car and drove off, and I walked back towards Wandsworth Bridge. After I'd gone less than a hundred yards I heard a car horn blow behind me. I ignored it until it sounded again and I turned. The car was a turquoise blue metallic Renault Clio with low-profile tyres. The electric window went down and Hunt was looking up at me. 'Want a ride?' she said.

'What the hell are you doing here?'

'I followed you. I guessed where you were headed and I waited.'

'Why?'

'Can't we have this conversation in the car?' she said.

I sighed, walked round to the passenger door and got in. The car smelled of her perfume, something light and flowery. 'Lunch?' she asked.

'Banks wouldn't be pleased.'

'What he doesn't know can't hurt him. Come on, it's only lunch.'

'Is it?'

She shrugged, put the car in gear, and took off with a scream from the tyres. 'We'll see,' she said, as she bounced it round into the Wandsworth Bridge Road, heading away from the river.

We ate in an overpriced bistro in Fulham full of arse-holes with portable phones and hairpieces all hustling for the same deal, but we got a table well out of the way so we could ignore them.

'What's your real name?' she asked before we got round to ordering.

'Just call me Hurst. I think that's safest, don't you?'

'If you like,' she said petulantly.

The waiter arrived and we both went for the dish of the day and she ordered a bottle of house red.

'Why did you follow me?' I asked.

'You looked interesting,' she said. 'And the rest are so predictable. London hard men – losers one and all.'

'Then why did you sign on?'

'I need the money. I do this one then split. I've got my eye on a little property in southern Spain. Raise horses and dogs and drink myself stupid.'

'It's an ambition.'

'You could come with me if you like. It's going to be pretty hot round here after the job's finished.'

'This is all so sudden.'

'You look like my type.'

'Which is?'

'An angst-ridden hooligan hiding a sensitive soul under a shell of bad behaviour.'

I had to laugh. She'd got it on the button.

'See,' she said, 'I made you smile.'

'Hunt,' I said as the waiter poured our wine, 'you don't know the half of it.'

41

As it goes, the meal was all right. And by the end, under the influence of a bottle of wine and a couple of large brandies, I was quite getting to like Hunt. And to fancy her.

Like, yes, fancy, yes. Trust, no. No chance.

It even occurred to me that she might be the other one on the inside. But I doubted it. Red had said that whoever it was wasn't that close to the real action, and Hunt was. Besides, if she *was*, that would mean two of the gang would be copper's narks. At least two. And that would never do.

She even paid the bill. I didn't bother to argue. The lunch had been her idea. 'You can pay next time,' she said.

'Who says there's going to be a next time?'

She smiled. 'There will be. So is it your place or mine?'

'Not mine,' I said.

'Why? Have you got a wife stashed away there?'

I looked at her hard over the small vase of freesias in the centre of the table. 'I don't talk about wives,' I said.

'Sorry. Did I step on a corn?'

'Forget it, OK?'

'OK. I only asked.'

'Don't ask.'

'So it's my place, then?'

I shook my head. 'No,' I said. 'I don't think so.'

'Why not?'

'Fraternization,' I said. 'It's out of bounds. That's the rules.'

'But we're supposed to be desperadoes. We don't obey rules.'

'Shit,' I said. 'You're right.' Then I laughed out loud. It seemed like ages since I'd done that. 'OK, Hunt. Your place it is.'

Besides, it might help me if I did find out her real name, and she didn't know mine.

42

She had a small flat in a purpose-built pre-war block in Farringdon. It was OK. When we got in she asked me if I wanted a drink, and I said that a beer would be fine.

While she was in the kitchen getting it I opened the top of an old-fashioned writing desk and picked up a handful of envelopes that were inside.

I read her name. It wasn't Hunt. Not that it was ever going to be.

I was still looking at them when she came back with two drinks.

'I wanted to tell you my real name,' she said. 'You didn't have to do that.'

'I wanted to make sure you told me the truth,' I said. 'And this way I don't have to tell you mine.'

'I don't know why I'm bothering with you.'

'My angst,' I said. 'And no one asked you to.'

I put the letters back, closed the top of the desk and took the beer. 'So tell,' I said. 'How did you get involved in all this?'

She told me.

She'd been working in shops, then moved into hotel management, mostly abroad. The Caribbean, Jamaica and the southern parts of the USA. She'd done well, apparently, but during the recession had lost her job and taken up hustling tricks. Eventually she'd moved back to the UK, met Banks in a casino in the West End and screwed him for eating money. 'He was vile,' she said. 'A pig.' But he'd been interested in her stint in the hotel business and asked her if she could take care of the telephones at the target for as long as it took to rob the place.

'I told him I could,' she said.

'So you've never done a robbery before?'

'Spare me,' she said. 'I worked for a pimp in Miami for six months. You wouldn't believe what I did.'

She asked me for my history, but I blanked her.

Finally, when we'd finished our drinks, she said, 'Do you want a fuck or what?'

'Or what,' I said.

'I thought . . .'

'Some other time,' I said. 'I've got things to do.'

'You're a bastard.'

'It's society's fault,' I replied. 'Society and circumstances. I'll keep in touch. See you.'

And I left.

43

I took a taxi back to South London. I kept looking over
my shoulder at the road behind but there was no sign of a
turquoise-blue Renault Clio. I didn't really expect there to
be. Red was waiting for me when I got home. 'I don't
remember giving you a key,' I said.

'I didn't have to ask for one. That junk you've got on
your door wouldn't keep a child of three out.'

'And you even locked it from the inside. Just so's I'd
have no idea you were here.'

'I like to keep you on your toes.'

'I'm not that crazy about surprises.'

'Get used to them. Now, what's been happening? You've
had two days.'

I told him about the two meetings I'd had with Banks
and what occurred, but not about Hunt.

'We've identified most of the faces involved,' he said.
'Not that it really matters as we intend to nick you all red-
handed, as it were.'

I looked at his hair but said nothing. Somehow I didn't
think he was in the mood for humour. 'Just like at the
pictures,' was all I said.

'Exactly. And you've got the leading role.'

'Bruce Willis, yeah?'

'Mickey Mouse more like,' he said.

Maybe he was in a joking mood after all.

'Do you know exactly when you go?' he asked.

I shook my head.

'It won't be long. The family are booked into the hotel

from Monday week for a fortnight. When are you seeing Banks again?'

I told him I didn't know exactly. Banks's last words had been, 'Stay close to the phone. We'll need to get together again soon.'

'So do it,' said Red. 'I won't be far. I'll be keeping an eye on you.'

And on that reassuring note he left.

44

Banks didn't call for two days. Nor did anyone else. That was OK by me. I just wanted to forget the whole deal. When he did call, the phone clicked as I answered it, and I knew that Red had put a tap on the line. Banks didn't seem to notice.

'Same time, same place tomorrow,' he said. 'Final briefing.'

'When do we go?'

'Not on the phone. We'll talk then.' He was careful, but not careful enough, and I felt my bowels clench. This was going to be a bad one. I had a feeling.

I drove to the boozer and the same geezers were on the door at the back. I didn't see anyone watching as I walked from where I'd parked my truck, but I knew they were there.

I was amongst the last to arrive and helped myself to coffee from the big silver urn on the bar. Banks was next to last in and Hunt was close behind him. She smiled a big white-toothed smile at me, got a coffee of her own but didn't speak. I sat in the back row next to Peters, who I could tell wanted a natter but was hushed by Banks when he stood at the front and faced us all.

'Right,' he said, after he'd led us through the plan one more time. 'We go today week. No dry runs. No practices. It's a one-off. I want you at the base at six in the morning. Peters, you know what you've got to do on the days before. You've got spare keys to the base. That's all. See you then.'

As simple as that, but I felt a palpable tension rise in the room.

We were on to a runner, and the colour was pink.

45

Hunt smiled at me and said softly, 'Changed your mind?'

I shook my head, although I was tempted and she knew it.

'Why not come round for a drink?' she said.

'When?'

'Now. You remember where I live, don't you?'

I nodded.

'Well? I've got champagne in the fridge. We could celebrate.'

'Bit early for that.'

'It's never too early for champagne.'

'Maybe,' I said.

'You do play hard to get.'

I hadn't forgotten the Welsh girl, or anyone else for that matter. 'I've been bitten before.'

'Not the way I bite.'

'I'll take your word for it.'

'Well, I'll be there in forty minutes if you change your mind. But I won't wait for ever.'

'I'll remember that.'

'Do,' she said, and with a wiggle of her finger she was gone.

Banks collared me before I had a chance to leave. 'You all right about this?' he asked.

'What's there to be wrong about? I go in with a gun, put the frighteners on some punters. The rest of you have the hard part. Getting the cash, the tom and the bonds.'

'No problem. When we turn up with shooters we'll have the bastards cold.'

'Armed bastards, remember.'

'So we shoot them.'

His voice was cold and I felt my bowels clench again.

'Could bring some attention, shooting bastards.'

'In and out, no problem.'

'I hope so.'

'Take my word.'

'No choice.'

'See you next week, then,' he said.

'I'll be there.'

'You'd better be.'

I left and went back to the motor and climbed aboard. Farringdon was roughly on the way home so I pointed the bonnet that way. I decided that if I couldn't find anywhere to park I'd head back over the river. But there were two meters vacant just round the corner from her place.

Fate, I thought, parked up, threw a few quid in, and went and knocked on her door.

She answered it dressed in jeans and a T-shirt, and I could tell she had no bra on underneath.

'I thought it would be you. The champagne's on ice.'

I walked in, shut the door behind me and she took me through to the living room where she'd closed the curtains against the sun and something with lots of bass and piano was playing on the stereo.

'Very romantic,' I said.

'Don't take the piss.'

I lit a cigarette and sat down whilst she busied herself with opening the bottle. 'What do you think?' I said.

'About?'

'The state of the nation. The bloody job, of course.'

'Getting cold feet?'

'I've got a bad feeling about it. It's going to be sodding dangerous. There's too many guns involved. Too many people. On both sides. Women, children. And our lot are too fragmented. Too many individuals, not enough team-work.'

'Too bad. Nothing worthwhile comes without a risk.'

'It could go badly wrong.'

'And it could go right. How many times have you been offered that much money for a morning's work?'

'If we ever get the money. If Ramsey and Banks don't vanish into the mystic taking it with them.'

'You're going to have to trust someone some time.'

'If you say.'

'Don't tell me you're scared.'

'Terrified.'

'You don't look like someone who scares easily.'

'Don't you believe it.'

'Banks said you were a bad man.'

'Define bad.'

She gave me a drink. 'I'll tell you later.'

'Do that.'

We sat and drank, comfortable together, and it re-minded me of happier days with other women, which was dangerous.

'Hungry?' she asked after a bit.

'No.'

'You're a weird man, Hurst.'

And getting weirder every day.

'Most men would've made a move on me by now. You're not gay, are you?' she went on.

'I don't think so.'

'Tell me.'

'What?'

'What's troubling you.'

'You got a week?'

'So it's not just the job.'

'No.'

'So tell me.'

'I don't think so.'

'I really don't know why I put up with you.'

'I think you've said that before.'

She sighed. 'So what about afterwards?'

'After what?'

'The job. Will you relax then?'

I didn't tell her that the plan was that she'd be locked up.

'Maybe,' I replied.

'I hope so.'

'Why?'

'Because I'd like to see you.'

'And my money?'

'It wouldn't hurt. We could go away.'

'You've got it all planned.'

'Not all. What do you say? We could watch each other's backs on the day. Two are better than one. Fewer individuals, as you put it.'

'We could.' Why rain on her parade?

'But not now.'

'This is nice,' I said, looking round the room. 'Let's not complicate things.'

'You're hopeless. But after?'

'Sure,' I said. 'Why not?'

And I sealed the devil's bargain with a kiss.

46

Red was waiting in my flat again when I got home. 'Had a nice time?' he asked from the comfort of an armchair.

'I don't know what you mean.'

'Don't fuck about. With the scrubber.'

He told me her real name, but I made no comment. 'You know fucking everything, don't you?' was all I said.

'It's my job.'

'We had a chat, that was all.'

'I bet. I hope you're not playing both ends against the middle. That would upset me greatly.'

'And we don't want that, do we?'

'You don't. That's for sure.'

I was growing tired of him and his comments, and the way he came and went in my life without so much as a by-your-leave. 'You've tapped my sodding phone,' I said.

'But of course. What did you expect?'

'A better job for a start. If it's obvious to me, it's obvious to anyone else.'

'Has anyone else commented?'

'Not so far.'

'There you go, then.'

'You're so fucking confident,' I said.

He grinned. 'It goes with the territory.'

'That's what I used to think. Don't count on it lasting for ever.'

His look turned mean. 'Don't lecture me.'

I was glad I'd got to him at least a bit. But it was a meaningless victory. He still had me where he wanted me, and we both knew it.

'So,' he said. 'Tell me all.'

I told him.

'Brilliant,' he said. 'Next week. So it's all going according to plan.'

'So far.'

'So far, so good. Now just be a good boy and make sure it stays that way.'

'I'll try.'

'See you next week, then, after the job. Don't worry, the boys will treat you nice. Maybe just a few bruises for show.'

A likely sodding story.

'And after that no more,' I said.

'We'll see.'

'I mean it,' I said. 'I've done my bit for Queen and country, and it's definitely over.'

'It's never over till it's over, son. Till the fat lady sings.'

'Then you'd better make sure she's got the right music.'

He came over and gently slapped me round the face. 'That's for me to decide.' And with a swirl from the skirts of his coat he was gone.

Part Three

Holy Mary, mother of God.
Pray for us sinners now and at the hour of our death.

47

The day itself dawned damp and dull. I had hardly slept at all and was up, showered and shaved by four thirty. I drank black coffee as I got ready, the thought of any food being repugnant.

I dressed as instructed in a dark two-piece suit, a pale blue button-down shirt and sombre tie, and a pair of high-sided Chelsea boots. On top I put on a voluminous tan macintosh and a pair of skintight black leather gloves.

For personal ordnance I chose a Dan Wesson Model 14 revolver in .357 magnum with a two-and-a-half-inch barrel which fitted neatly into a suede shoulder holster and hardly made any bulge under my suit coat. I'd spent some of the night modifying the six shells to dum-dum by drilling a small hole in the point of each, then cutting neat crosses in the lead and inserting the heads and a fraction of the shanks of six small nails into the holes.

Vicious, but fair.

As a back-up I slid a tiny FN Browning Baby .25 six-shot semi-automatic into the top of my right sock and pushed it down until it was held fast by the elastic of my boot.

I ordered a cab for five-thirty, and loaded for bear I locked up my flat for what could be the last time for a long time.

I got the cab to drop me off on the south side of Wandsworth Bridge and smoked a cigarette as I strolled across the river with the sun just rising on my right.

The outside of the old garage was quiet, but inside was full of people. Banks's Jag plus another half a dozen cars –

but no turquoise blue Renault Clio – were parked up at
one end. Her motor was slightly obvious, and Hunt had
clearly come by some alternative mode of transport – she
was leaning against the bonnet of a gleaming black,
stretched Mercedes limousine with tinted windows,
dressed in a modest dark suit, a white blouse, dark nylons
and black shoes talking to Peters who looked the part in a
black double-breasted suit with a chauffeur's cap perched
on his head. The Merc stood at the front of the garage just
inside the double doors, next to a Bedford panel truck in
Parcel Force livery, and an anonymous-looking navy-blue
Vauxhall Cavalier.

Hunt looked at her watch as I walked in. 'You're the
last,' she said. 'You're late.'

I checked my watch too. It said one minute past six.
'Hardly,' I said.

'All right,' said Peters. 'We was beginning to get worried.
Have a bit of first-night nerves, didja?'

'Six o'clock, the man said,' I replied. 'I don't believe in
hanging around waiting.'

I spotted Banks at one side of the building next to a
bench on which were laid out the weapons, state-of-the art
walkie-talkies and spare ammunition. 'See you in a
minute,' I said and walked over to join him.

He was dressed similarly to me, and talking to BC, also
togged up in suit and mac. The rest of the bunch were
sitting together on a collection of odd chairs by the office
door.

'Morning,' said Banks to me. 'You look pretty spiffy.'

'As long as it fits the part,' I said.

'Perfect.'

'Good.'

At the back of the bench stood a long slim parcel
wrapped in brown paper: Wilson's gun made up as the
decoy parcel to get him into the hotel.

'Everybody,' shouted Banks. 'Now we're all here, come and get your weapons and radios.'

Peters and Hunt joined us from beside the cars, and JC, Ball, Stiles and Moore, all dressed in leather jackets and jeans, hopped off their perches and wandered over too. Wilson was wearing a short-sleeved blue shirt, a red and black bodywarmer and navy-blue trousers and looked like a postman, and Cohen was dressed in baggy white trousers and a white shirt, presumably an approximation of what the truck driver wore.

The radios had numbers from one to eleven painted on their black plastic fascias and we each took one. Mine being eight.

'Now we all know how to use these,' said Banks. 'It's dead easy. They're all tuned into the same channel. Press the button on the side to speak, otherwise leave them alone. Kid's stuff. But it's not a fucking chat line. Don't talk unless it's absolutely necessary.'

'Are these affected by whatever fucks up the satellite links?' I asked.

'No,' said Banks. 'Totally different frequencies. Any more questions?' No one said a word, so he said, 'Good. Now get your guns.'

I took off my mac and picked up the closest Winchester pump and a handful of shells. I loaded five into the gun and an extra one for luck into the pipe, then slung it over my right shoulder by the carrying strap. Then I helped myself to one of the Brownings and slapped the thirteen-shot staggered-line clip into the butt and found another shell on the bench and slid it into the breech, cocked and locked the gun and put it under the belt of my trousers at the back. Then I shrugged into my coat again. Done up, the guns I was carrying on my person hardly showed. I picked up two spare loaded magazines for the pistol and a handful of shells for the shotgun and distributed them

297

about my person. Finally I clipped the tiny radio into the top pocket of my suit jacket. Perfect. I was ready for anything.

As I was arming myself the rest were doing the same, and before long most of the weapons from the bench had vanished.

'Right,' said Banks. 'There's thermoses of coffee in the office. Let's take a smoke break, people, then saddle up and fuck off out of here.'

48

After we'd drunk our coffee, BC, Hunt and I got into the back of the stretch, Peters behind the wheel. It was ten to eight and we were just right. Banks allowed the post office van and the Cavalier out of the garage before locking up all the doors tight and joining us in the limo. The back of the Merc was all leather and walnut with a TV and video, stereo and cocktail cabinet, and the whisper of air conditioning when the engine was running. It had plenty of room, which was just as well as it was not easy to sit down with three of us carrying shotguns, even the short Winchesters, under our coats. Hunt had put on a light mac and carried a large black leather handbag, inside which I knew was one of the Browning Hi-Powers.

I sat facing the front next to BC. Hunt and Banks sat on a pair of seats in the bulkhead that had to be pulled down. Peters rolled the dark glass partition between the driver and passengers down and said, 'I'll take a slow drive.'

'Make it the pretty way,' growled Banks. 'We've got plenty of time.'

And we had. Even at that time of the morning it took us less than thirty minutes to get to Harrods the way Peters drove the car, all twenty foot of it through some of the narrowest streets of the capital. We lost sight of the other two motors within a few minutes.

'I've done this journey twenty times at least,' he said from the front. 'And the drive they've gotta do. We all want to be there in plenty of time but not make a show by hangin' around.'

It seemed logical to me.

At first we parked on Montpelier Square, between Knightsbridge and the Brompton Road, with the engine running to keep the interior cool, and the Merc didn't stand out a bit as there were maybe half a dozen other limousines lined up in the street.

'Embassies,' explained Peters. 'Shockin' waste of money.'

'And you'd know,' said BC.

'Sure I would. Used to work for one as a driver. You see all sorts.'

'I'm sure,' said Hunt.

'Had a bit of luck the other day,' said Peters.

No one answered, so he went on, 'Had a win on the lottery.'

'Did you?' said BC. 'I've put in a fiver every week since it started. Not a sniff. How much?'

'A tenner,' said Peters.

'A fucking tenner,' said BC. 'Jesus. Was it worth it? I thought you'd had a real result.'

'Better than a poke in the eye.'

'I won the pools once,' said Banks, altering his position to make himself more comfortable.

'We *are* a lucky bunch,' said BC. 'How many points?'

'Twenty-three. I got a postal order for thirty pence. There were a lot of score draws that week.'

'Fuck me,' said BC. 'I hope we do better today, otherwise we'll be in trouble.'

''Course we will,' said Banks.

'Anyone watch TV last night?' asked Peters after a bit. He sure was a chatty bastard.

'I did,' said Hunt.

'EastEnders?'

'Never miss it.'

'What do you reckon to that Barbara Windsor, then? I'd give her one.'

'It's bread and bread to me,' said Hunt. 'I don't fancy women.'

'Too old,' said BC.

'Big tits,' said Peters.

'If that's all you want you should go out with a mummy elephant,' said Hunt.

'No, I like the other one. The one that runs the caff,' said BC.

'She'd give you a good blow job,' said Banks.

'Specially in a Range Rover,' said Peters with a dirty laugh. And then to Hunt. 'What do you reckon, love?'

'Don't look at me. I like a bit more comfort. I fancy the one who runs the used car lot,' said Hunt, giving me a look. 'Hunky.'

I looked at my watch and then out through the tinted glass at all the straight people going to work. 'Excuse me for interrupting critics' corner, but shouldn't we be going?' I said.

'Right,' said Banks, glancing at his watch too. 'Peters, let's go.'

49

We ended up outside the hotel at eight forty-five. All seemed quiet and serene. I'd taken time to check it out when Banks had finally relented and told us exactly where it was. It was a five-storey block of dark-coloured brick and tinted windows with a flat roof. Given the chance I might even have stayed there myself, but the tariff was rather high.

It was going to prove higher than ever that day.

The first part of the plan went exactly as planned. At eight fifty-seven Wilson, in his fake postie's outfit, drove the stolen Parcel Force van up to the front door, while Cohen turned the white panel truck into the service road, and chugged on round to the back of the building.

The five of us sat in the Mercedes and watched Wilson amble into the foyer, the long, brown parcel in his hand. He vanished through the doors, then after maybe half a minute we simultaneously heard through our radios his voice say the single word, 'Done.'

'Let's go, boys and girls,' said Banks, and we left the car and walked across the road to the hotel, our coats covering the weapons hidden beneath them.

We pushed through the doors and I saw Wilson with his shotgun on six people standing with their faces to the wall next to the lift, the parcel wrappings lying on the floor around his feet.

He was holding the gun on two heavy-looking dark-skinned men in lounge suits, a bloke in morning dress who I recognized from his photograph to be the manager, a pretty blonde girl in a blouse and skirt, who I took to be the receptionist, a bellboy in full livery with a little pillbox hat on his head, and another, older, skinny, swarthy-faced character who I assumed to be one of the entourage of the family. The phone behind the reception desk was buzzing.

Banks, BC and I opened our coats and brought up the weapons we were carrying. Hunt took the automatic from her bag.

'What the hell—?' said the bloke in the morning dress.

'Shut up,' said Wilson.

'You will die for this,' said one of the dark-skinned men.

I kicked him in the nuts. He fell to the carpeted floor, doubled up in pain. This was no time for conversation. The more we talked the more time we wasted and the more chance that some fucker would walk in holding a loaded weapon.

'The man said shut up,' I said. 'That goes for all of you.'

Banks nodded his agreement. 'Take over the desk,' he said to Hunt.

She went behind reception, put the gun out of sight, picked up a headset, put it on, pressed a button somewhere and said, 'Langton Hotel. Good morning. How may I help you?'

Banks gestured for the standing prisoners to move away from the wall, then he and BC frisked them all down, including the girl and the heavy still writhing on the floor. Their total haul was three big semi-automatic handguns, one each from the three Arabs. Wilson took one, which he tucked into his belt at the front, BC the second which went into the side pocket of his mac, and Banks the third which he put into his coat pocket also.

'Let's go into your office,' Banks said to the monkey in the suit. He hesitated and BC jacked a shell into the breech of his shotgun. It's amazing what effect that simple act can produce. The hotel manager went white and pointed in the direction of the office door, and Banks pushed him that way. Meanwhile BC had vanished through the door leading to the restaurant, and a moment later stuck his head back and shook it. Then he and Wilson took the others through the door and out of sight, the dark-skinned geezer I hadn't kicked supporting the one I had. When the place was empty apart from Hunt and me I took off my coat, slid the shotgun off my shoulder, laid it flat on the cushions of one of the overstuffed sofas that littered the foyer, and covered it with the mackintosh so that just the pistol grip showed and I could have it up and ready to fire within seconds. I winked at Hunt, undid my suit coat and tried to look as nonchalant as possible. For the next stage I was relying on other people doing their jobs properly. No wonder the palms of my hands were wet.

If all went well, Cohen, who had been messing around at the back of the delivery truck, would have got the word from Wilson and carried a box of Canaries into the kitchen. The guard on the door would hardly give him a second glance – till Cohen put the box down, removed his Browning from under the tomatoes and stuck it in the guy's neck. A quick word in his radio and JC, Ball, Stiles and Moore would nip out from under the cabbages in the back of the van. In a few seconds the guard, and the rest of the kitchen staff, would be snugly locked in the coldstore.

If all went well.

There was a whisper on the radio. Cohen. He was in the van again, watching the back entrance. The England attack squad had gone up to the top floor in the service lift and were collecting swag and guests en route back to the ground.

So far, so good.

All was quiet in the hotel and nothing much seemed to be going on in the street. I imagined that Red, or at least some of his cronies, were outside checking on the party, until two people walked up the front steps and into the foyer.

It was Smith and the driver.

Shit! I hadn't expected them of all people. They were both smartly dressed and walked past me without a hint of recognition and up to Hunt behind the desk. She looked at me and I walked over to them, taking the Browning from the small of my back. Hunt looked over Smith's shoulder and he and the driver turned. They acted surprised and frightened at the sight of me and the gun, the driver herself stifling a scream and putting one hand to her mouth, the other on Smith's arm as if for support. It was Oscar-winning stuff.

Now it was my turn. 'Don't be frightened,' I said softly. 'Armed men have taken over this hotel. You're in the wrong place at the wrong time. But you won't be hurt. Just sit over there.' I moved the Browning's muzzle in the direction of another of the sofas. 'And very soon this will all be just a memory.'

They stood transfixed as if in shock. I played along. 'What are your names?' I asked.

'Ballantyne,' said Smith. 'John and Angela.'

'Right, John. Right, Angela,' I said. 'Sit down and no one will be hurt.' And I pushed them towards the seat.

'Search them,' said Hunt. 'Just in case.'

'But naturally,' I said and frisked Smith quickly. He was wearing a gun under his left arm. I did the same to the driver, taking great satisfaction at the look on her face as I ran my hands over her breasts. 'Bag,' I said. She opened the handbag she was carrying, and nestling on top was a nickel-plated Colt Detective Special.

'They're clean,' I said as the phone behind the desk buzzed again. 'Come on, let's go.'

As we were moving away from the desk I heard Hunt speaking to the caller and I said quietly so as not to let her hear, 'What the hell are you two doing here? You took a fucking chance coming in here armed.'

'Change of plan. We take you all here. Someone you know had to come in. We knew your job was at the front as security,' Smith whispered. 'And we got the short straw.'

'Short straw is sodding right,' I said. 'We've got enough guns and people here to start a small war.'

'You want to see what's waiting outside, then,' said Smith.

'You bastards,' I said. 'You knew this was going to happen all along.'

Smith shrugged imperceptibly. 'There's things Special Branch need here. Papers and stuff. You're just opening the safe for us.'

50

I looked over my shoulder. Hunt was watching us with a puzzled look on her face. I gave her a forced smile, remembering the gun she had hidden under the desk top, as I turned back. 'She'll suss us if we're not careful,' I said.

'Then shut up and stay calm,' said Smith.

Calm, I thought as I glanced quickly out into the street. Calm. With what sounded like it might be half a sodding army outside ready to burst in.

'Sit down,' I said. 'Or by Christ I'll shoot you myself.'

I suddenly saw a quick flash of fear in Smith's eyes. Yeah, I thought. How does it feel, sucker? For once not to have the upper hand.

They did as they were told and, keeping the Browning in my hand, I picked up the Winchester from off the sofa and slung it over my left shoulder. There was no point in trying to be discreet any longer. It was crunch time and I needed all the hardware I could get.

'Stay there,' I said to them. 'I swear if you as much as twitch an eyelid I'll kill you.' Then I walked backwards over to Hunt.

'All right?' she said.

I nodded.

'Who are they?'

'Just punters looking for a room.'

'Bad choice.'

'You can say that again.'

Then, simultaneously, the door to the manager's office opened and one set of lift doors swept aside soundlessly as Banks, carrying a large briefcase in one hand and his shotgun in the other came into the foyer from the room, pushing the manager in front of him, and Stiles exited the lift holding his gun on three women and two children with one hand and swinging a bulging black garbage sack from the other.

Banks clocked Smith and the driver, and gave me a quizzical look, and I flashed him a thumbs-up sign to say that everything was under control.

Stiles began to push his charges towards the restaurant door and I saw the most frightening of all the frightening things I'd ever seen in my life. Through the glass door of the hotel from a window on the opposite side of the road, to the left and behind the limo which was still parked there with its exhaust burbling, and sited dead centre on my chest, appeared the tiny red spot of a laser beam rifle sight.

I looked down at it as it crawled like some malign insect from the centre of my tie down towards my groin.

The hotel door was shut and made of heavy-duty plate glass, and intellectually I knew that it would probably deflect or even shatter the bullet into a thousand pieces, even if the glass was not strong enough stop it completely, but that didn't stop me from almost pissing myself with fright.

I flinched at the sight, and then as quickly as it had arrived it winked out. I looked round and saw that Smith had noticed it too, although no one else seemed to have done so.

Then, as Stiles moved across the carpet behind his prisoners, the red beam appeared on the collar of his shirt, moved up imperceptibly, and the glass door broke into a million pieces as the sniper over the road fired. Stiles took the bullet just below his right ear and the left side of his neck exploded in a spray of rich red arterial blood. So much for intellectual thought. The bastard was using armour-piercing bullets or something similar. Stiles fell forward on to his face as suddenly as if he had been chopped off at the knees. There was no sound of a report from outside, just the noise of traffic in the street now louder since the door had been destroyed.

For a second, everyone in the foyer was still, as the glass tinkled across the floor and Stiles died before our eyes.

The women and children screamed and clung together as both Banks and I looked at each other, then Smith came out of his seat, his hand going under his jacket, and he pulled out a heavy automatic. Banks didn't hesitate and fired his shotgun point blank at him. The flechette round literally blew Smith's top half apart as the HE in the cartridge exploded on impact and Smith was hurled cartwheeling across the back of the sofa, his arm and half his head separating from his body and showering the driver in blood, skin, bone and body fluids. She yelled something I couldn't understand, stuck her hand inside her bag and came out with the Detective Special, which she emptied into Banks, knocking him down too. As he went down he fired again, and the round blew a crater in the ceiling, covering him, the manager, the women and children, and the driver in tiny pieces of plaster. The driver stood covered in gore and dust and looked at me. I raised my Browning in my right, and my empty left hand in a placating gesture, and she leaned on the back of the sofa for support, then threw up all over the Persian rug at her feet.

I looked round for Hunt and she was gone from behind the desk, destination unknown.

At precisely the same moment, the door to the restaurant burst open and BC crashed through, his Browning at the ready. He saw the tableau and fired at the driver, hitting her in the thigh. She returned fire, missing him by a mile. I knew it was decision time and made one in a second. I raised the Browning and shot BC twice. He was thrown back against the wall and slid down, leaving a trail of red on the cream-coloured walls.

'Thanks,' said the driver to me.

In the silence that followed the gunshots we stood like a tableau. It was decision time again. Now or never. On the side of the goodies or the baddies. But then, as I'd noted before, there wasn't much difference. So it was no contest. 'Don't thank me,' I said to the driver and shot her twice.

As she died she tried to bring up her gun to shoot me back, but didn't have the strength, and I finished her with a third shot.

51

The foyer was rich with the stink of blood, faeces and body parts, and the smoke from the guns that hung like a pall over the place.

Time seemed to stop as everyone still alive froze into position.

Then with an almost audible click, time started again as cars and men appeared outside, and from the sky I heard the clatter of a helicopter's rotors. Out of the corner of my eyes I saw the limousine peel away from the kerb only to be halted as two cars smashed into its side, and I knew that Peters was out of the game.

The briefcase that Banks had dropped when he was shot was just a few steps away from me. I looked round, saw the door behind the reception desk swinging gently to and fro, darted forward, expecting a bullet at any moment, picked up the case and dashed back towards the door, through it, and into the corridor beyond.

It was empty, and there was a dead end to the right. I stuck the Browning back into my belt, brought up the Winchester in my right hand and, carrying the case in my left, ran towards the door to the emergency stairs, just before the corridor dog-legged towards the locked emergency exit and another dead end.

As I ran I heard Hunt's voice through the speaker on my radio. 'It's blown,' she said. 'Hurst is one of them. Get out while you can.'

Charming, I thought.

I gently pushed open the door to the emergency stairs. The stairwell was empty and I headed upwards. Another door, another service corridor, also empty, Then Hunt stepped from cover directly in front of me, her Browning in her hand. I stopped short. 'Hi,' I said. 'How's it going?'

'You bastard,' she said. 'Those two were the law.'

There was no point in denying it.

'You sold us out.'

'It wasn't like that.'

'Put down your gun and the case.'

I looked at the Winchester, barrel pointing uselessly down at the ground, then at her again.

I heard gunfire from above and below. If there was fighting upstairs too, things were obviously getting interesting. But we remained in an oasis of calm.

'Put them down,' she repeated. I did as I was told, placing them both gingerly on the floor.

'Now the Browning. Slowly.'

I did as I was told again, taking the automatic out from the small of my back using just two fingers and dropping it next to the shotgun and the briefcase.

'Happy now?' I asked.

She nodded and brought up her pistol.

'You're not going to shoot me,' I said. It had never really occurred to me that she would. 'I've got the goodies. We can get out of here if we're clever. We can be together.' Being at the business end of a gun makes liars of us all.

'Aren't I?' she asked.

'Are you?'

'Believe it,' and she fired. The first shot missed, but came so close that I heard the crack as the bullet whizzed past my head and dug itself into the plaster behind me.

She aimed again and I was looking down the barrel, and the fucker jammed. I saw her finger working at the trigger and she swore and threw the gun at me. I dodged to avoid it and it hit the wall and went off. It felt as if someone had whacked me at the top of my left arm with a piece of two-

312

by-four and the front of my coat sleeve was shredded as the bullet went through.

'Bitch,' I said, took the .357 from its holster under my arm and shot her twice with its dum-dum bullets. Once in the left breast, once in the stomach. The bullets burst inside her and shredded her to mincemeat, exiting in chunks. She looked at me in surprise, tried to hold on to the wall, missed, buckled at the knees and went down on to the floor where she lay perfectly still.

I looked at my arm. It was a mess. Awkwardly I pulled out my shirt tail, tore off a strip and wrapped it as tightly as I could around my bicep above the wound and knotted it using one hand and my teeth. I could hardly feel any pain, but I knew that it would really start to hurt soon. Then I picked up the case, wedged it under my left arm, tucked the Browning away safely and lifted up the Winchester in my right hand. I stepped over Hunt's body just as the door was kicked open behind me and a figure in a blue boiler suit came barrelling through.

I fired back along the corridor one-handed, the narrowness of the space making it hard to miss and I didn't. His Kevlar flak jacket did little to protect him from the high-explosive blast and his torso exploded in a mist of blood and bone and he was blown backwards through the door again, leaving a long smear of red on the woodwork.

I pumped the action of the gun awkwardly, wedging the grip against my thigh as I did it, and headed along the corridor again, realizing that I was lucky. I was the only person in the whole place who had no one on my side. Everyone was my enemy, and somehow that made me feel better.

Through the corridor window that overlooked the service road at the back of the building I saw Cohen's bloodstained and bullet-riddled body slumped against the side of the white van surrounded by blue overalled troops.

I smashed the glass with the Winchester's barrel and fired three more high-explosive rounds down into the street, sending the police scurrying for cover and leaving one lying, writhing on the ground.

It didn't do me much good, but it made me feel better and let them know there was still someone around. By my calculations the most of the original eleven of us left by then was five. We were being massacred. Not that I gave a shit. They were no friends of mine, and after what Hunt had said, I was definitely infra dig with them.

At the end of the corridor was the door Hunt had come through. I eased it open and found myself in the cocktail bar. It was empty and dimly lit. I was in the serving area behind the counter. To my left was a mirror as long as the bar itself, engraved with flowers. In front of the mirror were hanging maybe fifty spirit bottles on optic and on the shelf below the glass probably another hundred or so standing upright. In front of the counter were swivelling stools with leather seats and little arms. Tables and armchairs were grouped across the carpet. Opposite were two sets of double doors for the guests to enter either from the reception area or the restaurant next door.

I took time to have another look at the wound in my left arm. It didn't seem too bad. The bleeding looked like it had more or less stopped, but blood had leaked down to my hand and I wiped it off on my trousers.

I opened the flap of the counter and started to walk towards the exits. Before I'd taken half a dozen steps I heard a commotion outside and one set of the double doors burst open to allow three armed men in civvies to come in, guns at the ready. I dropped the briefcase, turned, dived across the top of the counter, slid along its polished top, face down, and as they started to fire flipped myself off behind it. Something hit me hard low down in the back and a pain like fire ran up my spine. That was a bad one and I knew it.

The bullets from three Heckler & Koch MP5K machine guns on full automatic smashed into the wall behind the bar, destroying the mirror and exploding the bottles that hung and stood there. I was covered in liquor and broken glass and cowered away from the hard rain that poured down on me.

I took out the Browning and fired over the top of the bar. I heard a scream and the firing stopped. I emptied the magazine, slid it out of the butt of the gun and replaced it with a fresh one, then hurriedly reloaded the shotgun, put away the pistol and crawled towards the gap in the bar. I came round low and opened up with the Winchester, ignoring the pain in my left arm as I worked the action. I shot shit out of the room with the six flechettes. Armchairs burst in a snowstorm of foam rubber and fabric, and tables blew into matchwood. The doors were destroyed, and holes big enough to accommodate big dogs were blown in the walls. The three men who had fired at me all died or were mortally wounded in the small corner of hell I created with the shotgun and the high-explosive loads it carried.

When my weapon was empty I pushed open the door at the back of the bar and slid through the gap back into the corridor beyond where Hunt's body was still lying. Apart from her it was deserted. My back hurt like hell and every time I breathed deeply I felt a terrible pain in my chest. Don't breathe deeply was all I could think to help myself. I felt around and my hand came back covered in blood. I'd lost the briefcase in the commotion, but I didn't care. Whoever came out of this alive was welcome to it.

I stopped to think. Upstairs or down? Which way to go? I figured upwards. What the hell? I had to go somewhere.

52

I shoved at the door to the emergency stairs again, but it was stuck, and I shoved harder to move the body of the policeman I'd shot out of the way. I waited for a second to see if any of his friends had arrived to help him, but all was quiet. That suited me. He'd obviously come up under his own volition. That was fine. The more of them running around like chickens with their heads cut off the better.

I could still hear sporadic firing as I slowly climbed up the stairs, and as I went I discovered evidence of the firefight that had taken place.

The walls were scarred with bullet holes and great chunks had been chopped out of them from the Winchester's loads.

The noise of the gunfire got louder as I got closer to the top floor.

My wounds were starting to hurt badly, and I could feel something grinding together in my back. Every step was agony. As I went I reloaded the Winchester with my last six high-explosive cartridges, pushing each one home against the spring of the shotgun's action with an audible click that sent new waves of pain through my body.

I felt fresh blood running down my back, and when I got to the top of the final flight of stairs I peered through the emergency exit door and saw a police marksman lying prone on the floor in front of me behind the cover of a table that he had knocked over. Scattered across the carpet in front of him were a bunch of white roses in a pool of water next to a broken vase. He was aiming his pistol down towards the middle of the wide hall where there was an open door, and at a sign of movement inside the doorway he double-tapped his weapon, knocking splinters from the door frame.

As I took out the .357 magnum from its holster under my arm and gently eased back the hammer, he heard or sensed something, tried to turn and I pulled the trigger and shot him in the side of the head, the big gun's boom contrasting to the sharp cracks from the nine-millimetre pistol the policeman held.

His skull exploded like a ripe watermelon and his brain splashed across the back of the table and the carpet.

At the sound of my shot another copper darted out from behind cover at the other end of the hallway and let off a barrage of rounds that sliced into the walls, throwing dust into my eyes. I returned fire. During the crescendo of shots Moore jumped out of the doorway. He fired wildly in both our directions and our crossfire chopped him down. The other copper was hit too, by whom I had no idea, and I finished him with the last shot from my revolver. A deathly silence descended on the corridor and I dropped my empty gun on to the floor.

I took the Browning out of my belt and walked slowly up the hallway. When I reached the open doorway I shouted, 'It's me, Hurst, hold your fire.' Then I stuck my head round the jamb.

Inside was the sitting room of a suite. JC sat on the floor next to the body of a young boy whose throat had been cut. The carpet was stained with blood, and a gory, long-bladed knife with a serrated blade lay on the carpet next to him. Another child and a woman, both Arab-looking, cowered in the corner. The woman's face was tear-stained and she was making soft, keening sounds as she reached out her hands to the dead child. JC had his Browning pointed at the doorway. His hands and the cuffs of his jacket were stained with blood. 'Jesus,' I said through a swirl of gunsmoke from the shoot out. 'What the fuck went down?'

'I told them I'd kill the kid if they didn't let us pass.'

'But they wouldn't.'

He nodded.

'So you did it.'

He nodded again. 'You're hit. What happened downstairs?'

'It got fucked. Totally fucked.'

'You can say that again,' he said tiredly. 'Ball's dead in the other room with a couple of coppers. A slop shot. They came down from the roof.' Then realization dawned. 'Hunt said . . .' he said, and I shot him with the remaining bullets in the Browning's magazine.

I looked at the dead boy and the woman. 'Bastard,' I said, threw down the gun and left the room.

I walked down the hall again, avoiding Moore's and the coppers' bodies. Then I heard a sound from behind me and the Arab woman was standing in the doorway with what must've been JC's pistol in her hand. She fired and hit me in the shoulder, spinning me round and knocking me down. Before she could aim again I took the Baby Browning from out of my boot and emptied the clip into her. She crashed back on to the carpet and lay still.

Somehow I dragged myself to my feet and continued on my way, leaving the .25 automatic where I dropped it and armed only with the Winchester. The corridor faded in and out of my vision and I knew that I was close to being finished.

I stumbled through yet another door and saw a flight of wooden steps leading upwards again. Next to it was a sign saying: ROOF – NO EXIT.

I dragged myself up the stairs where a door in a sort of wedge-shaped concrete blockhouse opened on to the flat roof paved in black tar.

I felt weak and faint as I dragged myself round to the opposite side of the blockhouse and slumped down against the concrete, leaving a dark red trail behind me. I knew I was losing blood big time and I suddenly realized what it was like to be dying.

It was good.

Then I heard a terrific roar and from behind the building next door to the hotel which was maybe a storey and a half taller than the hotel itself came the shape of the helicopter I'd heard earlier. Its plastic bubble caught the sun, then swung round and I could see Red sitting in the passenger seat.

Was there no end to this fucking nightmare?

The chopper swung like a pendulum at the edge of the building and Red brought up a sniper's rifle and aimed it in my direction. I pulled myself slowly to my feet using the Winchester as a crutch and tried to dodge, but I was far too slow and a round hit me in the thigh just below my groin. I fell to one knee and crawled back towards the shelter of the doorway. A second bullet tore tarmac beside me and I turned and brought the shotgun I was holding round and fired, pumped, fired, pumped until the gun was empty. Which round did it I don't know, but one of them must have hit the fuel tank. I saw Red screaming something into the mouthpiece of the headset he was wearing as I fired, and then the helicopter exploded, blowing me flat and littering the roof with burning debris before it tumbled into the street below with a terrible crash followed by silence.

I dragged myself to the edge of the roof and looked down. The chopper and the two cars it had landed on were burning merrily and men who looked like ants from my vantage point were running in all directions. The smoke that reached me had that peculiar odour almost like roasting pork that meant human flesh was burning.

I was suddenly back on the roof of the nick after I'd pushed the suspect to his death. What goes round comes round. Only this time I didn't even have the strength to puke. I looked down at my ruined leg and knew that I didn't have long unless I got some medical help.

I dragged myself to my feet for the last time and started to hop back to the doorway when three police came through the door carrying automatic weapons.

'Armed police,' the front runner said, kneeling. The second stood behind him pointing his sub-machine gun in my direction.

'Put down your weapon and lie face down,' he ordered.

Once again time seemed to slow, and simultaneously I remembered two things. One was part of a prayer, or maybe it was the rosary from my brief Catholic youth, and the other was the black guy in Handsworth who'd smiled at me before he was blown into chopped liver by the men from the armed response group.

'Drop your weapon now or we'll shoot,' shouted the third copper, and I repeated the sacred words to myself as I smiled and slowly brought up the empty shotgun in my hands that were slippery from my own blood and smeared the shiny satin chrome red, and pointed it in their direction.

'Holy Mary, mother of God.
Pray for us sinners now and at the hour of our death . . .'